"Even if you don't usually read spy novels, you'll get sucked into this international story of intrigue and suspense and won't want to put it down. I know, because that's what happened with me."

—Donna Chacko, Doctor & Blogger

"New twists and turns in every chapter—a thrilling page-turner that keeps me guessing."

—Joe Roos, Pastor and Activist

"A smart thriller for smart people who enjoy knocking off a couple of martinis while taking a break from Henry James. Meet journalist Anna and her frenemy Raven who must join forces to solve an international scandal that ranges from DC, to Miami to Thailand. Take it to the beach and you'll forget about the waves."

—Kimberly D. Schmidt, Historian &
Author of *Magpie's Blanket*

Praise for *Source of Deceit*

"Bahren masterfully creates a cloak-and-dagger spy story that takes place at the nexus of international development aid and armed insurrection, in a part of the world that is not often in the headlines but has been the scene of political unrest for much of the past 50 years. Bahren skillfully weaves the various threads into a compelling narrative that is hard to put down. The writing evokes the sights and smells of a humid Bangkok night, the feel of a crisp February morning in DC, and the sleek elegance of a Miami Beach villa. A highlight for anyone interested in an intelligent novel!"

—Pilar Wolfsteller, Journalist

"*Source of Deceit*'s brisk narrative keeps you guessing—a much needed and perfectly safe escape from your pandemic world."

—Susan Hines, External Affairs Director

"Wolf has managed to subvert the typical thriller without pulling one over on the reader; delightful, deceiving, and whip-smart."

—Kevin Barrett, Programmer & Novelist

"Really brilliant! Absolutely love the style! Great that the main character is a woman. It's such a pleasure following Anna Jones around. Amazing how meticulously all the settings are described, as if Wolf had lived there for years. And it is a true thriller. Too bad it will be a while before there's another Anna Jones adventure."

—Elisabeth Binder, Journalist

"Anna Jones should be considered the new standard for a smart, modern protagonist. *Source of Deceit* is well plotted with engrossing prose and excellent attention to detail. Suspense thrillers don't get any better!"

—Michelle H., App Developer

"A fast and fun read that keeps the suspense going until the end."

—M. Jeffries, MS CCC-SLP

"*Source of Deceit* is binge-worthy. Wolf Bahren writes the sort of thriller that appeals to readers of any genre. The characters keep you entertained as the plot thickens and twists about Anna and Raven's search for the truth through a deceitful web of motives and power. A task that anyone living in the age of misinformation can appreciate."

—Mark G., English Teacher

"I love how the Anna Jones character from *Agents of Suzharia* has become the star of *Source of Deceit*. Her adventures as an intrepid, truth-seeking journalist, along with the 'you are there' locale descriptions make this a compelling, fun and satisfying read!"

—Renee Catacalos, Author of *The Chesapeake Table: Your Guide to Eating Local*

Source
of
Deceit

Also by Wolf Bahren

Agents of Suzharia

Source
of
Deceit

a novel

WOLF BAHREN

Pigeon Post Books

For the strugglers, the stragglers
and the underdogs

Chapter 1

Washington, DC – Tuesday, February 18, 2020, 12:30 a.m. EST

Nou Channarong jaywalked across Pennsylvania and 18th toward the World Bank. In the intersection, he glanced over his shoulder. Traffic was thin after midnight, even two blocks from the White House. A lone taxi slowed as it approached, but Channarong shook his head. The taxi sailed onward.

The main entrance of the Bank lay on H Street, a half a block more. When Channarong entered, he greeted the night guards and raised his hands to show he had no bags. Engrossed in a conversation, they ushered him through the metal detector. An Executive Director, he was one of the most important people in the building, and they knew who the tall, impeccably dressed man was. The guards bid him goodnight, failing to note the mild alteration in his gait, the result of too much scotch.

Channarong traversed the empty lobby and rode the elevator upstairs. As soon as he arrived on his floor, he heard vacuums growling. The cleaning team was still at work.

A janitor darted out of one of the doorways. Wearing grey coveralls and sturdy construction boots, he was carrying a bag of trash. "Oh. Good evening, Professor Channarong," he said. "Sorry we aren't finished. We can come back later. Please," he added, gesturing for Channarong to walk by. "We'll be heading downstairs shortly."

"Wonderful," Channarong said, mustering a smile for the kind, bear-like man. "Thank you, Mike."

Channarong unlocked his office, entered and loosened his tie. Then he poured himself another scotch from a bottle he kept stowed in his coat closet and sat at his desk. Leaning forward, he rested his elbows on the blotter and perched his forehead on his fingertips. His slumped posture bore no resemblance to the confident swagger of his public persona. His thick, straight black hair lay tousled, while sweat shimmered on his neck and cheeks. He sat back. Swirling the amber drink, he stared out the wall of glass. After a few minutes, he downed the more-than-double shot. His wrist shook as he returned the empty glass to its coaster.

He opened the top desk drawer and removed his fountain pen. Out of a side drawer, he pulled two sheets of letterhead and proceeded to write two letters. When he was finished, he folded the letters neatly in thirds, sealed them in World Bank envelopes, addressed them and placed them in his out box. More satisfied than he had felt in months, Channarong gazed at the city lights once more. He finally knew what to do.

Chapter 2

Washington, DC – Tuesday, Feb.18, 7:00 a.m.

As soon as Anna Jones saw the number on her caller ID, she knew something was wrong. Richard Tanner, the DC bureau chief of the *New York Daily Journal*, never called his reporters before the morning meeting.

"Hey," Anna answered, as the elevator doors rattled shut.

"Jones, where are you?" the old man barked.

"On my way up right now."

"How serendipitous," he said, clearing his throat.

"Why? What's wrong?"

"Nou Channarong was found hanging in his office."

"What? But I saw him last night."

"Well, he's dead now! Get in here."

"Right," she told him, but Tanner had already hung up. Anna frowned. The Executive Director for South East Asia at the World Bank, Channarong had been the keynote speaker at the annual gala of the Starlight Institute for Global Prosperity, off Dupont Circle, the previous night. A showman at Washington's endless stream of dry talks, he had

3

flung his arms around, twinkled his eyes, and flashed his perfect teeth in strategic spurts. He had pushed for increased disaster funds and development aid. The audience of policy wonks and journalists had stopped texting as he wove tales of adventure while making his case. How could he be dead?

The elevator doors opened. Anna glanced around—no one was there. She took off her coat and rested it on a chair. Facing the vestibule mirror, she swiped her ring fingers outward under her hazel eyes to blot her eyeliner. Her light skin still held its moisturizer. She refreshed her red lipstick, smoothed her blond hair and reviewed her outfit—shimmery light grey blouse, charcoal trousers, favorite drop earrings. She was glad she had bought the new clothes. And the heels? Sharp. At five-foot-six, she had to admit, sometimes she enjoyed the intimidation factor of the extra height.

Ready to face her new boss, she grabbed her coat, tapped out the combination to the bureau lock and strode down the hall to an open area called "the pen." Anna stopped in front of Tanner's office, a glass box in the center of the vast space.

The bureau chief was on his cell phone, nodding. He made eye contact with Anna and turned his hand in quick circles, signaling the caller was blathering. His tan crackled skin and cotton-white hair, thick and short like a bristle brush, announced his age—but they did not imply fading glory. Tanner pointed to Anna, then the chair.

Anna opened the door and sat down. "Right," he yelled at the phone, pushing hard with his thumb on the end-call button. Without blinking, he looked straight at Anna.

"Morning, Tanner," she said.

"Jones, here's the deal: A cleaning lady discovered the body. No note. Now, who do you know over there?"

"One of the flacks is an old friend—used to work for DMV News."

"Flacks!" he interrupted. "Those simpering mouthpieces aren't going to tell you anything. They're not even going to try to spin this one. And do you know why? Because they're going to do their damnedest to bury it!"

"She's not my sole contact. I have—"

"Wait until we see their official statement."

"Depression? Family issues? Are we sure it was suicide?"

"Who the fuck knows!" barked Tanner, a former Marine. He leaned back and stared at the ceiling for a few seconds. "This could be small potatoes, or it could go nuclear, Jones! Put your other stories on hold—I'll assign Fritz to cover Treasury and the Fed. Find Channarong's colleagues, relatives, neighbors, anybody he was doing anything with—church, mosque, kids, whore, whatever," he said, shooing her out with a mitt of a hand. "Get to the bottom of this, Jones! And do it before anybody else!"

"Got it," she said, walking out, pulling the door shut behind her as he got back on the phone.

She passed rows of desks. The DC bureau was much larger than the one where she had recently worked in Moscow, but it was small compared to the paper's headquarters in New York. Most desks were tidy, stripped of clutter, virtually interchangeable, like a hotel business center. A few workspaces brimmed with papers, spiral notepads and books. Reports and documents stood in stacks. Despite the reams of information available online, some journalists hoarded old-fashioned proof. For the older generation, it was force of habit. But there were practical considerations as well, even for her youngest colleagues: Given a crash or a hack, they would still have evidence, if emails or other electronic files disappeared into the ether. Unfortunately, everyone knew, they sometimes did.

When it came to the books, there were other excuses. For Anna, they held an irresistible allure. Concrete stores of knowledge that you could hold in your hand, books could be digested without extra apps or devices, and they represented tangible proof of a careful thought process. Treasures.

5

She made her way down an aisle toward the far end of the pen and arrived at her corner. Tanner hadn't said anything when she moved some bookshelves around to create a nook. It wasn't the droning of the TVs or her colleagues' talking on the phone that bothered her. It was the chest-thumping and the posturing that drove her nuts. Not all of the guys did it, but still, she worked better in a little oasis. Plus, she missed the intimacy of a foreign bureau. This way, her beloved collection of reference books and foreign-language fiction blocked the view.

Anna pulled out the ergonomic swivel chair and sat down. Who to call first? She knew the police and the Bank would soon release statements, but they would lack heft. In any event, they could be procured online, pro forma, and she could check the wires. For the juiciest meat, she wanted to see for herself. One guy stuck out in her mind: Sasha. She took out her phone and dialed.

Chapter 3

Miami – Tuesday, Feb. 18, 7:00 a.m. EST

Liberated from the morning traffic congestion on Biscayne Boulevard, Theo van Torenmaas sped along MacArthur Causeway to his emergency meeting in Miami Beach. The top on his sports car was down. Driving into the rising sun, he wore aviator sunglasses to protect his light blue eyes and a white baseball hat on his pink bald head, which burned easily. His Swiss watch and gold necklace glittered in the morning light.

On his left, the palm trees in the median flew by. Mansions with docks lined the edges of Hibiscus and Palm Islands. Glorified sandbars, he thought. On his right, the Main Channel of the Port of Miami lurked practically level with the road, as if it might rise up and bleed over onto the highway with the next rain. Cruise ships waited for passengers along the pier. Behind them, the real icons of adventure—cranes, ships and cargo containers—formed a backdrop to one of the busiest ports in North America.

When the street light ahead turned yellow, Torenmaas gunned it, blowing past tourists in a mid-size sedan. No matter how many times he heard it, the V8 gave him a thrill. Soon, the highway arched upward over Meloy Channel, the final body of water before the barrier island that formed Miami Beach. Torenmaas peered into the marina below the bridge and admired his yacht, the "Angelfish." At 250 feet, she represented the maximum vessel-length allowed, a jewel in the marina's crown.

Five minutes later, Torenmaas slid into the garage of his Art Deco townhome in South Beach, a crash pad near the hotspots—for times when he didn't want the seclusion of Key Biscayne. Listed on the National Historic Register, the place had been retrofitted with the latest fortifications and electronics, while maintaining period charm and authenticity. Torenmaas parked, jumped out and surveyed the beach clothes and bathing suits in the gear room. He kept his white polo and khaki shorts on, but switched from loafers to flip flops. He grabbed a beach towel hanging on a hook, threw it over his shoulder and marched out the side door, heading east on South Pointe Drive.

The neighborhood was still sleepy—no hip hop blaring, no partiers pulsing at the beach club. He passed a trailer that would sell tropical smoothies and gourmet tacos, starting in a couple of hours. The air smelled of salt water.

Where the road dead-ended, a thicket of sea grapes, native grasses and yucca blocked the view of the ocean. Cars were forced to U-turn, but pedestrians could trudge through the dunes to the water's edge, or walk along a promenade. Torenmaas chose the paved path. Soon enough, the boardwalk reached its southernmost point and dumped him onto the white sand for a few hundred yards. The Atlantic Ocean came into full view—clear and turquoise, like the Caribbean Sea. South Pointe Park Pier jutted out, demarcating the entrance to the man-made channel known as Government Cut, and a container ship headed out to sea, right there next to the public park and the tourist beach.

Slogging through the sand toward the pier, Torenmaas spotted a skinny, black-haired man with creamy skin wearing white pants, a short-sleeved light blue buttoned shirt and a straw Havana Fedora. The man was eyeing two women as they jogged by.

Torenmaas walked up to him and said, "What's the matter, jackass? Been stood up?"

"Theo! I didn't recognize you at first. You're, uh, tan. And you've gained...weight!" he laughed. "You look like one of those wealthy Germans seeking a 'single lady'."

"Ever the joker," Torenmaas said, shaking the man's hand.

It was true that Torenmaas had put on some kilos, but Jimmy Lin knew full well that Torenmaas was Dutch, not German, and that Dutch people despised being mistaken for their prominent neighbors. Most people couldn't tell Torenmaas' origins, especially since he had dropped the "van" whenever he was in the States—people never used it anyway and he got tired of explaining how his name worked. But a "d" sound when there was an English "th," and a "g" that came out like a cough gave him away to the attuned listener.

"You are as slim and trim as ever," Torenmaas added.

"Healthier than you!" Lin replied, smacking Torenmaas on the shoulder. "Good to see you in person."

Torenmaas smiled with his mouth closed, like a perturbed parent. "Listen, Jimmy, let's not discuss this on the beach. We can talk at my place. Better creature comforts. Better beverages. I could make you a cafecito."

"I don't need a beverage. Besides, the wind and surf will kill any attempt to record our conversation—by you or anyone else."

"Tiny microphones and cameras are everywhere now, my friend. Satellites. Drones. You can't hide in the public sphere anymore."

"My team has examined this area. Where the waves roll in, it is very difficult to record."

"So be it. You have always been quirky, Jimmy. I acquiesce in the interest of old times, but our next rendezvous will be according to my specifications."

"We'll see about that."

Discussing local real estate, they eased their way toward the water's edge. The jogger-yoga-health-nut crowd was circulating full-throttle, and a few early birds were lying in the sun. In some quarters, the two mismatched men might have seemed odd, but amid the global mix in Miami all year round, nobody looked twice as they sauntered together along the waterline.

Once they passed the first life-guard station, Lin changed the subject. "What's this all about, Theo?"

"Do you need me to spell it out?"

"Why don't you review the order?"

"Fine," Torenmaas said, rattling off every item in Lin's shipment.

"Alright," Lin said, nodding. "It's already in your possession?"

"Jimmy, you know I don't keep perishables in my facilities until the last minute."

"Not even among the coffee beans or the sugar?"

"Everything will remain in safekeeping until loading."

"And delivery?" Lin asked.

"Same as it ever was. My friends at the port here in Miami sign off on the departure; your friends at the port there oversee the arrival. Everyone is handsomely rewarded. A four-way win," he said. "Let's get to my concerns."

"You will have your money, Theo," Lin assured him.

"That's not it."

"What, then?"

"Even for you, the financing on this deal is unorthodox."

"What's not to like? The final payment will be in US dollars. We priced-in the forex fees and hedged against exchange rate shocks."

Torenmaas studied the hotels and condos stretching north up the coast as far as the eye could see. "We've always worked well together, Jimmy. You are no fool, and I know you believe this scheme is airtight. But I don't agree."

"You don't need to worry about the baht taking a nosedive."

"I don't give a shit about the value of the baht, Jimmy."

"So what the hell is your problem?"

"It's not the payment per se. It's the origin of the money. Where is the buyer originating the funds? Normally, I am happy to feign ignorance. It protects us. But usually I can read between the lines, and it comforts me."

"The buyer has connections in the international development community, aid agencies, NGOs. He's 'reallocating', as it were."

"A 'reallocation' I could have guessed. But why are you comfortable with this vague source? It's easier to deal with the Russians!"

"You're being paranoid, Theo."

"I'm asking again. Who the hell is financing the buyer?"

"What difference does it make? Why should this be any different from any of our other clients?"

"Because it is. Our deals have always followed a certain pattern, a straightforward duplicity, if you will: We source and prepare goods for shipping. We transport, deliver and negotiate. We utilize holding companies and secure offshore accounts at the best private banks."

"It's good, Theo. This Thai bank meets our standards. It's not on the Interpol watch list. They can handle the volume without triggering safeguards."

"What about that shit show, Global Transparency? Maybe it's a trap."

"You're having second thoughts," Lin said, straight-faced.

"Be serious for a minute. I want to conduct this business as much as you do, Jimmy, but only if it's not going to screw everything else up. We don't need this anymore. We're getting too old."

"I hear you. I wouldn't mind some time on the Angelfish, and that's precisely the point. This deal will secure you and me forever, Theo."

"That's what the old guys always say, Jimmy, right before they're locked up or blown to bits," Torenmaas said, facing the Atlantic. The surf crashed.

"My people have been all over this bank. Cybersecurity checks out. All the usual routing transfers and diversions will be in place, and the payments made incrementally. None of the transactions will trip the triggers. And I have a half dozen contacts inside Thailand who can help us out, if anybody gets too curious. Let me deal with this, Theo," Lin reiterated. "It's all under control."

Chapter 4

Bangkok – Tuesday, Feb. 18, 9:00 p.m. local time (9:00 a.m. EST in DC)

Striding across the roof deck of Heaven's Gate, located on the 67th floor of a bank building near the Chao Phraya River, Jesse Martin weighed which was worse—the unexpected call he had received or the restaurant's location. His wife Joanna, bronzed from pool-side sunbathing and all dressed up in her flowy dress, bounded ahead of him. Dining al fresco in the sky had been her idea, and he didn't want to disappoint her—they were supposed to be on vacation, after all.

Joanna passed the Italianate fountain that the tourists were using as a backdrop for their selfies, right up to the waist-high Plexiglas barrier on the edge. Leaning over, she looked down and reached out, as if she could touch the ground. She laughed out loud, her perfectly highlighted hair swirling in the wind.

Bangkok's lights glittered to the horizon—far more skyscrapers than 30 years ago. It was literally breathtaking. Stuffed into his navy-blue suit, Jesse wheezed, as the renewed realization of their place up in the air punched him in the gut. At six-and-a-half feet tall and over 300 pounds, his oversized body, calibrated for the frigid winters and scorching summers of America's Great Plains, betrayed him here. As his stomach turned, his skin acquired an unhealthy khaki cast. He imagined Joanna blowing away, although he knew she wouldn't abide such a thing. His woman might be light as a quail feather but she was also fearless as a mama cougar.

Joanna brushed her delicate hand by his ear, along the side of his crew cut. "Do you want to leave?"

"I'll be OK. You have your fun."

At the center of the rooftop patio, Jesse kept his fear at bay. By the time they finished their entrees, however, his stomach rebelled again, and he excused himself to visit the restroom. Upon his return, Joanna relieved him of his suffering.

"Let's go meet Ko," she said. "Right now."

"Wouldn't you like dessert?" he asked.

"Come on, dear, it's written all over your face. You need to get down from here—you're like a bull in a tree. Plus, you're anxious to see what he wants. His call was irregular, and now you're worried."

Jesse bit his lip. There was no use lying.

"Ask for the check," she said. "It's fine. I'll order dessert at Ko's."

"If you insist," Jesse said.

In a matter of minutes, Jesse had settled the check and slipped a tip to the attendant to maneuver a ride down without the usual wait. As soon as he set foot on the ground, he was restored. He had to wonder—would he be as uncomfortable in the real heaven?

Jesse guided Joanna down a marble hallway to a row of taxis under a portico. The bellman, wearing a black-and-gold uniform and cap with white gloves, hailed the next car. He asked Jesse their destination in English, wrote it down on a pad and handed the driver a slip of paper with the address written in Thai. The driver presented a different piece of paper to Jesse—information about taxi safety in Bangkok, also in English, including a warning about a legal requirement for the driver to turn on the meter. The attendant opened and shut the door for Joanna. Jesse walked around to the other side.

Once in the cab, windows closed and AC cranking, Jesse leaned forward. The meter was off. Addressing the driver in Thai, he negotiated a fare and described the route to Ko's hotel. The driver offered a cheap price and compliments on Jesse's language skills. Jesse leaned back, pleased.

Traveling on the left side of the road, as per Thailand's British-style traffic rules, they crawled toward the Taksin Bridge, and Jesse drank in the big city of his childhood. They passed shops selling everything from electronics to fruit to clothes and Buddha statues. The roads were narrow and lights bright. He observed a vendor selling noodle soup, another with kebabs. In an alley, a group of people were sitting and laughing. A bowl of pinkish shells on the table revealed they had been eating shrimp. Further down, a girl was doing homework in the back of a shop. Electrical and telecoms lines drooped from poles and were tacked along walls in thick bundles—some as low as waist-level. Metal gates protected a mansion, sandwiched between other structures, crumbling on one side.

The taxi came to a stop at a traffic light. Slowly a sea of scooters and mopeds engulfed them, headlights beaming. One by one they pushed to the front of the intersection to wait—as if the cars were boulders, stationary objects to be circumnavigated. The motorbike drivers crab-crawled along the pavement to maneuver tight turns around idling cars. Once the light turned green, their engines roared and poofed out a cloud of black soot.

Flood lights reflected on the gold roof of a Buddhist temple, illuminating the night sky. Dilapidated two-and-three story row homes decorated with fancy ironwork and shutters reflected faded colonial French influence. Sleek new high-rises cried out to the country's burgeoning middle class.

Joanna broke the silence. "Oh!" she chirped. "Look at those buildings. Some of their windows are missing. It's like they're abandoned. Kind of apocalyptic."

"They are. Abandoned, that is. They're called ghost towers," Jesse said. "Vertical scrap heaps."

Joanna grimaced.

"Some people even climb them," he said above the roar of a couple of tuk tuks, which raced by over the center line. "At least the advertising agencies have the sense to project images and unfurl giant banners on them. Nobody wants to pay for demolition."

"There are so many—once you notice them," she said.

"Developers went broke, after the collapse of the baht back in '97," he said. "An agonizing reminder—and a warning."

"It could happen again."

"You know how it is. Crashes come and go, like tornadoes and ethnic conflicts. Eventually there's another big one."

A vehicle that looked like a pickup truck with benches installed long ways in the back pulled up next to them. It was filled with women.

Jesse saw Joanna staring at it. "It's called a songthaew. Works like a bus," he said.

"Yes," she whispered.

Jesse clenched his teeth. The image of the abandoned towers stuck in his mind. Financial crises, storms, battles, what's the difference, he thought. All were subject to the same cycles of destruction and rebirth. Some areas—destined to recover, others to fester. Sad to think Bangkok might never rid itself of these wrecks. Would they crumble and take their squatters with them?

When they crossed the bridge, Jesse looked upriver. A water taxi zipped past a container ship. A million lights reflected in the water— midnight blue, red, yellow and white. How different from the browns, golds and greens of the Great Plains.

Suddenly, the taxi was pulling into a drive.

"We're there," Jesse said. "Ko's hotel. Let's find out what the hell is so urgent."

Chapter 5

Washington, DC – Tuesday, Feb. 18, 10:00 a.m.

Anna waited for Sasha Bolokov, assistant vice president for international finance and investment at the World Bank Group, to pick up the phone. She hoped he could get her onto the scene. Right before the fourth ring, he answered. "Hello, Anna! I gather you've heard our news," Sasha said in his proper BBC English.

"It's all over social media," she said. "I'm sorry for your loss. Everyone must be devastated."

"It is a tragedy," he said, pausing. "But I thought you might call—the silver lining. I'd love to see you."

"Thanks, I guess. I mean, I wish the circumstances were different, but do you have a little time? I could use your insider's view."

"It's a madhouse around here, and I've an important meeting at 1. But how about an early lunch? We could meet here at the Bank. 11?"

"Great. That would be perfect."

"I'm looking forward to it. It's always lovely to see you, Anna."

"You too. Thanks. See you soon." Anna shook her head. Sasha had always been such a flirt.

SOURCE OF DECEIT

Leaning her elbows on the desk and her head in her hand, she rifled through her memories seeking links to the dead man. People with an axe to grind liked to talk—but sources who gained from another's loss weren't reliable. Several leads came to mind. She sent emails and left phone messages, and despite Tanner's scoff, contacted Jennifer Reynolds, one of the Bank's best PR people, a woman with whom she had gone to journalism school. Anna also scanned the program from the Starlight gala, which included a list of participants. Guessing which individuals may have seen Channarong earlier that evening, she reached out to them too.

Soon it was time to go. She donned her coat, grabbed her bag, and wound through the newsroom past her colleagues' desks. On one of them stood a name plate announcing Raven Garcia. A pang of anxiety stabbed Anna's stomach. She tightened her left fist, like her father used to do, then rolled her eyes at herself, and went outside.

The World Bank was a dozen blocks away—close enough that a stuffy taxi ride wasn't worth it. Walking briskly, she passed one standard twelve-story structure after the other. That so many of Washington's office buildings looked simple had surprised her once—the first time she had seen DC was during a summer internship after her freshman year. Growing up in a small town in southern Illinois, she had expected more from the capital of the entire nation. Only later did she come to see that the lack of design belied the influencers inside.

Approaching H Street, she caught the Metropolitan Club in view, one of the exceptions. Imposing but not ostentatious, it flew a blue and yellow "MC" flag above the entrance. She crossed the street to walk right next to it, then skimmed her hand along the stone facade, paying homage to her deceased mentor, a well-connected old dog who had made a point of counseling upstarts, no strings attached. She had eaten lunch with him at the club a few times. His integrity and generosity had been unwavering. At the time, she had taken those qualities for granted. Looking back, she thought of them as rare. She wondered, had there always been a paucity of people of good character?

The doors at the main entrance to the Bank slid open automatically when Anna advanced. She placed her coat and bag on the conveyor belt of the X-ray machine, and a stone-faced guard signaled for her to pass through the metal detector. She grabbed her things and proceeded to the reception desk, where she offered the usual information. Expressionless, the receptionist printed a pass and told her to wait.

She sat down on a bench. Sunlight streamed into the atrium, reflecting off the white-washed walls. Anna had read that the architects intended the interior to symbolize light and goodness, and she admired the sentiment. Yet she wondered about the shadowy underbelly, especially in the wake of Channarong's death. After all, the World Bank office in DC was the global headquarters of what was arguably the most important international financial institution in the world. Its aim was to help poor countries afford development projects. Its detractors, however, argued it failed to alleviate poverty, maybe even stoked it. Protests were likely to flare up again in a few weeks for the semiannual meetings, but for now the demonstrators remained at bay. On balance, how was the Bank really doing?

Shifting her glance, Anna saw Sasha approaching from the far side of the atrium. By all accounts, he was a very good-looking man—and he knew it. He was almost six feet and three inches tall, or "one ninety," as he would say, and his facial structure was just the right amount of chiseled. He wore his dirty-blond hair slicked back and his beard trim. As always, his clothes were perfectly tailored. Today, he had on a white, collared shirt and a slim-line navy blue suit. A cerulean pocket square and tie perfectly matched his eyes, and his light skin was naturally flawless. Anna knew Sasha was an American citizen, but it was easy to understand why, between his accent and this City of London look, people often mistook him for English.

"Anna, darling! You look amazing," he announced, as he walked up and kissed her on the cheek.

"Thanks, Sasha," she said, smiling. "How are you? This is pretty difficult news."

"Yes, yes, yes," Sasha murmured as he signaled her to follow. "This way."

They ambled back through the atrium toward the elevator bank.

Half-way, Sasha stopped. "You were right to come and get a look. The coroner was here. Bomb-sniffing dogs and a homicide unit too. I saw them myself. Quite extraordinary." Moving again, he continued in a low tone. "It's been crawling with police—our own security service, the MPD, and a selection of clean-cut mystery men. Probably FBI." The elevator's bell chimed. "More outside the lift."

As they boarded, Anna nodded to the occupants—three well-dressed women, roughly her own age. The one on her left was petite, and wore red-framed glasses and a long brown braid down her back. She was feverishly typing on her phone with both thumbs. The second, a tall dark-haired woman in the middle carrying a stack of reports, nodded back at her, and the third, who had the white-blond hair of the Icelandic girls that Anna travelled with during college, stared down into the right corner, seemingly lost in her own thoughts.

Anna and Sasha turned their backs on the women, according to the demands of elevator etiquette, and faced the door. On the next floor up, all three women filed off. As the doors closed, they glommed on to one another, whispering as they walked. Anna wondered if they knew Channarong.

At the top, Sasha and Anna headed to the executive dining room, where Sasha had reserved a table. As soon as they were seated, a waiter offered wine and announced the daily specials at the buffet—grilled fresh wild Alaskan salmon with mango chutney and Swiss chard, pot roast of

100% grass-fed beef with French beans, and Rajasthani curried lentils with brown rice.

Anna scoffed at the prospect of mid-day alcohol, while Sasha ordered a Malbec. The two of them walked over to the buffet, and as she served herself, Anna computed what it would cost the newspaper to subsidize such an elaborate buffet for its employees. When they returned to the table, Sasha's wine glass was waiting. Classical music played in the background.

"It's good we're here early," he said, looking around. "No big ears."

"What about big eyes?" Anna said. "Are you sure this is OK? Being seen with me?"

"I can handle myself," Sasha said, smiling at her. "And you."

"I don't know about that."

"Besides, whatever I tell is on deep background," he said, drinking a sip of wine.

"Of course," she agreed. Sasha would never speak on the record about such a sensitive topic.

"Well," he said, voice faltering slightly. "It does...throw things off around here."

"I'm sorry. Were you two close?"

"No, no," Sasha said. "It's just, he was such a brilliant fellow. You've seen his c.v.?" he continued, pausing for a bite. "I mean, Phi Beta Kappa undergraduate, PhD in finance at the ridiculously young age of 24, five years at a top-tier investment bank in New York. Ten years in London, where he cinched his reputation as a star. By 40, he could have chosen to work at any hedge fund he wanted—could have easily founded one— maybe held a central bank or cabinet post at home. But he chose to come here! Settled in Georgetown."

"He was a scientist too, no?" Anna commented as she ate. "His bio says he had a double major in finance and environmental ecology, undergraduate. After he came to the Bank, he earned a master's degree in fisheries science."

"Agriculture is not my field," Sasha said. "But anyone could see he was the rare bird who could both walk the walk, and talk the talk. Agricultural development. Poverty reduction. Clean water and all that. He went around lecturing about giving back to community and country. People loved to hear him gab. People believed in him."

"He was here about eight years? I guess he was pushing 50?"

"Seems so."

"You know, I heard him speak at the Starlight gala—last night. Last night! Bizarre."

"I know. Huge event. I was there too. Everybody was."

"But what's the scuttlebutt around here? Does his professional prowess relate to his death?"

"I don't know. Maybe it does. Maybe it doesn't. But that's the thing. His c.v. was sterling, and yet, contrast that with his private life. A total cock-up."

"A total cock-up?"

"A total cock-up," Sasha repeated, looking straight at Anna. "It was an open secret he was having an affair with his assistant, for example. Like the women in the elevator."

"What are you talking about? Was she in there with us?"

"No, no. There are a lot of young women around here."

"What's that supposed to mean?" Anna cringed. "What are you trying to say? That they are sleeping around? Or that Channarong pressured his assistant? Or what?"

"All of the above," he said, shrugging. "You don't have to have much imagination to wonder."

"Ew," Anna protested. "But..."

"Look, I'm just saying," Sasha interrupted. "In private life, he was a one-man soap opera."

"Such as?"

"Such as: His son is a heroin addict; his wife Grace is the mistress of Senator Caleb."

"What! Senator Lucas Caleb? What does she see in him?"

"What does anyone ever see in situations like this? Think about that governor and his mistress from Argentina."

Anna groaned.

"He's estranged from his daughter, who went back to Thailand or something. A brother at home is involved in human trafficking. It could be basic child labor, without the sex trade piece."

Anna harrumphed.

"You wanted to hear what people say. There are lots of reasons why such a man might get in trouble."

"Or maybe lots of reasons why people are jealous and make things up."

"What if it's all true?" Sasha said.

"Sasha, the man is dead. Have some respect."

"It's easier to assume it's true."

"I'm sure you don't believe this stuff, at least not everything."

"Look, it's clear he had a dark side, his marriage was on the rocks, and he had financial problems."

"Any more details—either on the wife or the financial problems?"

"That's your job, I'm afraid."

"Mm-hmm," Anna said. "What about the investigation?"

"Three-ring circus."

"Have you gone to his office?"

"I peered down the hallway, but I didn't try to pass."

"Can we go there now?" Anna asked.

"By all means," Sasha replied.

Chapter 6

**Bangkok – Tuesday, Feb. 18, 10:30 p.m. local time
(10:30 a.m. EST in DC)**

The Martins' taxi pulled into the circular drive at the Royal Independent Hotel in Bangkok. Golden trumpet flowers, fan palms, and ginger plants—with their phallic red protrusions popping out of waxy green foliage—lined the entryway. Jesse overpaid the driver, aware the extra baht amounted to an outrageous amount by local standards. He didn't buy into the nonsense that his pocket change would "spoil" the drivers, or that he was being cheated.

Attendants bowed to greet them, and Jesse followed as Joanna floated through the main entrance, across the mosaic tile, beneath a crystal chandelier the size of a small car, and down a hallway. Passing the reception desks and expansive lounge area, she knew the bar Silk River lay hidden in the back. As they entered, they recognized Ko Maung Mai's distinctive bushy eyebrows and rimless eyeglasses from afar. His hand cupping a snifter of clear, viscous liquid, he was sitting at a river view table.

Joanna waltzed over. "Ko," she said, extending her arm to shake hands and turning her head coquettishly.

"Good evening, Joanna," said Ko, now towering over her, returning her handshake and kissing her on the cheek, American-style. "I'm honored to see you. Did Heaven's Gate live up to your expectations?"

"It was divine—although Jesse hated it." She laughed. "But he put up with me. Their chef is incredibly talented. Have you been there?"

"Not to eat, I'm afraid; just drinks," he said, shaking Jesse's hand as well and gesturing to the chairs across from him. "Please, sit down. What can I offer you this evening? A brandy? Their selection is outstanding."

The waiter darted over.

"Coffee for me," Jesse replied. "Joanna is thinking about dessert."

"Coffee too, please," she said.

"By all means," Ko said. "Coffee for my friend and this beautiful lady, and bring the dessert menu," he told the waiter, who scampered off.

As soon as the waiter returned, Ko ordered his second drink, while Jesse stuck with the coffee, despite Ko's encouragement to sample Silk River's finest French pear brandy. Joanna ordered a flourless chocolate cake with mocha ganache and raspberry coulis.

"Your timing is fortuitous, Jesse," Ko said.

"You can thank Joanna for that. She planned this trip. We're taking a hiatus."

Ko inquired about their vacation plans at length, but as soon as Joanna had finished her dessert, he changed tack. "Now," he said, looking at her. "I must inquire, would you, Joanna, be interested in exploring the hotel library—a rare collection on the penthouse level?"

"You're suggesting I shouldn't be privy to your conversation with my husband? I thought you were the liberated type," Joanna remarked.

"Ah, Joanna, I'm sure your opinion would enrich the discussion, but if you chose to avoid it, let me say, it would be for your own good."

"Ko, you don't realize how ridiculous you sound," she said, laughing and looking at her husband.

Jesse did not react.

A second later, Joanna capitulated. "Fine. Ko, I will go upstairs, and I don't even mind. But I won't do it because you are pretending to protect me. I will go as a favor to you, in the interest of your privacy."

"Thank you, Joanna," Ko said, reaching out to shake her hand again. "I didn't mean any disrespect."

"Of course not. It's getting late. You men stay out all night, if you want. I'll get my rest."

"Sure you don't mind, Joanna?" Jesse asked.

"The receptionist will call me a taxi. But don't let me catch you sleeping on our floating market tour tomorrow," said Joanna, smiling as she walked away.

Jesse looked at Ko, who was watching Joanna disappear down the hall. "You must have something serious to convey, Ko. This meeting comes as unexpected. I had no idea you were even here."

"Actually, I just arrived. I left early yesterday on that flight from Dulles through Dubai. I was on my way up north for a rendezvous with my cousin. But by the time I got here, all hell had broken loose. I was still at the airport, when I contacted you."

Jesse opened his eyes wide, but said nothing.

"You haven't heard?"

"What? I've been on vacation. Spit it out!"

"Nou Channarong is dead," Ko told him.

"The Executive Director at the Bank?"

"How many Nou Channarongs do you know?"

"Shit," Jesse said, making a low whistle. "Whoo-eee," he said, slapping his own knee. "Shit!"

"I don't need to convince you that discretion is of the utmost importance."

"Are you telling me to pipe down?" Jesse said, laughing heartily. "Nobody in here cares one whit."

"Let's not draw attention to ourselves."

"Son of a bitch," Jesse said, shaking his head. "What the hell happened to him?"

"Looks like suicide."

"Did you offer him a little help?" Jesse chortled.

"I was traveling, Jesse."

"Isn't that convenient? What an alibi!"

"Does this amuse you?" Ko asked, noting Jesse's jowls bobbing as he laughed.

"A car accident would look better," Jesse said. "More tragedy, less mystery."

"Maybe I should be asking you about it, then, Jesse," Ko snapped.

"I have been on vacation for a couple of weeks, my friend," Jesse answered. "Out of pocket. Same as you. Isn't that nice?"

"Oh so very nice," Ko said.

"Why were you coming over here now?"

"I have to check on things. I told you that."

"You're not trying to say that I could be behind it, of all people?" Jesse said, placing his right hand over his heart. "If you want to do that, I could point the finger right back at you." Jesse chuckled some more.

"Look," Ko said. "I don't see the humor in it. Now I have to explain this to Keng."

"Yes, you do," Jesse drawled.

"He will not be pleased. Why do you look so smug?"

Jesse sat back. He pushed his lower lip outward, and his eyelids drooped. "People are fragile. Sometimes they commit suicide. Tragic, sick, sad, what have you, but it's pretty simple."

"You are saying he just went and hung himself?"

"Sure."

"His death could draw attention to us, and everything we have worked for."

"You worry too much, brother. Go back to that mansion in McLean and take a load off. We are well-insulated."

"And how thick is that insulation?"

"Thick enough. We didn't have anything to do with it," Jesse said, drinking his coffee. "Right?"

Ko looked away.

"Any talk of a suicide note?" Jesse asked.

"One hasn't been released."

"You're not worried our operation has ties to this joker?" Jesse asked.

"Let's pray it doesn't," replied Ko, downing the last of his brandy.

Chapter 7

Washington, DC – Tuesday, Feb. 18, 11:30 a.m.

When Anna and Sasha arrived on Channarong's floor, Anna witnessed the hubbub that Sasha had been talking about. Several people tried to push into the elevator before she and Sasha had even stepped out. Uniformed officers from DC's police—known as the Metropolitan Police Department or MPD—as well as investigators wearing FBI badges, and others, crowded the foyer.

"To the right," Sasha said. "I'll follow you."

Stepping into the fray, she took stock. Two men wearing business attire and World Bank IDs were typing on their devices while leaning against a wall. Next to them, a woman was writing notes on a pad of paper—but Anna didn't recognize her as another journalist. An FBI guy was speaking on the phone and three other people were discussing something amongst themselves. The competing conversations seemed to cancel each other out. Two more officers walked past single-file, while a few women headed toward them.

Anna began to walk down the hall. Security guards stood near her, halfway down, and at the far corners, six in total, like sentries.

Channarong's office was about two-thirds down—she could tell, because people were entering and exiting like bees at a hive.

"Shoot," Anna said. "It is a madhouse."

"What did I tell you?" Sasha whispered into Anna's ear. He pushed against her.

Anna glanced behind her at him. Why the push?

"Excuse you," he muttered.

What? Anna was confused. She followed the sight line of his death stare and noted two women rushing off, one in flats, the other in spiked heels cradling a large pile of spiral-bound reports. One of them had evidently imbalanced Sasha, causing him to stumble into her.

"Idiot," he said.

"Forget it," Anna told him.

Sasha proceeded but was stopped by the first hallway guard, big like a linebacker. He held up his hand in a "stop" signal.

"Good afternoon," said Sasha, holding up his ID card. "As you can see, I'm…"

Before he finished, the guard said, "No access at this time."

"Alright, but I need to be over there," Sasha protested. "On the other side of the hallway, down there. We won't touch anything."

"Sir, no access to this hallway at this time," the guard said.

"There must be some exceptions. I'm Sasha Bolokov, assistant vice president for international finance and investment, and I'm going to be late."

"No, sir. No access," the guard repeated the third time. "I don't care who you are."

"It's fine," Anna added. "We'll go around."

"No," Sasha said, resting his hand on Anna's forearm and directing his attention at the guard. "All those people are already over there. Are you going to make us go all the way around?"

"What's wrong with you, man?" the guard said, raising his voice and striding toward Sasha. "Those people are assisting with the investigation. You are not. Go a different way. Or come back later."

Sasha turned around.

Anna tutted at Sasha's obstinacy. "He's just doing his job."

"Come on," Sasha said. "Let's go."

Anna followed Sasha, checking her text messages and voicemail as she went. Back at Sasha's office, they sank into his arm chairs.

"Was that long enough?" Sasha asked.

"For what?"

"For information gathering?"

"I don't know. I saw the 'circus,' as you put it."

"Did you see that woman—the one when I bumped into you?"

"The tall one in the spiked heels?"

"No. The one in the flats—it was Channarong's assistant, Sara Reedman—the one I was telling you about."

"Remind me what she looked like," Anna said, fiddling with her phone.

"Tall. Thin. Pretty. Long, straight dark-brown hair in a low ponytail. Brown skin. Parents from India, if I'm not mistaken."

"Here," Anna said, showing her phone to Sasha. "Ever since I got here, I've been checking my messages—and taking pictures."

"You are slightly clever, after all."

"One can only hope. Now, see if she's in the photos, and tell me if you notice anything."

Sasha swiped through the photo gallery. "Here she is—from behind—white skirt, black sweater. It seems you shot some great photos, but none of them captured her from the front."

"Oh, white pencil skirt, black cardigan, cute shoes. I remember that. It's alright. I'll find her on social media or the Bank's website. I'm sure I can find her face."

"Also," said Sasha, pointing at a sallow man in his early 60s in a white button-down and khakis.

"Your regular computer guy?"

"Officially, yes. His name is J.D. Smith. People around here say he's a spook."

"CIA? What's he doing here?"

"God only knows," Sasha said.

"Fine, I'll check him out," Anna said, noting a World Bank directory on the coffee table. "Hey! Can I borrow that?" She pointed at the booklet.

"That old phone directory? Sure."

"Great," she said, snapping it up. "It's time I got back to the office to make some calls."

Sasha stood up. "I hate to see you go. But I suppose I should take care of a few things myself. I'll escort you downstairs."

When they had returned to the atrium by the main entrance, Sasha bid Anna farewell with a kiss on each cheek. "Let's get drinks together soon," he suggested. "I'll tell you if I find out anything more, and you can update me on Sara and that dodgy one, Smith."

Chapter 8

Washington, DC – Tuesday, Feb. 18, 7:00 p.m.

Anna was pacing in the lobby of the E Street Cinema, when one of its six doors flew wide open and crashed into a tall metal garbage. A stunning young Black woman tumbled into the place. She had long straightened black hair, dark brown skin, arched eyebrows and bright brown eyes, and she was visibly out of breath, as if someone had been chasing her. Wearing a black thermal puffer jacket and ripped stone-washed jeans, she looked like a supermodel ready for an outdoor photo shoot.

Looking around, the woman mumbled, "Sorry, sorry," and then rushed toward Anna. "Excuse me, I'm so sorry. Could I use your phone to text my boyfriend? My phone died," she said. The woman stood there doe-eyed.

"Sure," said Anna, shrugging. She unlocked the phone and handed it to her. "Here."

"Thank you so much," said the woman, who began texting.

Anna drifted up to the three sets of double doors and gazed toward the old FBI building for her friend Mel—still no sign of her. Mel hadn't warned Anna she would be late, but that wasn't really unusual. Mel refused to conform to the norms of constant electronic communication. Anna thought about leaving, but after a long afternoon of open questions and unresolved leads, she stuck with the plan to meet Mel in hopes an outing would clear her head.

Movie posters in gilded frames decorated the lobby. A Norwegian spy movie, coming soon, seemed promising. The box office attendant chatted with the trickle of customers as he swiped their credit cards. Still no sign of Mel.

The model was still using Anna's phone, and she was emanating a nervous vibe.

Anna wondered what was up with her boyfriend. Second thought, I don't want to know, she said to herself. I have my own boyfriend troubles—if only Viktor weren't a ten-hour flight away.

"Thanks!" said the woman, interrupting Anna's thoughts and handing the phone back with a flourish, as if presenting a prize.

Anna took the phone back. "No problem," Anna murmured.

"Thank you so much," the woman repeated, squinting, cocking her head, wrinkling up her nose. "I really appreciate it. I guess he got held up. I'm going to wait outside," she said, smiling more, backing off and rushing away.

"No big deal," Anna said. Why so coy?

The woman left as quickly as she had arrived, just as Mel's spikey hair and excellent posture came into sight.

"Who was that?" Mel asked, first thing.

"Who?"

"That woman you were talking to."

"Some woman. I don't know. Hello to you too."

"What do you mean? Some woman? She had your phone," said Mel, giving Anna a hug. "I saw her."

"A random woman whose phone died. She had to text her boyfriend."

"Are you sure? I saw her leave with a woman."

"That's what she said."

"She's quite the specimen," Mel said. "Goddess-type."

"Do you need a matchmaker?" Anna asked.

"I'm still officially single, but no, not really. Things are going well with Saloma."

"Duly noted. So, 'Mayhem,' is it? Are you sure about this film?"

"It got great reviews. Why?"

"I don't know. I feel pretty wound up."

"Want to skip it?"

"Kind of. I'm sorry."

"No worries," Mel said, raising eyebrows expectantly. "Karl's?"

"Thanks," Anna said, spotting a couple waiting on line. "Hey!" she said, holding the tickets up. "Want mine?"

The couple accepted the tickets, and Anna turned back to Mel, who was already halfway out the front door. Anna appreciated how Mel knew what she was thinking. Hanging out was never straining. Ever since they met playing soccer at Illinois State, it had been that way. Mel called Anna the "perfect sibling," the kind that didn't exist in real life, because they didn't fight. She was one of only a few people in the city who knew Mel's real name was Tiffany Melissa Allen.

"Do you mind if we walk?" Anna asked.

"No, it's fine."

They passed Ford's Theater where Lincoln had been shot. A group of high-schoolers herding toward a tourist-trappy rock-n-roll café engulfed them and ebbed, like a human flood.

"Rough day?" Mel asked.

"Need to clear my head," she said.

"The World Bank story, I presume. Want to talk about it?"

"Yes. And no. Not yet. Let's talk about Saloma."

Mel told Anna about her recent date. They turned north and passed the ice hockey/basketball arena in Chinatown. The surrounding stores and restaurants announced themselves in English and Mandarin. Chinese New Year animals looked up from the "zebra stripes" of the crosswalks.

"It's a good thing they put these signs up in Chinese," Anna said.

"Now who's being snarky?" Mel replied. "It's worth paying homage to this old place. Besides, it draws people in. It's reassuring to see the old businesses thriving, even if they have evolved into tourist attractions."

In a restaurant display window, an elderly man rolled, cut and stuffed dumplings with the precision of a celebrity chef. A line had formed in the narrow entryway, as a couple of hostesses escorted people down the steps.

Anna and Mel zigzagged, continuing northward on 5th. Talk of Mel's job carried them to the former industrial yard where the lights and picnic tables of Karl Maria Schachholzer's Restaurant and Beer Garden sprawled along the railroad tracks. Nestled near three universities—east of Howard, west of Gallaudet and south of Catholic—Karl's was the baby of a German economist and an American TV journalist, Lisa Markelli, who had covered the White House. At first Karl and Lisa had offered only coffee and booze, but they rigged the place with free high-speed wifi. When they stabilized, they served the German basics—sausage, potato salad and strudel—and later added the best finger foods the world has to offer—falafel, samosas, kebabs. People couldn't resist. In summer, they put up umbrella tables. In winter, they erected a tent and outdoor heaters. Instead of barges floating by on the Rhine, their customers watched trains trundling along on the rusty tracks.

Karl's quickly became a home-away-from-home for an incestuous in-the-know crowd.

"Maybe we'll catch Garrett Zarribe again," Anna said.

"The guy who used to work on Iran at the National Security Council?" Mel asked.

"Yeah. I'd like to pick his brain on where the White House is going with that new so-called carrot-and-stick approach. He's at that think tank now, the one in Georgetown."

"He won't tell you anything of merit."

"Why not? He doesn't work at the NSC anymore. He can share an opinion—based on his own current independent research and analysis. I'm not asking him to divulge anything he's not supposed to. He's allowed to give us his general understanding."

"He's not the type to talk in public. And he wouldn't tell the *Daily Journal*—even on 'deep background' in a completely secret cave."

"No, he would. He'd be helping me stay informed, which helps him too in the end."

"He's a horse's ass. He doesn't care about educating journalists."

"But he has to keep up his reputation—you know, maintain status as an expert."

"I don't trust him. He has all kinds of ulterior motives—especially with a blonde bombshell like you," she said. "Come to think of it, he probably would talk to you, but what would he want in return? Do you want that type of information?"

"What is that supposed to mean? Blonde bombshell? Ulterior motives? You sound like my grandfather."

"I'm realistic. You shouldn't ignore the fact that people are attracted to you."

"That's not a good enough reason to avoid him. His perspective could be valuable, especially if I keep ulterior motives in mind. You know I won't take his word for gospel. I'll double, triple check, corroborate. Besides, we have mutual friends."

"Sorry to hear that," Mel said. "Wait, who?"

"Rick Nadyam."

"Your old boyfriend—from freshman year? How would they know each other?"

"Rick was best friends with his son, Coho, at boarding school."

"Gross. When was the last time you saw Rick? I didn't know you kept in touch."

"We don't. Not really. Just social media, holiday greetings, that sort of thing. But Rick works in DC. He heard I had moved here and called me. Since you told me about Karl's, I suggested we go there—and that's where we ran into Coho's dad, Garrett Zarribe. Coho is a lawyer now, and he and his dad recently took a giant tour of China. They were pretty informative. I told you about it, Mel. What's the matter with you?"

"I didn't catch that, Anna. Sorry. Rick was not my favorite person. Maybe I wasn't listening."

"Whatever you think of Rick, Coho's dad is a solid contact." Anna glanced at her phone. "Shoot."

"What's the matter?" asked Mel.

Amid the usual churn of her news feeds, emails and messages, Anna saw an unexpected text. She shook her head. What the hell? Do a simple good deed, screw yourself over. "Check this out. It's from that 'goddess' of yours." She showed her phone screen to Mel.

Mel looked at the text.

"Need to see you in private," it said.

"You are such an idiot," Mel told her.

"Ugh," Anna said, dragging out the word. "You know I never give out my private number. Stupid, stupid, stupid."

"Maybe it's a game, a secret-admirer thing."

"Come on, Mel. Even you don't think that."

"Maybe she hacked your phone, inserted malware and tracking."

"Here I thought she was a lost puppy."

"But she was actually a troll."

Anna showed her phone to Mel again. "Look. She sent a message that says, 'Hey, at the theater. Hurry up. I'll get tickets.' But then she sent this other message back to me from the same number that she texted. So was

39

she texting herself? Or is she using someone else's phone?" Anna shoved the phone in her pocket.

"Have tech check it out," Mel said. "And get a new phone."

"It's not that nefarious."

"How do you know? Anna, have the tech department look into it. Maybe she's benign, but maybe she's not."

Anna tilted her head.

"Look, I can't believe I'm saying this, me of all people, but you need to be more careful. Don't forget all that hate you collect in your social media feeds—'bitch,' 'whore,' 'slut'?"

"You forgot 'wench'," Anna said, rolling her eyes and moving her hand in quick circles. "And 'stupid idiot,' 'fucking snowflake,' 'dumb blonde'..."

Mel made a face. "You're a complete fool, Anna, but you're also the guru running the global conspiracy!"

"Yeah, that's why I should be raped and shot, right?" She shrugged. "People say it so often, I'm getting used to it."

"Might as well admit it, Anna. You're an omniscient moron, a slut and a hack for an international cabal."

Anna's phone vibrated just as Mel said "cabal." Both of them flinched.

Anna laughed and pulled out the phone again. "This time she tells me to meet her—like now."

"We're almost at Karl's."

"True, but check this out," she said, showing Mel her phone display again. "She says, 'Really urgent. Have info 4 U'."

"Oh, come on!" Mel laughed. "She has *in. for. ma. tion.* And it's *uuuur-gent!*"

"What's your name?" Anna typed.

"Doesn't matter," the woman texted.

"Does matter. Who are you?" Anna asked.

"Evy. Hurry up."

"Evy what? What info?" Anna wrote.

Standing still now, about a block from Karl's, Anna and Mel waited for a reply. A few moments passed, but nothing came.

"Hang on," Anna said to Mel. "Let me check something." Anna typed and stared, typed and stared at her phone.

Mel made a face.

"Hang on," Anna repeated. "Another text popped up, and it's from her. It says, 'You work for the NYDJ'."

"She knows who you are," Mel said, raising her eyebrows.

"So what?" Anna texted as Mel looked on.

"It's about New deals," Evy wrote. "URGENT!!! Meet me on the patio at the Egyptian."

"New deals?" Anna texted.

"Nou & sketchy deals" Evy replied.

"Why didn't you talk to me at the theater?" Anna texted.

"Will explain. PLEASE NOW! Meet NOW," Evy replied. "I'm being followed."

Anna turned to Mel. "She says 'n-o-u,' as in Nou Channarong—my story."

"She could be bullshitting you."

"True, but even a lie might turn out to be useful. And maybe this is important. I won't know if I don't go. Besides, let's face it—you want to go to Karl's, but you weren't going to hang out with me. Saloma will be there."

For once Mel was quiet.

"I don't want to be a third wheel," Anna told Mel. "On my way," she texted to Evy.

A car pulled up, and Anna raised her hand to it.

"You already ordered a car, didn't you?" Mel asked.

Anna nodded and gave Mel a quick hug. "Thanks for hanging out," she said, jumping into the back seat.

"You go get that scoop!" Mel yelled, as Anna sped away.

Chapter 9

Bangkok – Weds., Feb. 19, 7:30 a.m. local time (7:30 p.m. EST on Tuesday, Feb. 18 in DC)

In a crisp white shirt, slate-blue suit and tangerine tie, Giovanni Salazar approached the marble concierge desk at his hotel in the Sathon district of central Bangkok. Handsome and dark-haired, he was blessed—or cursed, depending on your perspective—with the type of ethnically ambiguous look that fit in equally well in Bangkok or Lima, Madrid or L.A.

The concierge, a middle-aged Thai woman who had seen myriad businessmen come and go, bowed and offered a wai, the traditional Thai greeting of palms pressed together in a prayer position. "*Sawat di kha*," she said. "*Bonjour!* Good morning," she added, unsure which language he preferred.

Salazar nodded and smiled in reply. "Good morning. I'm Salazar. Room 2323. Could you point me toward the restaurant Sathon Stars?" he asked in English.

"Wouldn't you like to try our extensive international breakfast buffet, Mr. Salazar? You will not be disappointed."

"Sathon Stars has excellent online ratings."

"We too have outstanding food and service. Our dining room also offers a traditional Thai garden in the back."

"I'm sure it's wonderful," he said, smiling and nodding at her. "But I have a breakfast meeting."

"Well, then, sir. You may stroll down the soi to the main road. There is a taxi stand on the corner. Otherwise, I am happy to call a car for you."

"What about on foot? I like to meander, better to explore the city."

She tilted her head slightly, puzzled at the high-class foreigner who preferred to walk amid Bangkok's smog and traffic, but she told him the route. He thanked her and, grabbing a complimentary paper copy of the English-language Bangkok Sun from a rack by the revolving door, he departed in the direction she advised.

Several blocks later, where the concierge had told him to turn right, he turned left. He ducked through an alley and entered a luxury shopping mall, snaked through and continued northeast along Silom Road, then Ratchadamri. He passed through a parking lot and the gates of Lumphini Park on the northwest side.

Locals and expats alike were taking advantage of the cooler morning air to run around the lake; some people were cutting through the park for a respite from the heavy street traffic on their walk to work. The music of an outdoor exercise class blared. Not far off, a six-foot monitor lizard lounged along the water's edge. Like a deer in Central Park—but not—he mused. Salazar passed an open-air gym, where several men and women were lifting weights. He kept moving until he reached a bench under the trees on the west side. He sat down and, holding the newspaper up, pretended to read.

Soon, a man wearing a Niagara Falls T-shirt and Orioles baseball hat jogged toward him. Old enough to be Salazar's father but still strong and fit like a bodybuilder, he stopped by the bench, removed his hat, wiped the sweat from his brow and sat on the other end. He brushed his hand through his black hair and put the hat back on. Then, he turned to Salazar briefly and nodded.

"You've been to Niagara Falls?" Salazar asked.

"Oh, yes," the man replied. "Great place to visit."

"I've never been there myself. People say it's for honeymooners."

"Anybody would enjoy it," the man said, again nodding but avoiding eye-contact. "You weren't followed?"

"That's what I'm saying, right, Mr. Gold?"

"Are you sure?"

"I'm sure I convinced the hotel concierge I'm crazy. She thinks I walked all the way to Sathon Stars."

"Better than Soi Cowboy or Patpong," said Mr. Gold, smiling without opening his mouth. "Isn't that where an American man of your age is expected? Farang!"

Salazar remained silent, looking down. Mr. Gold was knowledgeable about many things. Why did he say things like that? The slur farang was vulgar, at the very least old-fashioned. Also, it was unfounded. It was Mr. Gold who went to the go-go bars.

"Very well. You see, if anyone quizzes her about where you went, she will know, and she will not know," Mr. Gold said.

"I used your techniques. I know the drill."

"These precautions are very important," the older man said, leaning over, resting his elbows on his knees and looking at the ground.

"What's wrong? You scheduled this meeting abruptly," Giovanni asked.

"Complications," Mr. Gold said, studying his jogging shoes. "Mr. Channarong is dead."

Giovanni forced a straight face. "That comes as...unexpected."

"Yes, plans have changed. Now, you are to bring the girl here."

"Just like that?"

"Buy her a ticket. Tell her you can't stand to be alone. Something like that. We don't have the time for you to start all over. I'll be in touch," Mr. Gold added, jogging off. "Good day."

Chapter 10

Washington, DC – Tuesday, Feb. 18, 8:15 p.m.

It proved more difficult than expected to reach the Egyptian, a bar and restaurant in a turn-of-the century mansion near Dupont Circle. Anna's driver cut over to Rhode Island Avenue and headed southwest past a development of two-story garden apartments. Brownstones—some boarded up, others with renovated turrets and manicured mini-yards—filled the next blocks. She counted three liquor stores, an organic market, a dry cleaner and two coffee shops. A sign commemorated an Eritrean cultural center, which had recently been knocked down.

At Logan Circle, as they turned west on P Street, Anna took out her phone and ran through her social media feeds, messages and emails. So far, her contacts had said nothing she didn't already know. A text from Sasha read, "Investigation extensive, secretive and atypical. Still working. Will get back to you." Great. Useless update, Anna thought. If this Evy woman provides any ideas, it will be a welcome lead.

"There's a jam up ahead. Looks like a wreck," said the driver, pointing to a map on his phone screen.

"We're almost at Dupont Circle. You can stop here," she told him.

Getting out near the Iraqi Embassy, she walked toward the circle and continued on the outer loop. Not far from the fountain, a few people were setting up a tent. In another section, a group of student types were smoking—a sweet vaguely skunky scent was wafting her way—and a range of others were traversing the park for unknown destinations. She walked a quarter of the way around the circle and continued north on Connecticut Avenue up the hill. Traffic was inching along, one lane in each direction. Emergency lights flashed, sirens blared, and a helicopter circled, low.

Then she knew: The problem was not an accident.

Anna picked up her pace. The police activity was by the Egyptian, which was on a corner where three roads came together—one of those six-way DC intersections where the grid pattern of streets overlaps with a diagonal avenue, creating corner lots like pie pieces. A block away now, she counted five parked police cars and a van, as well as two ambulances and a fire truck. At least a dozen police officers were on the scene. The usually-crowded patio bar was devoid of customers.

She ventured closer. One of the officers was stretching out yellow tape marked "police line do not cross." A few figures were moving around inside the restaurant. Where was Evy?

For a second, she wondered if there was a bomb scare. Anna surveyed the area but didn't see a canine unit. A crowd of onlookers had gathered on the west side of the building across the narrow street from the patio, and the police had not removed them. Probably not a bomb.

A news truck with a satellite on the roof pulled up to the curb.

Anna raced ahead. She overheard a witness talking about a gunshot and a speeding car. A few people were crying. More than once Anna heard someone utter the word "terrorism." She walked up to a woman and said, "Do you know what happened?"

"Some lady got shot!" the woman said.

The man with her added, "We were walking by when we heard a pop. Then all the people ran."

"Did you see who did it?" Anna asked.

"No," the man said. "No, we didn't."

Anna took another few steps and asked a different woman the same question.

"I heard a bang," she said. "I saw people scattering and dropped to the ground, but it was quiet after that."

"Thanks," Anna mumbled. She snapped pictures of the scene and texted them to the bureau.

When she reached the corner opposite the Egyptian, where the cross streets both intersected Connecticut Avenue, traffic was blocked. She pushed through the crowd and skirted the property. An ornamented wrought-iron fence secured the mansion's backyard garden, which bordered the street. People were standing along the fence, pointing and talking. One woman held her cupped hand over her mouth. Garden lights illuminated the patio.

Anna snapped more photos. The patio must have been busy. Now empty of people, it was still full of their things—partially eaten meals, half-full drinks, a baby stroller, knocked-over bottles, a dropped serving tray. Patio heaters in rows like trees in an orchard contrasted with the disarrayed chairs and errant napkins.

Three police officers stood talking in the corner closest to her. Anna gasped. At their feet was a supine woman, arms splayed, face to the side. She was so near that Anna had missed her before. A dark splotch marked the beige patio stones beneath her, and a chair next to her body lay tipped over, an obscene sculpture. Was the woman dead? In an instant, the truth became obvious. There was no question. Perhaps even more shocking was the woman herself. Long black hair, jeans, puffer jacket—she was the woman from the theater. The woman was Evy.

Bile gurgled in the back of Anna's throat. Closing her mouth, she looked away. Guilt washed over her. What if I had been here earlier? Could anyone have prevented this? Why the whole charade with the cell phone? Weren't they going to cover her up?

Anna's mind turned to personal safety. She used to think it was paranoid to worry someone might try to kill her, but now she knew her fears were not unfounded. She had personally met reporters and whistleblowers who were jailed or murdered for truth-telling, and terrorists had tried to kill her boyfriend Viktor while he was covering a plot in Chicago.

Doing her best not to draw attention, Anna backed up and walked off. She headed east, north, east, peering behind her occasionally. Many of the homes' interior lights were on, but there was no time to admire their artwork and antiques. Her phone blipped and vibrated more than usual, but she ignored its cries for attention. She didn't want to appear distracted—or actually be distracted.

At 16th, she turned south again, and when she reached the corner of S, she sat down on the front steps of a church. Checking her phone for the first time in a half hour, she stared at the screen in disbelief. There were many notifications, including 23 text messages from Evy. The final one said, "If you get this, I'm dead."

Chapter 11

Washington, DC – Tuesday, Feb. 18, 10:00 p.m.

Oh my God!" Anna gasped. She knew Evy must have used an app to schedule the texts, but she had never received messages from a dead person before. What a strange new brand of secret! Anna quickly scrolled back to the beginning.

The text messages said: "phone under cedar here; pw = your office address with caps," "corruption at WB," "collected docs, spreadsheet & video," and "can't fit pieces together." The subsequent texts were hyperlinks to web pages. Anna clicked through and saw statistics and legal documents, which could be combed through later. Finding the phone was more urgent.

Anna jogged south and then west on Corcoran, a charming cobblestone street—passing more exquisite brownstones. As she ran back to the restaurant, she tried to figure out what Evy was getting at. What could be on the phone? Was it on the patio? Would it still be there?

Where Corcoran hit 18th, Anna looked right. The police were still blocking R. She went the other way, looping around by the Argentinian

Embassy toward the Dupont Circle metro stop. She retraced her earlier steps up Connecticut Avenue toward the Egyptian.

Most of the emergency vehicles had departed, and traffic on Connecticut was flowing again. The news truck was gone, but the corner by the restaurant was still cordoned off. Where could the phone be? Where were the cedars? Anna found the potted plants, but the bushes in the pots were holly, not cedars. The hedge along the side was boxwood. Anna drew a blank.

Then she spotted a faded mural across the street on a wall near a dumpster at the back of a defunct copy store—and the scene featured a cedar. Anna crossed nonchalantly and walked up to the mural. Something was wedged into a crevice between the wall and the sidewalk beneath the image of the tree. She reached for it—something wrapped in soft paper, the shape and feel of a cell phone. She shoved it into her bag.

Anna hailed the taxi that had been hovering at the corner and directed the driver to the office. En route, she unwrapped the paper. Indeed, inside was a phone. The paper turned out to be a napkin with a note written on it: "AJ - Giving this to a bystander for delivery. Thank God for crumbling walls – EP."

A calm washed over Anna—an autopilot she experienced in extreme stress. She folded the napkin and stuck it in her bag.

The phone she held in her hand. As per Evy's text instructions, Anna typed her office address into the password field in every possible variation. Nothing worked. She worried she'd never figure it out. She wondered what she'd missed. Perhaps I'm thinking too much, she thought. Then, she typed the actual words "YOUR OFFICE ADDRESS" using all caps—nothing. Finally, she tried, "Your Office Address"—and she was in!

"Evy, you rock!" Anna said, regretting her outburst, as Evy could no longer receive the compliment. She clicked on Evy's email app, but Evy wasn't logged in. Still, the phone itself was bound to contain significant information. Anna was anxious to explore its files, but the taxi was pulling up to Anna's office building. She put the phone away, paid and went inside.

The receptionist had gone home hours ago, but Tanner was still at his desk.

"Hey, Jones," Tanner yelled from his glass box. "You look like crap. But your crime scene pictures are good."

Anna walked over to the open office door. "I try. What are you doing here?"

"A bureau chief's work is never done, Jones. You know that. What have you got?" Tanner said in a paternal tone.

"You really want to know—now?"

"It's a hot story. And my wife's not going to miss the wheezing of the C-PAP." Tanner leaned forward, placing his right elbow on the desk and his temple on his right hand. He fixed his eyes on Anna.

She brought him up to speed and showed him the napkin and the phone.

Tanner wasted no time in saying: "Watch your back, Jones."

Anna assessed Tanner's face.

"Yes, I'm serious. I want you to be careful." Tanner reclined, and his chair squeaked. "Local TV and social media have been blowing up over that homicide scene tonight. People are connecting the dots, even if the police aren't."

"Dots?"

"You didn't see? Evy—full name Evy Poole—worked as a program assistant at the World Bank—in the same division as Channarong." Tanner cocked his head back and forth. "Two separate and grizzly deaths at one rarified financial institution in one day equals a lot of very public social media paranoia."

"Shoot. Evy said she had information about Channarong, but she wouldn't tell me anything else. Why didn't she tell me who she was? Why didn't she talk to me at the theater?"

"And what is her direct link to Channarong?"

"Love triangle? Spurned lover?"

"Maybe," Tanner said, scrolling through the sources. "Channarong was charismatic, and he had money. But some are speculating a drive-by or stray bullet."

Anna shook her head.

"I agree. Evy's death wasn't coincidental. If we say she was targeted, it could have been jealousy. A few other reasons also come to mind—punishment, silence. You saw her body. What do you make of it?"

"Witnesses on the scene said they heard one shot. Nobody was talking about stray bullets, gang activity or a melee."

"Very 'professional.' No?"

"As absurd as it sounds, yes. It looks like a hit. But who would want to assassinate a twenty-something World Bank assistant?"

"She alluded to corruption."

"Maybe something will come up in these links," Anna said. "Or in the files on this phone."

"That's your next task. Copy everything—contact list, phone log, text threads, downloads, photos, everything. Then we'll share it with the tech team."

"That's why I came in here. Maybe Jeff or somebody else in tech will see something I don't. And, just so you know, we can't access her email—I already checked; she's not logged in on the phone, and I only have the phone password, not the email one."

"Can you copy the contents in half an hour?"

"Less."

"I'll wait for you," he said. "When tech is finished, I'll call my friend over at MPD and hand it over."

"I didn't think we were obligated to give it to them," she said, frowning.

"We're not. They have to do their own work. But this girl's family will want to know what happened. It doesn't hurt us to tell the police we found the phone."

"Aren't they going to wonder why I had it?"

"So what? You found it and brought it to the office tonight. Jones, listen, you cover a financial beat. This is a little more than you bargained for. Are you alright?"

"I'm fine. This stuff never sinks in until later."

"I mean it, Jones. I don't want you getting hurt. If anything changes, tell me."

"Alright, sir."

"And when you're finished with that data dump, get some sleep, Jones. You're going to need it. Tomorrow, you can have that intern, John Carlston, assist you," he said. "Let me know when you find something."

Chapter 12

Washington, DC – Wedsnesday, Feb. 19, 7:30 a.m.

Carrying a chocolate croissant in a brown bag and a large coffee in a paper cup, Anna walked into the bureau pumped at the prospect of deciphering the story. Tanner saw her coming and waved her inside.

"Get any sleep?" Tanner asked.

"Barely," Anna said. "But it was worth it."

"And?"

"First, I checked out the hyperlinks. Mostly, they go to World Bank project pages—publicly available stuff on the Bank's website. Clues, probably. Then, I downloaded the contents of her phone. On the surface, it looks pretty basic—a couple of podcasts, some music, the usual standard apps, plus a few word games. Then it got weird. Most of the private stuff was wiped—contacts, text log, phone log, downloads, photo history. Nothing, except for one call—somebody called her twice after the shooting from an unlisted number. We need to look into that."

"Alright. Is that it?"

"No. In her text to me, she had mentioned a spreadsheet, video and documents, so I kept looking. Inside of 'playlists,' I found them—contracts on shipping and trade, bank statements, bills of lading, Custom's forms, as well as a thing called 'master spreadsheet' and a video."

"I can have Jeff help dig into that too, if you want," Tanner said.

"Definitely. Thanks. It's a lot to digest."

"Did you watch the video?"

"Yes," she said. "It's of Channarong."

"Channarong?"

"Yes, Channarong. The audio is bad, but it's him. He's dining outdoors at a busy restaurant with palm trees and a beach in the background. He's talking to a man—pale guy, ruddy complexion, maybe in his 60s. If you zoom in, you can see the name of the restaurant on the menu. It's on South Beach in Miami."

"No kidding. Maybe tech can decipher the audio. Who's the dinner partner?"

"I wondered that too, so I went back to search for clues. In this so-called master spreadsheet—which lists details about World Bank projects in South East Asia..."

"This is a World Bank document?" Tanner interrupted.

"Not sure. It might be a draft—no letterhead, no header. It could've belonged to Channarong or someone else with detailed knowledge of these projects, but there's no evidence it was ever released. My sense is it would never be released, either, because it's too detailed. If someone prepared this for the Bank, I think it would have remained internal."

"What's in it?"

"Right, so in this spreadsheet there's a lot of information. Much of it is also posted on the Bank's website—things like project locations, inception dates and total loan amounts, nothing special. But it includes other details I couldn't confirm or cross-reference—notes on hybrid financing, commercial banks, aid agencies, sovereign loans, even potential alternatives. There are also columns of data on currency rates, forex trades, fees, products, and possibly ID numbers."

"Hmm," Tanner nodded and frowned.

"Double books?" she said. "But get this. At the bottom, a little chart shows contacts and coordinates—first and last name, salutation, title, phone number and email."

Tanner made a face.

"Right. And then I noticed the phone numbers have the same area code plus the same first three digits. Turns out they all route to the Miami offices of Theo van Torenmaas."

"Dutch shipping magnate and commodities trader," Tanner stated.

"Also philanthropist—with a reputation for keeping a low profile."

"I know the one. Avoids the party scene, hates charity balls, even when he's the big donor," Tanner said, nodding in recognition. "Well, he could be working with the World Bank."

"It's possible. I called a friend of mine to find out more. She's the assistant director of development at a charity based in the Hague."

Tanner bugged out his eyes a little, leaned his head down and moved his chin into his neck.

"She said even though he's seen as a recluse on the global stage, he's known in society circles. He spends most of the summer and fall in Amsterdam—lives in a beautiful turn-of-the century villa near the Vondelpark, the city's central park. He even has a stable there—actual horses—but he winters in Miami."

"And?" Tanner asked.

"And I had a hunch, so I showed her the video of Channarong with the unknown guy at dinner. She took one look at it and said it's him."

"Is she sure?"

"Yes," Anna said.

"Torenmaas and Channarong knew each other," said Tanner, pressing his lips together. "And the evidence is right there on Evy's phone."

"Yes," Anna said.

"I'll have people here scrutinize the data. Meanwhile, why don't you go to Miami and see Torenmaas?"

"I already booked a ticket."

Chapter 13

Washington, DC – Weds., Feb. 19, 11:00 a.m.

When Anna heard the airport announcement that her flight to Miami would soon board, she rose to wait in line at the gate. In doing so, she noticed a familiar woman making a beeline toward her. Then Anna watched the crowd watching the woman.

She wore a white coat with a waterfall collar, wide white belt, spike-heeled shiny black boots and sleek black pants. A black designer bag hung from her left shoulder, and on her right, she cradled a black teacup Chihuahua. Her lips were coral, eyeliner winged. Gold hoop earrings bounced against her ivory chin, offset by her shoulder-length black hair and dark brown eyes. The outfit was over the top, but Anna had to admit, she pulled it off.

The way Anna saw it, most people fit into categories, especially at airports—personnel, vacationers, IT types, lawyers, military, students, retirees. Even artists tended to display a formulaic "artsy" look. Anna made a game of identifying people outside the box, the folks of mixed semiotics, and this woman was one of those.

Anna caught her eye. "Raven Garcia. Hey."

"Oh, Anna," Raven said, inspecting Anna's simple skinny jeans, ballet flats and blazer. "I heard you were around."

"Bound to land in the same bureau eventually, right?" Anna said.

"Maybe so."

"Where you headed?"

Raven stared at her for a moment before pointing to the monitor at the gate. "What does it look like?"

"Miami," Anna said, trying again. "That's where you're from, right?"

"I grew up there."

"Looks like we're on the same flight."

Raven nodded.

Anna reached out to the creature, who lifted his chin to accept a neck-scratch. "Cute guy. What's his name?"

"Apollo," Raven said, finally breaking a smile as she turned to him. "He loves to fly."

"I see," Anna said, withdrawing her hand. "Have a nice flight."

"Take care." Raven sauntered away.

Anna kept a straight face but did a mental eye roll. The loop of stories on the airport TV repeated itself—pets, natural parks, art exhibit, pets, natural parks, art exhibit. A few minutes later, an announcer called "Group A," and Raven boarded the plane. Anna put her earbuds in and waited for "Group E."

Filing down the aisle, Anna looked at Raven buckled into her first-class seat. Apollo was already sleeping on her lap, and Raven was immersed in a pile of documents. Anna slogged to her window seat in the last row by the bathrooms, where the seats don't recline—the only one left by the time she booked her ticket.

Two-and-a-half hours later, after the pretzels and the ginger ale, Anna was craning her neck, trying to distinguish landmarks. A cumulus cloud occasionally dimmed the light, but for the most part, the bright Florida sun did not disappoint. Tan and brown rectangles of agricultural land, which filled the state's interior, gave way to green lawns and blue pools. The sand traps of a golf course flashed by, and the plane bounced down the tarmac.

As they taxied, the din of the passengers speaking on their phones rose. When the aircraft parked with a jerk, the unclipping of seat belts pinged around the cabin. Too many people stood to remove their bags from the overhead bins at once, even though no one had left the plane. Anna shook her head. Why did most people attempt to leave before it was physically possible?

When she walked up the jet bridge and into the terminal, Anna was surprised to find Raven waiting for her.

"Anna. I have a favor to ask. Could you hold Apollo while I go to the women's room?" she asked, pointing to the doorway. "He hates this bag, and he barks incessantly in public restrooms."

"No problem."

Raven handed Apollo to Anna. "Be right back."

Anna sat down with the dog, who licked her neck as she pet him. "Don't worry, I'm a dog person," she told him.

After a few minutes, Raven rushed back toward them. "Much appreciated," she said, scooping up the creature. "What are you doing in Miami?"

"Work."

"Come on, Anna. I'm making an effort here."

"Researching that World Bank thing."

"The hanging?"

"That's the one."

"What's the Miami connection?"

"I don't know yet," Anna said, weighing how much to tell her. "I've got to meet this shipping guy Torenmaas"

"The philanthropist?"

"The same."

"Hmm," she harrumphed. "He's a big wheel in Miami. Notoriously hard to catch."

"Thanks for the tip."

"I used to work for the paper down here. I should know."

"Really."

"Yes. First job. Local news. Before grad school. So, tell me, what does Torenmaas have to do with it?"

Anna hesitated. "That's what I'm investigating. I've got some leads."

"Like what?"

"Ah," she said, deliberating how much to elaborate. "Like a video of him having dinner with Channarong."

"How did you get that?"

"Twisted mess. Long story. Anyway, what will you be doing this weekend? Beach, art show, club scene?"

"Funeral," Raven said, grimacing.

"Oh," Anna said. "I'm sorry."

"My Cuban side is down here. There's always something."

"Right," Anna said, giving Apollo a pat-pat-pat on the head.

"Well, then, good luck," Raven said with a forced smile. She walked off. After a moment, she called over her shoulder. "If you can't figure it out, call me. I might have a connection."

"Sure," Anna said, trying not to sound facetious. "Thanks," she whispered. Wouldn't you just love that?

Chapter 14

Miami – Wednesday, Feb. 19, 3:00 p.m. EST

Once inside the airport terminal at MIA, Anna bought a couple of empanadas at a kiosk and followed the moving walkways to the rental car complex. She approached the only counter where no one was waiting and had a contract within 10 minutes. Her ride was gutless but cheap—Tanner would appreciate that.

Driving south on Le Jeune, she turned east on the Dolphin Expressway toward the Azure Ocean, a boutique hotel she had booked online. She would have preferred to stay in Miami Beach, near the shopping on Lincoln Road or directly on the ocean, but the Azure Ocean was close to Torenmaas' office in the financial district.

As Anna drove, she thought about her game. How were the deaths connected? Why now? What if Torenmaas wouldn't agree to an interview? Carlston, the intern, had attempted to arrange a meeting, but nothing had been set up yet. What if the interview didn't pan out?

At the hotel, Anna left the car with the valet and checked in. Happy to see her room included a desk overlooking the Miami River, she sat down and returned to the task of securing an audience with Torenmaas.

Carlston had continued attempting to set something up while she was in flight, but the mogul's gatekeeper had rejected every potential permutation. Apparently, there was no reason for the busy and important international shipper to waste his time talking to the press. Anna again made a few cold calls and crossed her fingers.

With nothing else nailed down yet, Anna knew a stake-out was in order. She grabbed her laptop, slid it into her bag and walked the few blocks over to Brickell Avenue. Within minutes, she stood facing the building where Torenmaas ran his affairs and assessed the situation. Where is the best lookout point? What are the chances he's still here? Anna checked the time: around 4 o'clock. It was possible.

She pushed through the revolving door and eyed a seating area, complete with fake magenta orchid. She smiled at the concierge, a muscular well-coiffed guy who nodded in recognition, and sat down on the couch, as if she waited there every day. "My associate seems to be late," she said. Yawning, the man nodded again.

Methodically analyzing each man who entered or exited, she simultaneously mulled over all the times she had been in a similar position early in her career, doing stakeouts to question finance ministry and central bank officials. A split screen ran in her mind, one of the people before her eyes and the other of her past self, trying to wheedle information about currency movements and interest rates out of officials and bankers. The waiting wasn't all bad. It produced interesting thought patterns. Boredom scrambled her brain, then spit out new ideas. Eventually, the awaited individual usually showed up and she got her chance to pose her question. Even a "no comment" stood for something.

After an hour, Anna knew the concierge might ask her to leave. If questioned, she could simply explain her associate hadn't shown up. Avoiding awkward conversations was better. She considered waiting in another building, watching from a café, wandering around outside or pacing. The latter seemed too weird. Don't want to cross the line between staking out and stalking, she thought.

As Anna stood to leave, the elevator bell rang again. She turned to look. False alarm—it was a woman. Glancing outside, however, Anna spotted a man of the right age in aviator sunglasses bolting toward the building.

Eyes straight ahead, he rammed his arms against the revolving door. It jerked to life and flicked him into the lobby. Dressed in tennis shorts and sneakers, he flew past Anna toward the elevator.

"Excuse me," Anna called from the waiting area. "Mr. Torenmaas!"

The man turned to look. "Who are you?" he demanded.

"Anna Jones, with the *Daily Journal,*" she said, striding toward the elevator. "I wanted to talk to you. I've..."

Torenmaas shook his head. "Apologies."

"Let me tell you about the subject of my story," Anna added, now much closer to Torenmaas. "I think you will want to provide input."

"No, I don't do interviews," Torenmaas said, backing up. "And my assistant already told your assistant that, which you must know."

"Please, let me explain."

"No need to explain."

"It's about Channarong's death."

"You'll have to excuse me," Torenmaas said, as if Anna had asked him about his preference for still water or sparkling. "I have a game, as you can see," he said, pointing to his shorts. "I left my racket."

"But you knew him...," Anna pushed, hoping for some form of expression to register on Torenmaas' face.

"The answer is no! If I want to be in the news, I have friends at the good papers," he said, backing into the elevator. "Horatio!"

Anna froze. What? Oh! The concierge was rushing toward her. Anna backed off.

Horatio stared at Anna.

65

I've lost this round, she thought. She delivered a quick pursed smile and walked out.

Upstairs, Torenmaas unbolted the main door to his suite, unlocked the interior door to his personal office, took a glance at his racket case on one of the guest chairs, and dialed Lin on the landline.

"Theo?" Lin answered.

"I need to see you," Torenmaas commanded.

"You miss me that much?"

"Meet me tonight. Usual location."

"What's wrong with the park? It's beautiful," Lin replied.

"Jimmy, listen to me," Torenmaas repeated. "Cut the crap."

Lin laughed. "Alright, I'll be there," he said. "Can't wait to see you, you beast."

Torenmaas grabbed the racket and ran downstairs, with just enough time to play the game before Lin would show up.

Chapter 15

Washington, DC – Wednesday, Feb. 19, 4:00 p.m.

Sara Reedman stood in the kitchen of the Georgian mansion in Spring Valley where she was cat-sitting—way out Massachusetts Avenue in Upper Northwest, past American University—and emptied the bottle of cabernet sauvignon into her water glass. She took a gulp and banged the glass down on the counter.

She steadied her gaze on the door to the butler's pantry. Her phone was in there. She had stowed it in a drawer that morning, after calling in sick and reassuring her mother back home in New Jersey that she was fine—as if stashing it away would hold off both the problems in her head and the events outside. Neutralized, like someone had turned her emotions off, Sara sat stuck, cycling through a series of questions: What am I supposed to do on the day after my boss was found hanging and my best friend was shot? Will the police call me? Will they find the killer? What if they don't? Am I in danger? Should I leave town? An oblivion awaited.

The orange tabby rubbed against her pajama pants and padded off. Sara had taken the gig to help her aunt's friend, a recent widow soothing her grief in Sedona. It had seemed like a perfect retreat opportunity for Sara too. Off the beaten path, the enclave of ambassadors, corporate titans and political elites was beautiful. Now, she was thrilled it was well-patrolled, way more secure than her sublet on Capitol Hill.

Still, the butler's pantry irked her. Something about a whole room of cabinets, cubbies, drawers and containers seemed more absurd than any other aspect of the manor house, a symbol of the lopsidedness of society. I'll never get used to a kitchen closet the size of a bedroom, she said to herself.

Sara went in and opened the drawer. She stared at the powered-down phone. After a few seconds, she snatched it up, fetched her wine again, and moved to the TV nook at the back of the house, off the chef's kitchen. The long rays of February's afternoon sun streamed through the antique windows onto the Persian carpets. Taking refuge in the corner of the sectional, she stared not at the big screen but out the French doors at a slate patio framed by a low stone wall, which doubled as a bench.

Wisteria vines, well-pruned but leafless, snaked up and across a pergola. Even in winter, the garden looked perfect. Despite appearances, however, it was not. She had recently learned the neighborhood was infamous for its contaminated soil, the result of weapons testing at A.U. during World War I—and decades of incompetent, inadequate cleanup. It had been in the news again lately. She was dumbfounded to discover the environmental disaster was in her own proximity. Lewisite, mustard agents and arsenic were lurking in the soil. How could that be? How could influential people of means fail to clean up a poisonous, carcinogenic mess in their own yards? In America?

She picked up the remote and turned on the TV. A news anchor was reporting on the spread of a new respiratory virus that had apparently started near Wuhan, China. She flicked through the options and settled on season 14 of Grey's Anatomy, her favorite. The theme music played, and she fell under its spell. After a while, she dozed off.

SOURCE OF DECEIT

When she woke up, the cat lay on the opposite couch. She fed him his custom-blended chicken-liver mixture, microwaved a can of soup and sat down to watch more episodes. First, though, she turned her phone on. She scrolled through her photos, not realizing what they would unlock.

It was a recent image of Evy laughing that brought the tears. They had been drinking margaritas after work on the roof deck of the District Hotel, across from the Treasury Department. The view was great, even if the guys hadn't turned out to be. As tears dripped down her cheeks, Sara remembered their silly banter. She didn't try to stop them. Her chest heaved, and she bawled, fully consumed.

Eventually, her body ran out of steam. Sara wiped her face. Her nose was stuffed up, like when she had wailed as a child, outraged by some infraction that adults could not comprehend.

Yesterday she had met Evy at the mall. Sara put her hands on her temples. In her mind's eye, she saw herself wearing her comfortable flats with her favorite white pencil skirt and black cardigan.

She had arrived at the souvenir shop shortly after 1 pm. Evy was standing beside a rack of USA stickers, key chains and plastic toys. Sara pretended to shop as Evy had instructed.

From across a rack, Evy whispered, "Thanks for coming."

"Oh my God, can you believe Nou is dead?" Sara whispered while rifling through the T-shirts.

"Sara, don't show your emotions here. People will notice," Evy said.

"This is all crazy. I can't believe he's dead. Dead," said Sara. Her eyes watered.

"Whisper, OK? Hold it together."

"I guess. I got your note. Why did you want to meet here?"

"Keep looking down, as if you're on your phone," Evy instructed, looking around again. "I was afraid. I didn't want anybody to hear us or know what we are talking about."

"I don't even know what we are talking about. Why meet in a store, and at Pentagon City mall, of all places!"

"No one from work would come here."

"Like why not talk on a coffee run?"

"We might be overheard. Now, listen, someone tried to kill me this morning."

"What?"

"I was at Fort Totten waiting for the Red Line, and this guy rammed into me. Really hard. I'm telling you, he tried to push me onto the tracks—when the train was coming."

"Are you sure?"

"Yes!"

"Maybe it was a mistake. He was probably texting or something."

"It was supposed to look like that. But it was not a mistake."

"How do you know?"

"I could tell. Trust me. I saw his expression. And it was a major shove exactly when the train was coming."

"How come you didn't fall in?"

"I tripped—too soon, I guess. I ended up half-on half-off the platform. I screamed. I was scrambling," she said, faster. "A random guy grabbed me out of the way."

"That's horrible," Sara said, assessing an American flag T-shirt. "This is so messed up, Evy. I can't shop and talk about this at the same time."

"I have to go soon. Listen."

"But did you see the guy?" Sara interjected. "Like, what did he look like?"

"Brownish hair. White. I don't know. He was big, like a football player. Casual clothes. He disappeared—and that's the thing. If he did it by mistake, he would've stayed."

"Yeah. Maybe. I don't know. I'm sorry. What about the other guy, the one who helped you?"

"I was upset and had smashed my knee. I glanced at him, and then he was gone. He was older, 50 maybe, Black, short hair, no grey, wearing a suit. That's all I remember."

"Not much to go on," Sara whispered.

"Listen. What if it has to do with this new gig? Maybe I shouldn't have taken it on."

"Not to say I told you so, but...it sounded weird from the get-go."

"I've got to get in touch with Giovanni. I'm waiting for a call back."

"Why not go to the police? Tell them someone tried to push you. Maybe a security camera caught something. You don't have to say anything about the side job."

"I already did that, Sara, and guess what? My problems aren't the biggest ones on their list. I am not injured or dead. I don't think they even believed me. For now, I have to investigate myself, and gather evidence. What am I missing? What's at stake? Who's paying for what—you know—'follow the money'?"

"Can't someone at the Bank help you? What about Ko?"

"Or you. I need you to do some things for me."

"Me?" Sara said. "I don't know."

"What do you want me to do?"

"Call my old grad school friend Charles de Jeanbourg. Ask him what he knows about Giovanni."

"Now I'm lost," Sara said. "Like, why? I thought you were in love with Giovanni."

"Yeah. We've had a pretty good run. But I don't have time to explain everything now. Look, I wrote Charles' number down for you," Evy said, crumpling up a receipt and dropping it under a clothing rack.

"Why ask Charles about Giovanni?"

"Charles is our connection."

"Why don't you do it yourself?" Sara asked, bending down to pick up the paper.

"I'm being watched. I've got viruses on my computer, and I think my cell phone was hacked. My texts get dropped, and it randomly cuts off calls."

"I'm on your side, Evy, but you sound kind of...crazy. If it's so weird, why don't you tell the police that?"

"What? That my phone is tapped or a guy follows me sometimes? That I am suspicious of my boyfriend—who treats me well? For God's sake, Sara, guys beat their girlfriends to death and the police don't lift a finger. They're not going to believe me if I tell them I have a bad feeling, or if I think someone tried to fling me into the metro tracks. I have no proof at all. None whatsoever."

"When you put it that way," she said, tilting her head. "So, walk away from the job, from Giovanni, from all of it, even the Bank. Go teach English in Spain or something."

"No," Evy said. "There's too much at stake. I will figure it out, and I need you to help me."

"By calling this guy Charles?"

"Please do this for me. OK? Trust me."

Sara frowned.

Evy swallowed hard. "Charles told Giovanni about me, right? The connection was supposed to be for work, but you can tell him we're dating. Tell him you're helping me check out my new guy. Say you think Giovanni is strange."

"Fine," Sara sighed. "I'll see what I can find out."

"And I might need you to come with me on an errand—tonight."

"What, when?"

"I'll let you know. I'll get another note over to you, OK?"

"How did you do that, anyway?"

"Easy. The cleaning staff. I talk to them all the time—they're super nice. You'd be surprised what they know. They are privy to pretty much everything, but most people don't notice them. It's like they're invisible," she said, catching Sara's eye as she walked away. "Just call Charles, OK?"

Sara brought her mind back to the present. Outside, beyond the pergola was a yard, complete with a towering oak, fire pit and mini-Victorian playhouse. It was symmetrical, tidy, tucked in. And yet. Was the soil safe? Or were there still blister agents festering in the ground? People could be like that too—harboring toxic messes below the surface. What might Charles dig up?

Chapter 16

Miami – Wednesday, Feb. 19, 6:00 p.m. EST

After striking out at Torenmaas' office, Anna meandered down the wide-open sidewalks past the bank buildings and luxury high-rises along Brickell Avenue, jammed with commuter traffic. The setting Florida sun and ocean breeze taunted her. She half-wished dark clouds would roll in so the weather would align with her mood. Anna weighed Raven's offer. *If she helped me, what would I owe her?*

At the Azure Ocean, Anna headed for the hotel bar, which included a patio. Blue and orange hammocks hung between palm trees. The bar also offered a "beach," a sand box for grown-ups, where several people were well on their way to forgetting their troubles. Anna sat at a bistro table near the hammocks. A chalkboard announced the cocktails of the day, and she ordered a cosmo with fresh lime juice and a twist.

Waiting for the drink, she checked her email and messages, while the people in Channarong's division cycled through her mind. Anna had left a voicemail message with every person there, including Channarong's own program assistant, Sara Reedman. Interviewing those who knew Evy, especially anyone Evy considered a friend, would be amazing. But so far, no one had replied. Bank employees weren't supposed to talk to reporters without clearance from PR, but still. She hoped someone might. What might shake the Dutch kingpin out?

The sound of the waiter placing the cosmo on the table startled her. He asked about dinner. Anna ordered beef sliders and fries, and he returned to his shift. Sipping the drink, she contemplated her professional obligation to leave no stone unturned and the one pretty obvious boulder. Swallowing her pride along with the remainder of her cosmo, she dialed the phone.

"Anna?" Raven answered. "Already?"

"Raven, listen, I know you have this funeral to attend, and a million other family things to manage, but I need to take you up on your offer."

"I expected you to take at least 24 hours to come to that conclusion."

"Well, I'm eating humble pie today," Anna said. "Look, I staked out Torenmaas' office and...."

"And let me guess. He put you off?" Raven interrupted.

"Yes."

"Otherwise, how did he seem?"

"Composed. Unfazed. I don't know," Anna said. "Why?"

"Did you tell him about that video—of him and Channarong together?"

"I didn't have time."

"Right. Hey, I'll call you back." Raven hung up.

Ire rose in Anna's gut. Why did Raven have to be rude? Before her annoyance had time to fester, the waiter delivered the food, and Anna allowed the distraction. She was biting into her third slider when the phone rang. "Raven?" Anna said.

"It's all set," Raven said. "We can meet him at 10."

"You got an appointment?"

"Yes. At 10."

"Tonight?"

"That's what I said. What's wrong with you?"

"We?"

"You and me. You didn't think I'd miss this, did you?"

"I hadn't thought about it."

"Some things never change."

"No, I mean, it's fine. He's your contact. I get it. Come with. How did you do it?"

"That's my little secret," Raven said.

"Uh, OK," Anna said. "So, where?"

"Out on Key Biscayne. I'll pick you up at 9:30."

"Is that safe?"

"Nothing to worry about."

"How can you be sure? I don't want to drown in a mangrove swamp."

"Stop being paranoid."

"No, you stop being naïve. I'm sure you get as many of those misogynistic hate messages as I do. We have to be careful."

"Alright. I get that. But this guy isn't going to hurt us."

"I don't agree," Anna said. Her phone vibrated, indicating new text messages.

"You trust me. And I trust him, which means you have to trust him."

"To be honest, Raven, I don't trust you," Anna said. "I called you, because Tanner needs this connection, and I hit a dead end. But I don't want to risk my life. We'd be idiots to assume Torenmaas is trustworthy."

"Thanks a lot, Jones. Nice to know how you really feel," Raven said. "Be ready at 9:30. Cheers."

Chapter 17

Miami – Wednesday, Feb. 19, 8:00 p.m. EST

Anna fumed at Raven's audacity, but a string of urgent text messages diverted her attention. Apparently, the office tech Jeff had been the person disturbing her call with Raven, and now he had more to say.

"Check your email ASAP," Jeff texted. Twice more: "URGENT CHECK EMAIL!"

Anna switched over to her email. One of the most recent items was Jeff's. She clicked. His email stated: "We've examined the links. No obvious conclusions. Review them yourself in Cloud Bin, if you want. I'll keep sifting through this stuff, and alert you to any that seem interesting. BUT. Check this out: You missed a couple of photos, which weren't in 'Photos,' but in a file within a file within a file under 'Ringtones.' Diary entries? See jpg, attached."

Anna opened the attachment and found a photo of some hand-written pages. One glance at the script and Anna felt Jeff's guess at diary entries seemed on-target.

They served cava. Weren't there rules about procuring American products for embassy events? What was up with sparkling wine from Spain and not California—at the American Embassy? No one under forty. I caught myself yawning and decided to meet Mirale at Bonfire in Sukhumvit. Chugged my margarita and went to slip out when a man bumped right into me. What an ass! I didn't want to draw attention—I apologized profusely, and put on my best demure act. I wanted to duck out quietly. Then a strange thing happened. "I believe you're the woman I was looking for." OMG. Seriously? I told him I was on my way out, though I did think twice, because he was totally hot— well-dressed, fit, thick dark straight hair. Then, "Please don't go. You are Evy Poole, right?" More bizarre: I asked him how he knew my name. "I was looking for you, Evy. Your reputation for great beauty precedes you." I laughed straight in his face. What an idiot! "It's true," he cooed, smiling. "Let me introduce myself. My name is Giovanni Salazar." He said Charles de Jeanbourg mentioned me. I squinted at him. He knew my friend from grad school? Charles told him I'd be "the perfect person to hire." I told him I already have a job—am tired of projects that sound fantastic at first blush, end up with same pathetic pay. He insisted it was a "consulting opportunity." He said it would be "on the side" and "handsomely remunerated." Practically begged me to discuss it at the Three Dragons. How did he get a reservation there? "My company's got a standing reservation." I relented. Told him if they're false pretenses, I'd never speak to him or Charles again. Hahahaha.

Giovanni ordered a bottle of champagne. "I hope you don't mind switching to something French." Or something like that. "It's far superior to that imitation they serve at the embassy." Did he think he was sophisticated? I told him I prefer cava—"the Spanish aren't as uptight as the French, and their food and wine are better." He insisted French products are better. I spread on the snark: "I see you feel strongly about that." He laughed with a twinkle in his eye. Only then did I realize he was aware it was a game. Maybe he wasn't such a jerk after all. I think he preferred the French champagne, but he also liked my opposition. Something sparked in me. I had assumed he was Italian or Spanish, but the France comments made me wonder. I asked if he was French. "My mother was French, but I'm American. Like you." Hmmmm. What else did Charles tell him about me? We drank the champagne.

He told me Charles is with the CIA—not surprising, now that I look back. Oh God, one of those infamous meetings, where the suave spook lures in the protégé. I asked him if he thought he would get me, hook, line and sinker. Giovanni laughed. Exact words: "What I'm here to ask you is serious, but it's not like that. I'm not luring you, and you're not prey. It's a side job." I told him, "What a relief. You were starting to look like the Big Bad Wolf." He reached across the table, caressed my hand and said, "You would make a delicious Little Red Riding Hood." So cheesy and inappropriate! Yet, when he touched me, I felt that jolt. "What if I am the wolf?" I asked. "Even better for me," he said—such an obvious charm offensive, but he had me going. "Sorry to disappoint you," I told him. "I would never work for the CIA. That's the whole reason I put up with this research position at the Bank.

It's a stepping stone, but not into intelligence work." I picked up my glass, licked my lower lip and looked him right in the eye. "Fuck the CIA."

Adrenaline rushing, Anna sent a message back to Jeff: "Can you find more of these?" The waiter delivered another cosmo, which she downed. Fuck the CIA indeed.

Chapter 18

Miami – Wednesday, Feb. 19, 8:58 p.m. EST

Two minutes early, Lin drove his German luxury sedan up to the twelve-foot wrought-iron fence surrounding Torenmaas' main property. On a little peninsula on the bay side of Key Biscayne, the villa lay at a dead end off Harbor Drive—as secluded as one could get. An armed guard left the security booth and approached the car. Lin pressed the button to lower the window and announced himself. Two additional guards observed him from the booth.

"He is expecting you," the first guard proclaimed, glancing at Lin's license. The gate retracted, and Lin drove toward the house.

When Torenmaas bought the property, he had razed the previous home and hired a world-renowned architect to design a stormproof eco-friendly masterpiece, along the lines of the new art museum downtown. Tree-hugging eco-fascists, Lin had thought. But as he gazed upon Torenmaas' lair, he conceded the results weren't bad.

Lin took inventory of Torenmaas' security measures: iron perimeter fence, cameras, motion detectors, Doberman Pinschers. He also knew that, though unseen to him at the moment, a patrol boat cruised the mangroves and a cybersecurity team kept vigil. Beyond that, Torenmaas housed a small arsenal in a safe room, also filled with booze and cigars. Torenmaas had bragged about it once. He had said it was like the closet-style bomb shelters in the luxury apartments in Tel Aviv, only better. Torenmaas' security team even prepared scenarios to head off drone assaults. At his own home, Lin had a security system like everybody else, and he had enough semiautomatic weapons to defend his team, but Torenmaas' obsession with seclusion was over the edge, even for Lin. "Chacun sa merde," he muttered out loud.

Lin parked in front of one of the closed bays of Torenmaas' six-car garage, then walked across the permeable pavers, and past rows of prickly pears, scrub palms and statuary. An eight-foot replica of the Louvre's Winged Nike caught his eye. I'll never understand why they make the replicas without the heads, he thought. They should just restore the head.

Torenmaas' butler Hendrik, wearing a black three-piece suit, opened the front door before Lin had the chance to ring a bell or knock.

Lin gazed behind the butler, where a modernist light fixture illuminated a vase brimming with birds of paradise on an antique Javanese table. He nodded at the loyal servant.

"Good evening, sir," said Hendrik, a towering Dutch man with cloudy blue eyes and a high forehead that blended into his hairless scalp and crown. Grey stubble horseshoed around his freckled head. "Your electronics, please?"

Lin handed over his phone with a grunt.

Hendrik pointed to his left. "Mr. Torenmaas will see you by the pool."

Lin walked through the main entrance hall, past the library and out the side door, where Torenmaas was nursing a brandy.

"Evening, Theo," he said, taking a chair next to Torenmaas. "What's all this about?"

"We've got a problem," said Torenmaas, still in his tennis shorts.

"I gathered. Tell me what the hell is going on."

Torenmaas poured Lin a brandy and passed it to him across the side table. "That guy Channarong from the World Bank."

"What about him?"

"Maybe you missed the headlines, Jimmy, but yesterday Channarong was found hanging in his office."

"So what?"

"Today, a mere one day later, I have a *Daily Journal* reporter chasing me at my own office building, asking me about him!" Torenmaas yelled.

"What does that have to do with us?"

"This woman claims to have a video of me dining with Channarong on South Beach last year," Torenmaas said, regaining his composure.

"Is this a joke?"

"I am afraid not."

"What the hell did you do that for?"

"Right now, I have no fucking idea. He was in Miami promoting philanthropic projects in Thailand and Indonesia. At the time, I took a page from your rule book, Jimmy, and agreed to meet in public."

"Don't blame me for your lapse in judgement. Incriminating videos are not in my rule book."

Brooding, Torenmaas stared at the pool. "Who the hell took that video? And why?"

"Did Channarong have it taken?" Lin asked. "And how did the bitch reporter get it?"

"Now, I can't answer those questions," Torenmaas said. "But I might be able to later. She's coming over here later—with her colleague."

"Here! Why?"

"Why not? I have complete control in this environment. I can size her up, see what she's got."

"When?"

"In an hour."

"An hour!"

"Help me come up with a plan."

Lin shook his head quickly, as if a mosquito was buzzing his ear. "This isn't my fault."

"I don't care whose fault it is! We should agree on what to do. If the *Daily Journal* investigates Channarong, they'll be thorough, and it will branch out. Who knows what they might uncover. And if I go down, you do too."

"Well, you want my advice?"

"Yes!"

"If you think this snooping is so detrimental, get them out of the way. It's simple."

"Jimmy, that's like using a sledgehammer to kill an insect. And besides—the colleague is my niece."

"What the fuck are you talking about, Theo?"

"The second one, she's my niece, technically my step-niece. Her name is Raven Garcia."

"You're shitting me!"

"Afraid not."

"You are fucked," Lin added, taking a couple of cigars and a book of matches out of his jacket pocket. He offered one to Torenmaas, who accepted. Lin lit a match and puffed—the cigar glowed orange. He flicked the match into an ashtray on the table, as Torenmaas twirled his cigar and scowled. "Fine. Then just scare the shit out of them. Fucking hacks! Assign one of your teams to take care of it—ASAP," Lin said, blowing smoke. "Be clear. Black eye, bloody nose, broken ribs. Like that," he said, taking a sip of his brandy with his left hand, still holding the cigar in his right. "For now, spin the story. You can always kill them later."

Torenmaas stared past the foliage beside the pool at the twinkling lights along the mainland.

"That's my advice," Lin repeated, fidgeting.

Torenmaas signaled Lin to pass him the matches and joined him in smoking.

"For fuck's sake, Theo," Lin continued. "I will take care of it, if you don't. We can't have these people digging around."

"Something is wrong," Torenmaas said, exhaling cigar smoke.

"No fucking kidding. Channarong, that imbecile! Wife probably found out he was keeping a mistress and hired a P.I., or he had financial problems, or both. Standard shit. And I hear his son is running drugs," Lin said. "Any number of people could have been following him, filming him. There was a lot wrong."

Torenmaas took a deep breath.

"Snap out of it, man," Lin replied. "If you're not going to eliminate the reporters, throw them off. And get something out of them."

"They're going to refuse 'to reveal their sources'," Torenmaas said, using air quotes. "But you're right. They might slip up, or I might convince Raven to do a trade," he said, dragging on the cigar and holding the smoke in his mouth, then releasing it in one puff.

"If you don't deal with them, I will," Lin said, standing to go. "This isn't my fucking mess, but I won't hesitate to clean it up. We don't need any glitches."

"No. I'll deal with it."

Lin downed the last of his drink and stood. "Call me later," he said, leaving the cigar burning in the tray. "Hendrik! I need my phone!"

Chapter 19

Chiang Mai – Thursday, Feb. 20, 9:00 a.m. local time (9:00 p.m. EST on Wednesday, Feb. 19)

A half hour from the Chiang Mai airport, Ko was already nearing the meeting point. Dust flew, as the driver raced down a narrow road flanked by overgrown grasses. They passed an orchard—lychees—then rows of marigolds, ensuring steady supply for the temples. Beyond lay intermittent forest and farmland, bamboo and an occasional palm.

The car came to a rolling stop at a village intersection. Two small but sturdy houses had been built since Ko was last there, the modern kind with tight windows, colorful siding and a corrugated metal roof. A café with its menu on a hand-written sign occupied one corner. The scene was quiet—three tables, each accompanied by two plastic chairs, empty. With only a sleeping mutt to avoid, the driver sped off again. They passed a lane unfamiliar to Ko. According to a billboard, it led to a new condo development.

After a winding curve, a modest but solid gate came into view. The driver punched a code into a keypad at the entrance, and it opened.

A rooster and a few hens scattered as the car blew down a driveway and pulled into a dirt yard—large enough for a tour bus to clear a U-turn. Several buildings, including a mechanic's repair shop, its garage doors open, rimmed the yard, and a dozen mopeds stood lined up along a cinder-block perimeter wall, as if prepared for rental.

Ko's impulse was to jump out of the car, but he knew he was expected to wait. The driver sat still, keeping the car running, cool and dehumidified. Ko tapped his foot and surveyed the scene. A sniper was patrolling on one of the roofs.

Ko heard a commotion. Three boys had burst out of a concrete house opposite the garage. Laughing, they began playing soccer and kicking up more dust. A couple of panting dogs frolicked beside them. As the boys continued to play, one of the dogs stood there and watched, moving its head back and forth like an elderly referee. The other dog was more energetic, bounding here and there. The contrast between the normalcy of the boys' game and the unusual circumstances of the meeting was not lost on Ko, but he remained composed.

After a few minutes, two armed men emerged from a ramshackle building next to the main garage. They approached either side of the car and signaled Ko to open the door and step out. Once he did, the taller one, who was closer to Ko, pointed toward the house with his machine gun. Ko headed over, the younger dog at his heels.

Inside, Ko removed his shoes and placed them in a rack. The light was dim; his eyes took a moment to adjust.

Ko's cousin, Keng Maung Mai, was sitting at a table, grinning at him and smoking a cigarette. He was wearing colorful, immaculate American sneakers, jeans and a black short-sleeved T-shirt, snug against his bulging biceps. The lower portion of his tattoos—the clawed feet of a tiger on the one side, the open jaws of a crocodile on the other—stuck out. He had the shiny head of a man who re-shaved it every morning.

Ko knew his younger but more powerful cousin eschewed the traditional wai, so he simply offered a greeting. "Cousin Keng. Sawadee khrup."

"How the hell are you?" Keng said in barely accented American English. Snuffing out his cigarette in an ashtray, Keng came over and looked down on Ko, who at six-foot-one was already much taller than the average Thai man. Keng shook Ko's hand, crushing hard, then gave him a pound on the back. "Little Cousin," he said, chuckling.

"It's an honor to see you again," Ko said, annoyed at the "little" comment, but perennially impressed by his cousin's English. After all, Keng had learned it on his own, watching TV and talking to tourists.

"Yes," said Keng, jerking his gaze down at the dog, which had begun sniffing his ankles. In a sudden flash, Keng kicked the unsuspecting animal hard in the ribs and yelled, "Get out!"

With a high-pitched yelp and a hard tuck of its tail, the young mutt retreated to the yard.

"You look better than ever," Ko said, hiding his disgust.

"I do, don't I?" Keng laughed, showing off his biceps. "I work out! Soon, you will come see my new house—and new gym and new salt-water pool. I have a retractable roof—great in the rainy season. Today, you will have to be satisfied with this," he said, waving at the room around him. "I am grateful to my friend Waddy, always generous with his property. Tell me, how are you feeling?"

"Very well, thank you," Ko said, lying about the jet lag.

"I hope you enjoyed the flight from Bangkok."

"Yes, Cousin Keng. Thank you very much."

Keng scrutinized Ko, as if we were a child. "I don't offer my jet to everyone!"

"It was an honor, Cousin. Thank you."

"Sit down," Keng demanded.

Looking down at the floor and nodding, Ko complied.

A young woman in a fitted lavender silk dress emerged from another room with a teapot on a tray. Placing the tray on the table, she poured two cups of tea. "You must be hungry," she said in Thai, motioning to two women behind her. "Here we have congee, pork soup, pork skewers and omelets with rice. Please enjoy."

"Your hospitality is outstanding, as always," Ko told Keng. "Thank you again."

"Excellent," Keng said, now more satisfied with his cousin's obeisance. "You may begin."

While they ate, the cousins continued in English, catching up on family developments—who was getting married, who was studying abroad, conducting business, joining law enforcement. Determining who could be of assistance to their cause stayed in the forefront of their minds.

"Now, Cousin Ko," Keng said, as he finished eating. "Your efforts have been extremely successful."

"Thank you."

"The resources you have organized have allowed me to operate above the usual patronage schemes—both here, and north of the Thai border. Your contribution has paid off handsomely," said Keng, allowing a slight smile.

"That is what I had hoped for, Cousin."

"All the faction leaders have seen the wisdom of accepting my authority as head of the New Northern Territories."

"Of course! Your strategy is brilliant," Ko said, ever careful to offer the right balance of strength and submission. "You have shown great prowess in gathering the NNT forces, long stifled by their own skirmishes. I admire your vision!"

"We are fast approaching the pivot point," Keng said. "Our recent order of armored vehicles and helicopters has been delivered. The drone swarms and their systems are set. Tell me, is the final shipment of small arms ready?"

"Everything has been taken care of. Rifles, pistols, ammunition, grenades and launchers, detonators and explosives. Consider it done."

"Outstanding," Keng said, nodding. "Just as I expected. Is there anything else you'd like to tell me?"

"No."

"No? I have heard some interesting news out of Washington, Cousin Ko. Did you think I wouldn't notice?"

"No. I mean, yes, I assumed you would bring it up, if you wanted to discuss it."

"The timing of Nou Channarong's death is curious, Cousin Ko. Wouldn't you say?"

"How so?"

"He died while you were en route. A girl from the Bank also died the same day—after you left."

"Yes, that's the news," Ko said.

"And you don't know anything more about this?"

"No, Cousin Keng."

"People must not take matters into their own hands!"

"Of course not."

Keng stood up, towering over Ko, who was still seated. "You do not have the situation under control!"

"That is not true, Cousin. This is a coincidence."

Keng stood up even taller. "Think carefully, Cousin. If my vision comes to pass, you will be rewarded." Keng paused for effect. "But if you threaten my vision, you will be eliminated in a slow and painful manner! Is that clear?"

"That will not be necessary," Ko said, bowing his head. "I remain your loyal servant. You can trust me."

"You will stay in Chiang Mai until further notice. You will have the usual assistance and security at your disposal. But you will refrain from using the phone or the internet. Until now, you have not posed problems for me. On the contrary, you have been my most-trusted ally. It would be unfortunate, if that changed," he added, pounding Ko on the back again. "My driver will take you."

Chapter 20

Miami – Wednesday, Feb. 19, 10:00 p.m. EST

Minutes after Torenmaas' gates had closed behind Lin's fine German vehicle, Raven pulled up in a QuickRent car. Anna rode shotgun. They showed their IDs to the security guards, as Lin had, and were similarly sent through.

"Modest little shed," Anna said, as the villa came into view. "Are you going to inform me how you pulled this off?"

Raven just smiled as she parked.

"What did you say to get him to agree to the interview?" Anna pushed. "Do you have something on him?"

"Anna, Anna," Raven added, shaking her head. She got out and slammed the door.

Anna followed her up the pebble path to the front door.

Once again, Hendrik had been watching from the window and appeared at the door before the arrivals had a chance to ring the bell. "Greetings, Miss Raven! It is a pleasure to see you," he said, holding out his arms to welcome her.

"Thank you, Hendrik. It's good to know you are still here."

Anna took note. Hendrik knew Raven well?

"Who else would employ me, Miss Raven?" said Hendrik, showing them down a hall.

Raven laughed. "He needs you, Hendrik. We both know that."

Hendrik stopped for a moment next to a small office. "Now I must ask you to leave your phones and bags here. They will be safe in my care."

Raven placed her phone on a tray and bag into a cabinet.

"I guess we don't have a choice?" Anna said.

"I'm afraid not, Ms. Jones," Hendrik said. "But you are exempt from the pat-down, because you're with Raven."

"Awesome," said Anna sarcastically, following suit with the phone and her bag.

Hendrik showed them to the pool area.

As soon as Torenmaas heard footsteps, he rushed over and kissed Raven on her left cheek, then the right. "You look beautiful, my dear!"

"Thank you!" Raven beamed.

They sat down, and Raven got straight to the point. "Thank you for agreeing to meet us. I know you prefer not to conduct interviews."

"We have always gotten along, haven't we, Raven?" Torenmaas said. "You have my best interests at heart."

Raven smiled. "We're grateful you have changed your mind. It will be best for both of you, if you have a chance to set the record straight."

Turning to face Anna directly, Torenmaas said, "This is 'off the record'—'deep background,' as you put it in your world."

"That's fine," Anna said.

"To be crystal clear," he bellowed. "You do not quote me, and I do not wake up and find you called me a 'source' or an 'official.' Consider my information a brainstorm from God."

"Got it. If I attempt to quote God, my career will be over anyway," Anna said, trying to make light but garnering no reaction. "But I understand. Right. If you clue me in on something, I will not publicize it until I find corroboration from other sources."

"And you may not record the interview. You left your devices in the other room, yes?"

"Yes," said Anna, watching Raven nod. She was acting oddly compliant, Anna thought.

"One more thing," Torenmaas said. "You want to ask me why I had dinner with Nou on South Beach, and...."

Anna interrupted, "Raven discussed that with you already?"

Poker-faced, Raven did not look at Anna, but kept her eyes on Torenmaas.

"She was right to do so," Torenmaas replied. "I doubt I would have agreed to meet with you otherwise."

"And why is that?" Anna asked.

"Depending on how it's used, the video might compromise my reputation, Ms. Jones. You know that, or it wouldn't interest you. Nou is dead, and people are wondering what's behind it."

"So why did you have dinner with him?"

"I want to clarify one more stipulation before we continue."

"What else?"

"You need to tell me how you came upon that video."

"Interesting demand. I could agree to that—in this case," Anna added, dragging out her reply. "But let me preface this by saying that under normal circumstances, I would never reveal a source—in fact, I never have."

"Get off your high horse, Ms. Jones," Torenmaas interrupted. "I'm not here to discuss your journalistic ideals."

"This is different, because the source is dead."

"Nou?" Torenmaas asked.

"And in that light, nothing worse can happen to her," Anna continued.

"Her? Who are you talking about?"

"Didn't you hear of the murder of that young woman at the restaurant in DC yesterday?"

Torenmaas stared.

"Evy Poole, an assistant at the World Bank, was shot to death on the patio of a popular restaurant near Dupont Circle yesterday evening. She worked in Channarong's division," Anna said, observing Torenmaas' reactions. "And she sent me some information right before she died."

"So?" said Torenmaas.

"It included the video of you and Channarong dining together."

"You got this video from a World Bank secretary who is now dead?"

"Her title was program assistant, but yes."

"That is astonishing," Torenmaas replied.

Anna assessed Torenmaas. He appeared genuinely shocked. Maybe he actually hadn't known about her. "Perhaps you can shed some light on the situation," Anna said.

"Do the police know about the video?"

"They have her phone, so they must have the link to the video, but even if they saw it, they probably don't know if it matters. And I doubt they identified you yet."

"Indeed. How did you figure that out?"

"In some areas, humans work faster than AI," she said, noting Torenmaas' intense stare. He wanted more detail. "OK. I have a friend in the Netherlands who works in philanthropy—with elite private donors, art world. After that, it wasn't very hard. You are well known over there. So, now that I told you I received the video from Evy, you need to finish your end of the bargain. Why did you meet with him?"

"It was simple. We were discussing our philanthropic projects," Torenmaas said. "Nou wanted me to put more money into Thailand."

"Come on. Do expect me to accept that as an answer?"

"Why not? I can't dream up a more interesting story, because the truth is too plain."

"What projects?"

"My foundation has been financing an art museum linked with a series of community centers, which would simultaneously promote traditional crafts and boost economic development."

"Then why be cagey about it?"

"I'm not. I have a policy of not discussing my activities with journalists. Much of the news is...distorted. I don't want to have anything to do with it, or with you," Torenmaas said. "When—now, if—the satellite centers open, you'll hear about it officially."

"What do you mean 'if'?"

"Can't you see? If Nou Channarong is dead, the financial backing may be in danger. He was a big champion of the cause."

"I thought Channarong worked on rural health, agriculture and fisheries, things like that. What's he doing with an art museum?"

"Traditional crafts and the local art scene are an engine of growth. He wanted to support that. It was a slightly different direction, but not unrelated."

"Why did you have that video taken?"

"Me?" Torenmaas said, standing up. "It was not by me. How could such a video possibly do me any good? When you figure out where it came from, I expect you to fill me in. Let's count that as a part of our little information exchange here," he said, waving his hand back and forth between them.

Raven also stood. "Thank you, Uncle Theo. We appreciate your time."

Anna was dumbstruck. Uncle?

"My dear niece, you must stop by more often," said Torenmaas, ushering Raven out.

Anna jumped up. "Uncle?"

Stopping in her tracks, Raven smiled without showing her teeth and tilted her head at Torenmaas, who darted a look at Anna.

"Didn't you know Raven is my niece?" he asked Anna.

"No, no," Anna stuttered.

"That's why I wasn't worried about this meeting," said Raven, eyes wide. "I've known him for most of my life."

"Why didn't you tell me that before?" Anna snapped.

"You wanted to find your own connection. I thought I'd see if it panned out."

Torenmaas stood with an amused expression on his face.

"Great," Anna said. "Thanks. And thanks for relieving me of my self-flagellation."

"Any time," Raven said with a laugh. "He's my step-uncle, technically. Right, Uncle Theo?" she added, facing her uncle.

Torenmaas nodded.

"My father died of cancer when I was six," Raven offered. "Later, my mom married a man named Harrison, and his sister Poppy was married to Uncle Theo here."

"I see," Anna said. "What do you mean, 'was'?"

"She died too. Also cancer," Torenmaas replied.

"Oh," Anna said. A sour taste took over her mouth. "I'm sorry."

"Anyway, Uncle Theo was always good to me and my cousins," Raven said.

Torenmaas put his arm around Raven. "We should get together more often." Facing Anna, he added, "Raven is a wonderful person."

"Right," Anna said. "Thank you. And, wait, can you give me a lead on who else to talk to about the art center? Maybe I can get it on the record."

"You don't believe me, Ms. Jones?" Torenmaas said, walking toward the front door.

"It's my job to verify, Mr. Torenmaas. If I can substantiate the truth, everybody wins."

"Call Alex Ice," Torenmaas said. "He's a well-known artist in Chiang Mai—easy to find. It's his brainchild. You'll find what you're looking for."

"OK, then. Thanks."

Hendrik, who had been hovering in the background, returned their electronic devices and wished Raven well.

"One more thing," Anna said.

Ignoring Anna, Torenmaas hugged Raven and kissed her on each cheek once again. "Make sure this young lady knows she owes you," he told her. "And now, I must attend to some other business. It's late morning in Asia." Torenmaas stepped away.

"Mr. Torenmaas!" Anna called.

With a wrinkled brow, he turned and gave Anna a don't-push-your-luck look.

"Evy saved a spreadsheet of World Bank projects in South East Asia on her phone," Anna said. "Some of the phone numbers on it were repeated, and they are for your office here in Miami. Why?"

"My number?" Torenmaas said, raising his eyebrows. "That is curious, but I have no idea. Be sure to let me know. Good night."

Chapter 21

Miami – Wednesday, Feb. 19, 11:00 p.m. EST

Anna followed Raven down Torenmaas' front stairway, out past the statuary and the fountain, and through the pebbled parking area. They got back in the car.

"See? I told you he's a good guy," Raven said.

"We didn't get much, Raven," Anna said.

"What do you mean?"

"I mean, I gave him the info about who sent me the video, and what did we get out of him?"

"All kinds of things," Raven said. "He said he didn't know who took the video of him with Channarong. He told us he was involved in Channarong's philanthropy, and he explained all about the art center. He gave you that contact, Alex Ice, and he told us he doesn't have anything to do with that list or document or whatever you have."

"Even if we believe him, how useful is that?"

"Very. This guy Alex Ice is obviously the next step."

"It's a lead. But it's not much."

"You can't seriously have expected a smoking gun, Anna," Raven said. "Maybe you should be a little more grateful. Without me, you wouldn't even have this. You'd have nothing."

Raven's comments tweaked Anna—she had much more than the Torenmaas interview. She also had Evy's diary entry, the spreadsheet, the other files on Evy's phone, and the hyperlinks Evy sent. But she didn't want to share that with Raven right now. It was true, however, that Anna owed Raven for the meeting with Torenmaas. She kept quiet.

In their silence, the crunching of the tires on the pebble driveway became more pronounced. As they approached the security gate, it opened, and Raven smiled and waved at the guards. They emerged onto the road that led to Harbor, Crandon and eventually Rickenbacker Causeway to the mainland.

Anna went over the meeting again in her mind. Theo van Torenmaas hadn't revealed who made the video or why. He could be conducting activities that were illegal or on the up-and-up—whether they were commercial or philanthropic. If legit, they could be straightforward or a cover. Using legitimate businesses as a cover was an old trick—clever and yet run-of-the-mill. Either way, what if Torenmaas was a sidetrack, and didn't have anything to do with the deaths? Evy's information seemed to point to Torenmaas, and a nervousness swirled around the man. But the cause could be unrelated. And what about Raven? If her uncle was legit, the point was moot. But if he had something to hide, she was either in league with him or she wasn't. Anna's eyes swept over Raven, who was, at the least, biased in her uncle's favor.

"That's where the Miami Open takes place," Raven said, breaking the silence. "The Tennis Center at Crandon Park."

Anna wondered at Raven's remark. She didn't usually offer an olive branch. "Cool," Anna said. The tennis center's parking lots disappeared behind them, and they drove into a less developed part of the island. "Amazing how in an urban area of three million people, you can be surrounded by nature," added Anna—a feeble effort to return the good-will gesture.

As Raven drove, it grew darker. Dense vegetation formed a corridor for the road. Hardly anybody headed toward them from the opposite direction. After all, the island was a dead end without a boat. Then bright headlights approached from behind.

Anna turned and saw a vehicle gaining fast. It was a large pickup, clearly moving above the speed limit. It began to pass them, suddenly appearing on their left.

Raven waited for it to go on ahead, but it didn't. Instead, it sideswiped their little rental. The car jerked into the shoulder.

"He's probably texting, that idiot," Raven spit out as she swerved back onto the road. "And I'll be responsible for the damages."

Raven righted the car in their lane, but the pickup jolted sideways once more, smashing into Anna and Raven again. "What the hell!" Raven shouted.

Anna screamed, "Slow down!"

Raven jammed on the brakes, but her maneuver did no good. The truck fell back and sideswiped them a third time. Raven could no longer control the car. An invisible force seemed to propel them off the road. The pickup sped away, but the car crashed into the dense plant growth. When they landed, the airbags deployed, releasing a foul chemical smell.

Raven whimpered.

"Are you OK?" Anna asked.

"In one piece," Raven stammered. "My left wrist is killing me," she said, trying to hold it up by her right shoulder, above the airbag balloon. "What about you? Oh my God!"

"I'm calling 911," Anna said, dialing.

"You have blood all over your face! And it's dripping down your neck!"

"I have a cut," Anna said, touching her forehead. "But it's not that bad."

"Ew! You're bleeding like a pig, Anna," Raven said, recoiling. "Look at your shirt!"

Anna gingerly patted at the wet, sticky blood on her cheek and forehead. She tried to sop it up with her shirt, then opened her car door. "Hey, does your door work?" Anna asked, getting out. "911 is answering." Anna redirected her attention to the emergency services dispatcher. "Someone ran us off the road," she said, examining the damage to the car. "Newish full-size double-cab pickup—I'd say 2018 or 2019. Black. Florida plates, the one with the oranges in the middle."

Guarding her left hand and arm, Raven also stepped out of the car and walked over to Anna, still on the phone. "The first three characters were PJT," Raven said on top of Anna's phone conversation.

"OK," Anna said, nodding. She passed on the information and continued: "No, it could not have been a mistake. Front left tire blew out. It's shredded," she said. "We'll need a tow truck. The pickup must show damage—can you look for that?"

Shaking, Raven leaned against the back of the car, listened to Anna making the report, and nursed her arm.

"The driver was a male Caucasian, about 40, brown hair. Maybe 250 pounds," Anna said. "He wore a white sleeveless T-shirt, you know, that thing some people call a 'wife-beater.' Tattoo on his right forearm—couldn't see the details. And he was wearing a dark baseball hat," she said, pausing. "No, not really.... A sticker or a magnet on the truck's rear left bumper said Florida Everglades.... Alright, thanks." Anna hung up and leaned back against the car, next to Raven. "They'll be here any minute."

"He pushed me off the road," Raven said.

"He was determined, wasn't he?"

"Did you see him staring at us and laughing? It was like he was having fun."

"Maybe he was."

"What a nightmare. If he wanted to attack us, why would he speed off like that? I mean, why would someone do something like that?"

"To slow us down."

"What do you mean?"

"I mean, if we are injured in an accident, we can't work."

"But no one even knew we were coming out here!"

"Except your uncle."

Chapter 22

Bangkok – Thursday, Feb. 20, 11:00 a.m. local time (11:00 p.m. EST on Wednesday, Feb. 19 in DC)

Overlooking the city through the floor-to-ceiling windows of his suite, Giovanni was arranging Evy's trip to Bangkok when the news caught his attention. Something deep in his brain alerted him that the chatter in the background should supersede the conversation in his ear. He put his call on hold and shifted focus. The anchorwoman on the British World News broadcast had announced something about "the mysterious deaths of two World Bank employees in Washington, DC."

Grabbing the remote, he turned up the volume and walked toward the flatscreen.

The anchorwoman continued, "Nou Channarong, an Executive Director, was found dead in his office at the global headquarters of the renowned international financial institution. The cause of death was suicide, according to police reports. Later in the day, an assistant in the same division, Evy Poole, was shot at a restaurant in a drive-by."

Giovanni crumpled and knelt down on the Persian carpet, gaping at the TV.

"Authorities say the incidents are unrelated. At least one local expert, however, is questioning the official line," she reported.

The broadcast panned to a man who, according to the caption, was an expert on South East Asia at the Potowmack Endowment. "A coincidence, probably not. Same division. Violent ends. High-security, low-crime areas of DC," the talking head said.

The clip ended, and the anchorwoman switched to news about record-breaking heat around the globe.

It took Giovanni a minute to think straight. Luckily, he was in his own place, and not at a hotel or in some rental for one of Mr. Gold's missions. He darted to his antique teak desk and opened the hidden compartment where he kept his extra sim cards and phones. Grabbing two of each, he took his wallet and keys, put his loafers on, and left the building via the back staircase.

After riding in two separate tuk tuks, backtracking and powerwalking down a deserted lane, he emerged at the Temple of the Golden Mount. Luxury buses, taxis and tuk tuks filled the parking lot, while their drivers milled about waiting for their tourists. Giovanni stood against a wall, installed a sim card into one of the burner phones and called Mr. Gold.

"What the hell is going on?" Giovanni yelled when Mr. Gold picked up.

"Remain calm," Mr. Gold said.

"What did you do to her?"

"This was not my doing."

"We had a plan. I protected the asset and bought her a ticket. She would have been fine!"

"You misunderstand. I am not responsible."

"When did you give the order? Before or after we had that bull-shit conversation about bringing her here for a romantic getaway!"

"I was not behind her death."

"I don't believe you!"

"Why would I want her dead?" Mr. Gold asked. "For our own sake, we need to know who targeted her, and what they knew, or thought they knew. Who would go to such lengths? It's imperative that we determine the truth before anyone else."

Pacing, Giovanni let the conversation pause.

"Be professional. There is no logic for me to want her dead," Mr. Gold reiterated.

"Then who killed her?" Giovanni said. "Don't you know?!"

"An investigation has been opened."

"An investigation?! This never should have happened! You told me she wouldn't be in any danger!"

"I will handle the investigation. Now, you must take one of your usual trips to the States and salvage the operation. Get one of the other girls to replace her."

"That's impossible."

"No. It's not. You can, and you will. You must convince one of the other office girls to take her place."

"She can't be easily replaced, not just like that. She's been preparing for a long time," Giovanni argued. "And not just anyone could do this job."

"You can convince another one of the office girls to help you," Mr. Gold insisted. "Use your outstanding 'powers of persuasion'—and the money."

"Even if that were possible, they will be scared by what happened. Not one of them would agree to it. I should do it myself."

"No. Someone at the Bank needs to do it. They are the most credible. 'Bullet-proof,' as they say. Start with her best friend. You can recruit her now. Tell her that continuing the work and exposing the corruption is the only way to honor the dead. Say once the bad actors are caught, the girls will be free. Tell her the groundwork has all been completed and this will be over soon. Go."

Giovanni didn't reply, but he didn't hang up either.

"You have no choice," Mr. Gold added. "You must salvage the operation. She started this job, and it needs to be finished. She would want you to do that. Contact me when you get back to DC, but until then, keep your mouth closed."

Chapter 23

Bangkok – Thursday, Feb. 20, 11:30 a.m. local time (11:30 p.m. EST on Wednesday, Feb. 19 in DC)

After Mr. Gold shut down their conversation, Giovanni took off on foot. When he reached a canal, he removed the sim card from the burner phone and chucked both pieces into the water. Consumed by anger and disgust, sadness and self-hatred, he kept walking. The rich colors, sounds and scents of Bangkok's crowded streets failed to register.

Floating in a stupor, Giovanni recalled the first time he had approached Evy at the embassy—back when she was in town to evaluate Bank projects in the region. He envisioned her laughing. He saw her walking down the dark alley that night toward the Three Dragons. Then he pictured her in DC. She was in her apartment in Columbia Heights, lounging around in her favorite prairie skirt. He remembered her body, intertwined with his on Karon Beach in Phuket. He saw her reading the newspaper, the printed kind. She was preparing French food for him in her tiny kitchen. Then she was riding her bike in Bangkok. She was lying naked in bed after they had made love, asking him about his childhood.

He heard her explaining her future working in international development, having kids someday.

Bringing her on board had seemed a stroke of genius, and not only for their operation. He hadn't known his personal life could be that good.

"How did it come to this? How could I allow her to be killed?" he muttered.

When Giovanni finally got home, he went straight to his liquor cabinet and filled a tumbler with vodka, dispensing with the ice and lime. Then, he connected his laptop to the flatscreen, sat on the couch and downed half the glass. He scrolled through the files, and when he located the videos he had taken for Mr. Gold, he clicked play on the one when Evy had started to soften.

Her face came up on the screen—unknowingly, she had been looking straight into the camera—and a specter of his former life filled the suite:

> "My project fits with your principles," he said. "Charles told me you were brilliant, and that you care about the truth. This is exactly what we need."
> "I remain dubious," she said, raising her right eyebrow.
> "This is sensitive information, Evy. Do not divulge it to anyone else."
> "Or what? You'll eliminate me?" she said, laughing. "Giovanni, do you think you're in one of those spy movies I watched as a kid?"

Giovanni heard the sound of her laughter as she joked about the spy movies. The fact that she didn't take him seriously had confused him.

> "There would be consequences, Evy, if you jeopardized national security," he told her.

"You mean, I wouldn't get to enjoy these extravagant dinners?"

"Evy," Giovanni said. "We can stop talking about this right now if you want to. But I think you should hear me out. Remember, I am offering to erase your student debt if you complete the contract. That's almost $100,000."

"It's creepy that you know how much debt I have. Also, I'm not sure I want to know what I have to do. For that much money, are you planning a hit?"

"I told you it was important, and it is."

"Shouldn't I be top secret or something to talk to you about this?"

"Eventually, yes. If you choose to proceed, we will set all that in motion."

"So, if I listen to you, and you tell me what exactly you have in mind, I still don't have to do what you want, if I don't want to? You will let me go, if I say no—as long as I keep quiet about what you asked?"

"Exactly."

"I can say no?"

"You can say no."

"I should probably walk out right now," she said, darting her eyes at him sideways. "I'm pretty sure you're full of crap. But I guess I can listen to your ask. I am not necessarily saying yes."

Giovanni remembered that flirtatious glance well. He recalled sitting back and placing his hands on the table in an attempt to show gravitas.

"Got it," he said. "Good. We need you to pose as a whistleblower."

"What?" She gaped. "Where?"

"At the World Bank."

"But I have nothing to expose."

"You would take evidence to a particular journalist, someone we have in mind."

"I wouldn't know where to begin."

"Let me finish."

She cut him off: "You want me to be a whistleblower or pose as one?"

"We don't need you to gather the evidence. We already did that—mostly. You'll obtain certain documents and electronic files, but we'll tell you where and what to extract. From the vantage point of the journalist, you will be the whistleblower."

"I would lose my job, maybe worse," she said.

"No, you won't. You'll demand that the journalist does not reveal your identity—you may have to tell the editors at the newspaper, but they'll agree to protect you. That's how it's done. Your name won't get into the press unless you authorize it. The Bank won't know it's you, and your reputation won't be at risk."

"What am I supposedly exposing?"

"Wrong-doing."

"A little vague, wouldn't you say?"

"We'll get there."

"Why not expose it yourself?"

"Indeed. It might seem easier—at first. But if the CIA comes out and says that the World Bank is doing something untoward, it's not the same. We need the whistleblower to make it authentic."

"You could deliver the evidence anonymously," she added.

"It's a thought. But the journalist needs a known source, and that source is you. Otherwise, he—or she—is less likely to believe the story is true," Giovanni said.

"Maybe it isn't."

"But it is. It is true," he said. "And you will be convincing."

"How do you know I'll be convincing? You can't be sure of that. You are willing to pay me $100,000 to pick up a few documents and tell people about it? Sounds too good to be true. So—you know how the saying goes—it probably is."

"You don't have to believe me. You will see for yourself, once I show you where to find the details. You might have done this without a payment, but we didn't want to take any chances."

"Chances?"

"That you would refuse. This needs to be done right, and it needs to be done by a credible person. That person is you."

"You can't believe I would do this without knowing more about the so-called wrong-doing?"

"I am prepared to tell you."

Evy stared at him. It felt like she was present. She was right there!

"Someone is skimming off millions for their own purposes," he said.

"For what?"

"It relates to the Golden Triangle."

"The Golden Triangle!?"

"Northern Thailand, Myanmar, Laos, west and southwest of the Chinese border. At least 135 ethnicities and distinct languages."

"I was expressing amazement, not ignorance," she said. "I work in that division. I know the region. It's famous for its natural resources, gems and textiles—but also opium, heroin and meth."

"Precisely," he said.

"Which projects?"

"You name it. Water filtration, rural roads, telecoms, education, fisheries, women's health initiatives. Projects all over South East Asia—Myanmar, Laos, Cambodia, Vietnam—are supposedly getting this aid. In reality, they never see it. Most of it, that is—enough financing trickles through to ensure the projects don't die."

"That's awful," she said.

With that, the recording ended. Giovanni remembered wondering if she possessed a photographic memory. Ebullient, brilliant Evy!

Giovanni's nostrils flared. Crying out in agony, he grabbed the tumbler and hurled it at a print on the wall. Shards rained onto the floor—broken crystal mixed with picture frame glass. The base of the tumbler landed with a thud. His head pounded. He crouched on the floor and sobbed.

Chapter 24

Miami – Thursday, Feb. 20, 4:00 p.m. EST

Scowling, Torenmaas waited in his car, idling in a strip-mall parking lot along Coral Way. It was rush hour. People were picking up groceries, stopping at the ATM, grabbing take-out on the way home. Headlights, brake lights and traffic lights formed an impromptu show, as competing music escaped car windows.

Lin pulled into the spot next to his, facing the opposite direction. He parked half-in, half-out of the space, and lowered his window.

"I hate this place," Torenmaas said. "And you're five minutes late."

"I love it—no security cameras. You know that," Lin said. "Now, what's the urgency?"

"I told you I would handle the reporters."

"What the fuck are you talking about?"

"My niece's accident out on the Key last night?"

"What?"

"Let me be clear: If you do anything like that again, your business in Miami is dead, and if anything happens to my niece, you will be too."

"Hold up, Theo, you're pissing before your pants are down. No need for such an attitude. I didn't touch your niece, and I don't know what you're talking about."

"The hell you don't."

"I told you I'd leave the reporters to you, and I did."

"You are the only one I told that they were coming," Torenmaas hissed. "If you didn't arrange the accident, who did?"

"How should I know? You keep blaming me for things I didn't do. First that video. Now this. Maybe I should be the one threatening to kill your business in Miami—or you." A pedestrian holding a flimsy plastic bag of groceries bumped into Lin's car on the passenger side. Lin startled at the noise. "Pull out of the deal. I'll find another shipper."

"Is that what you want?"

"It's what you want, apparently."

Torenmaas glared at him.

"Look, Theo, we completed all the groundwork. You have the bulkers, logistics, customs agents and dock workers. The banks are on. The products are ready to move, and the buyer is demanding the shipment. But you're dragging your feet. Why throw it away? What I want is to finalize the deal—or I waste a lot of time and money. If we're going to move now, you have to be on board. What's wrong with you? What are you doing, Theo? Until your niece entered the picture, we weren't having problems."

"No, until Channarong showed up dangling in his office, we were not having problems. She's a symptom of the problem, not the problem."

"We need to get this deal done."

"OK, Jimmy, let's say you are telling the truth. If I accept that you didn't have anything to do with Raven's accident, then you need to accept that something is off. Find the son-of-a-bitch who did this. Then we'll know whether to go through with this deal."

"Alright. I'll ask around, and see what I can find, but if you're still dragging your feet after the weekend, I'm going to find another cargo guy," Lin said, zipping his window closed. "Later."

Torenmaas watched the luxury sedan glide away. If this deal isn't done in a few days, it'll be for good reason.

Chapter 25

Washington, DC – Friday, Feb. 21, 6:30 a.m. EST

Anna dried off, wrapped herself in a towel and gazed into the bathroom mirror. She tenderly removed the two damp bandages on her head and inspected her new stitches: thirteen in all—five on her right eyebrow and eight above her hairline, complete with a sliver of shaved hair. Having lost a full 24 hours in Miami due to the car accident, she was glad to be home.

She splashed water on the stitches and patted them dry with a clean towel. Then she parted her hair to disguise the wound. The doctor had said a bandage would not be necessary, as long as Anna kept out the dirt. She figured she could pull that off, at least in a literal way.

They had been lucky, she knew. Both she and Raven had been discharged by dawn the previous day. Raven's hand was sprained, not broken, and Anna's lacerations weren't too deep. Anna had caught a late flight to DC, but Raven decided to rest with Apollo and her family in Miami for a few days.

As Anna considered what to wear, the phone rang. Tanner's number flashed.

"Morning, boss," Anna answered.

"The *DC Mirror*," Tanner said. "Their headliner. How much truth is there to that?"

"I haven't seen the news yet today," she said, booting up her laptop.

"I don't know what game you are playing, Jones, but I don't like dirty pool," he hissed. "Get in here. We need to have a meeting with editorial—and I don't mean the usual one. Executive conference room! 8 a.m.!"

As Tanner hung up, Anna read the headlines on the webpage of the *DC Mirror*. One of the leads included a photo of her standing near Nou Channarong during the reception at the recent Starlight gala. It was by a reporter she didn't know, Jordan P. Green.

The article read as follows:

> Daily Journal *Reporter in Cybertech Deal with Dead World Bank Exec*
>
> *Documents reveal that World Bank economist Nou Channarong, recently found dead, formed a consulting firm with* Daily Journal *reporter Anna Jones and computer science professor Lois Canter Wang six months ago. The LLC, known around Washington as a "lobby shop," may shed light on the reasons behind Channarong's death, which was officially ruled a suicide but continues to raise questions.*
>
> *Neither the authorities nor Channarong's family have offered further information about his state of mind or health history. In a brief press release, his employer stated, "The World Bank Group regrets the tragic loss of a talented economist. Channarong, a native of Thailand, was a steadfast champion of rural development in South East Asia."*

SOURCE OF DECEIT

Channarong's new company, officially named Baltimore Export Assistance Team (BEAT) LLC, "supports foreign information technology firms in navigating the complexities of US export control and intellectual property laws and streamlines the legal environment to maximize cooperation," according to its mission statement.

Financial and family problems had been piling up for the economist, according to sources at the World Bank, who asked to remain anonymous for fear of losing their jobs.

Former colleague, Rose Gibson, said, "What happened to his son was sad." Robert Channarong was admitted to the Lindenflower Center for addiction recovery last year, sources said.

BEAT would have brought in significantly more revenue, relieving him of financial pressures, the sources said.

"If he left the Bank, he could have avoided these persistent personnel conflicts and earned ten times as much, and things would have been much easier for him," said Walker E. Maslow, an economist in London, who had also previously worked with Channarong.

BEAT was the pet project of Channarong, who apparently approached Jones and Wang more than a year ago. With the venture, he said he intended to capitalize on their complementary skills. BEAT opted for a soft opening to give the principals time to line up clients. It was due to launch officially in three months, according to Jeannie Fields, a realtor who was working with Channarong to secure a K Street office suite.

Jones, an investigative reporter with experience conducting long-term research projects and Freedom of Information Act requests, also holds expertise in terrorism, arms trade, foreign affairs and international finance. Previously a foreign correspondent for the Daily Journal *in Moscow, she has long-standing ties to Channarong, as the two have moved in the same international finance circles for years.*

Lois Canter Wang taught computer science at Hudson College in Upstate New York until last year. A Chinese national with "green card" permanent residency status in the US, she is currently an independent consultant living in Rhinebeck, NY.

Neither Jones nor Wang could be reached for comment.

Anna laughed out loud when she read it. What a lousy story! Someone was indeed playing dirty pool! But who?

Confident Tanner didn't actually question her integrity, she calmly finished getting ready. Careful not to jab her stitches, she smoothed her hair into a low ponytail and stared at the clothes in her closet. Her royal blue blouse, black trousers and favorite Italian booties called out to her. After dressing, she took the time to eat a bowl of cereal and carefully apply her eye makeup and lipstick. Then she collected her things and left.

When Anna arrived at the bureau, she headed to the top floor, where the meeting was set to take place. Tanner sat at a conference table with a local editor and two higher-ups based in New York—she could see them through the glass walls. They must have hopped on the 6 a.m. shuttle. Getting such an early flight was not a good sign. They've wasted no time, she thought. Worse, no one was smiling, and the door was closed. Mouths were moving, but no voices penetrated the walls. Anna paced in the hallway.

Tanner spotted her and came over. "Jones," he said, holding the door open.

Anna went in.

"You know Paul Eng from this bureau, and these are our colleagues from New York, Angela Derwint and Boris Painter," Tanner said.

Anna shook hands with each of them, all of whom she'd met previously. They greeted her with mechanical nods and "mornings," as if they had never seen her before. Tanner gestured toward one of the chairs, and she sat down. Despite the beautiful panoramic view southward toward the White House, the atmosphere was claustrophobic.

"Jones," Tanner said, containing the anger that had spilled into their phone conversation. "We trust that by now you have read the *Mirror*'s piece."

"You can't possibly believe there is any truth to it," Anna said, turning to look each of them in the eye.

"We would like to think not," Tanner said.

"This meeting should be about countering this nonsense," Anna said.

"Are you saying you are not involved in this 'venture,' shall we say?" Painter said.

"Of course not," Anna said.

"You don't need extra money?" Derwint said.

"What kind of question is that?" Anna asked.

"Answer it," Derwint demanded.

"Of course, I could use more money," Anna said. "Who couldn't? But I'm a journalist, not a lobbyist. I would never even work for a place like BEAT, no less co-found such a thing. It's out of the question."

"Jones, you have to come clean," Tanner said. "No bullshit."

Anna did a double take. Was Tanner hot under the collar, or was this for show? Did he have to speak that way?

Derwint took over. "There are some complications with your version of the events, Ms. Jones."

"Complications?" Anna asked.

"Look at these," said Derwint, passing over a pile of documents.

Anna pulled them toward herself along the table. They were articles of incorporation for the company Channarong had supposedly formed, and Anna's own name was indeed on the associated paperwork. Her signature looked reasonably accurate.

"These are falsified, obviously," she said. "Where did you get them?"

"Why should we believe they are fake?" Derwint said.

"Because they are! Because you know me!" Anna said. "Where did you get them? That should tell you a lot."

"They were dropped off at the editorial office in New York yesterday," Painter said. "They stand up to our authentication process."

"We need to update our authentication process, then, because these are forgeries," Anna said. "Who dropped them off?"

"You don't need to know that at this time," Painter said.

"Oh, right," Anna said, gazing at Tanner, who was studying his hands. "My professional future and personal reputation are on the line, my editors are betraying me, and I don't need to know who is trying to ruin me. Is that all?"

"No," Painter said. "I would not be flippant, if I were you, Ms. Jones. You have put yourself in jeopardy by mixing sources and business associates. We may be living in 'the gig economy' now, but in our line of work, your involvement with BEAT is a conflict of interest—which is strictly off limits."

"You think I don't know what a conflict of interest is?" Anna shot back at him.

"Ms. Jones, when you recede into the dark recesses of some sleazy internet café, and put your earbuds in and lick your wounds, we will still have a problem. You have put our venerable newspaper in jeopardy, and that we can't allow...."

As Painter droned on, Anna zoomed in on his face. The skin on his forehead creased into four or five windrows. Red pouches buoyed his eyes. His hair was thin and grey. Had this man ever been interested in the truth? Anna's heart pounded, but her mind was laser-focused. Derwint and Painter might be idiots, but they were in charge, she thought. I'll have to get around that.

Painter stopped talking. Anna heard an echo of what he had last said: "Bank statements show $20,000 was transferred to your bank account three separate times, once each month since these documents were finalized—the retainer stipulated in the documents."

"I don't know anything about that," Anna said.

Derwint and Painter scoffed.

"Don't you think I would notice $20,000 extra in my account—three times?" Anna asked. "All you have to do is verify the account. It's not mine."

"Look," Tanner said. "We're not going to come to an agreement now on your involvement in Channarong's venture, Jones. You're being put on leave."

"Leave?" Anna said.

"Under the circumstances, we don't have a choice," Tanner said. "To protect the reputation of the newspaper, we have to do something. Be happy you aren't being fired."

"I'm supposed to be happy I'm not being fired?"

"Yes," Tanner said, standing up. "I've spent the last hour convincing our New York colleagues there must be some explanation. For now, pending the investigation, you have to be happy you are not being fired.

You have a half hour to clear out your personal effects. Leave the laptop on your desk, or you will be charged with theft."

"This is a joke, right?"

"I am afraid not," Tanner said. "Don't worry about your books—I'll watch over them—but otherwise you have to clear out."

"What the heck, people! You should be ashamed of yourselves! You want my freaking phone too?" she yelled. "Oh, I forgot," she said under her breath. "The company's too cheap to distribute phones. Guess I get to keep it, huh? After all, it's mine!"

Chapter 26

Bangkok – Friday, Feb. 21, 6:30 p.m. local time (6:30 a.m. EST in DC)

Giovanni finished packing and called his car service for a ride to the airport. The flight through Tokyo didn't leave until late. Earlier in the day, he had informed his employees he needed to fly to the States at sudden notice to court a heavy-hitting client, who would simply not be satisfied without a face-to-face meeting. The cover story, which reflected the reality of his company, Cutting Edge Forex, was plausible.

Giovanni picked up his decanter and drained what remained of the vodka into his other tumbler. The broken one from the previous day still lay on the floor in a pile of shards with the picture-frame glass. He didn't care.

Evy's face haunted him. He saw her holding the tumbler up to her lips, licking the edge of the glass, and smiling.

Once more, he sat down on the couch, opened the laptop and scrolled through his files. He clicked on another video that he'd made for Mr.

Gold. They were in a restaurant again. This time the angle showed both of their faces from the side.

"The embezzled funds flow directly into the pockets of the arms manufacturers and dealers. The weapons end up with the rebels," Giovanni said.

"And these rebel groups want the weapons for what?" Evy asked.

"Venture a guess."

Evy tipped her head to the left. "Could have to do with the drug trade, the poppies—or the competition for natural resources—natural gas, minerals, gems. Maybe timber," she said, pausing. "But in this case, there's something more. Control, probably. It's not only about the goose that lays the golden eggs, is it? You're talking about sovereignty."

"I can see why Charles recommended you," Giovanni said.

"But why do you care? I mean, what does the CIA care if some region claims more control in that part of the world? Maybe that's even good for the US—it surely would piss off China."

Giovanni winced. "No, aggravating China is never good. And instability in the region would be detrimental all around," he said.

Giovanni remembered trying to sound professorial.

"Getting back to the Bank," Evy continued. "Who is in charge of the transfers? I mean, this 'funneling' can't happen all by itself. Is Channarong in on it?"

"The corruption is widespread, which brings me to another reason why we need you, in particular, why you are the critical actor."

"I am the critical actor," Evy repeated.

"Yes, you are critical."

"Right."

"Evy, forgive me—but you are 'low' enough that we know you are not involved, and yet 'high' enough that you have access to the people and the material. You are intelligent and knowledgeable. You work for an economist in the division, and you know the other people too. You are perfect for this contract."

"Why not ask Channarong's assistant, my friend Sara? She's in a position to do this too."

"Your psychological profile fits for us. But there are other reasons too. Your boss isn't in the limelight, so you are under the radar."

Watching himself with her, Giovanni almost smiled. He had admired her thoughtfulness.

"How did you figure this out?" she asked.

"Good question. We have a team focusing on international financial crimes and money laundering, and in the course of its regular operations, it detected irregular money flows. We looked into it further, and discovered this. It would have been close to impossible for the legal and accounting auditors at the Bank to pick them up. The routing is sophisticated, but the concept is not: It's a shell game."

"I don't know."

"You've heard of the Panama Papers, the Paradise Papers, and so on?"

She nodded.

"You know how it is. The rich and famous, corrupt and not, they use these mechanisms—offshore accounts, tax havens, holding companies, private equity funds. Sometimes, they are within the letter of the law. Other times, loopholes are...exploited, shall we say."

As she finished her champagne, the waiter placed red wine glasses down on the table and poured the Syrah. She picked up her glass and swirled the wine. The legs reflected the light.

"In France, they call those the tears of the wine," he said.

"Sounds better than legs," she replied, allowing her stare at him to linger.

He proposed a toast to Evy's future. She clinked his glass and drank slowly.

Giovanni recalled his tactics from that precise moment, which he had sensed was pivotal: She needs space to make up her mind. If I push too hard, she will never help. Though battling both sexism and racism, she has still managed to earn impeccable credentials. Nevertheless, she remains underappreciated in her job, so recognition of her intelligence and professional worth will be highly satisfying. She is motivated by "doing the right thing." She doesn't care about her own debt, but she wants to relieve her parents of financial woes. He had calculated when to recap.

"Evy," he said. "With your Ivy League debts paid off, you wouldn't be beholden to this paycheck. You wouldn't be stuck in a windowless interior space at a giant bureaucracy in DC. And you wouldn't be a financial burden to your parents. You would be free, free to take any social justice warrior job you wanted—and the best part is, you would get all this for telling the truth."

"OK," she said. "I'll do it."

When the video ended, Giovanni sat staring at the blue screen. He had been thrilled, when she had accepted the contract—a mixture of pride at his spycraft and intense arousal. That dinner had marked the start of their affair as well. Sex was all part of the game. Mr. Gold had told him in no uncertain terms to exploit that angle to their benefit. And Giovanni had assumed that part would be easy—success in the bedroom was hardly new to him. His own feelings had never entered the calculus.

Now, Giovanni's mind whirled like a carousel again—Mr. Gold's instructions, images of Evy, mundane logistics—around and around. He walked over to the windows and looked down. People were skittering about, scavenging materials at the enormous demolition site of an old embassy compound. So far below, the figures looked tiny, but he could see they were wearing gloves and masks to protect against the toxins and dust. Some had wheelbarrows. They had apparently driven there in a van, which they were loading. Did they find scrap metal or something else? What could they earn? They seemed so far away, so different, and yet Giovanni wondered the same thing about all of them. Were they the masters of their own fate or pawns in a game?

Chapter 27

Washington, DC – Friday, Feb. 21, 9:00 a.m. EST

Clenching her teeth, Anna peered inside the top drawer of her desk to look for anything she might need during her hiatus. She grabbed two flash drives and slammed it shut. From the paper files in her lower locked drawer, she extracted her lease, passport and birth certificate, originals she stored at work, figuring it was safer inside the multiple security layers of her office than her own home. She tucked the only other items of merit on her desk in her bag: a small rock from the grounds of a winery in the Kakheti region outside Tbilisi, and two framed four-by-six photos, one of her family and one of her boyfriend Viktor. Then she glanced at her books, promising them she'd be back soon, and walked down the aisle, passing all the other desks, including Raven's.

In the main lobby, the security guard wished her a nice day. She mustered a "thanks, you too" with a half-smile. After the revolving door discharged her onto K Street, she headed to the Proving Ground and ordered a latte to go. The other people requesting extra creamy macchiatos, dirty chais, and skinny iced double soy Americanos got on her nerves. Her mind raced. Why did it take this long to prepare a simple order? Why do I mind if other people want sweetened, adulterated, complicated caffeinated drinks? So what, if it takes all day, since no deadlines are looming and I might lose my job for no apparent reason?

When her latte was finally ready, she grabbed the cup and left without sampling it. She continued up 19th Street toward Dupont Circle, crossed into the park and sat on a bench facing the fountain at the center—her favorite spot in DC. Her shoulders relaxed. She finally tried the latte, but it was no longer hot.

Resting the cup on the bench, she stared at the white marble Beaux-Arts fountain. It was like a giant vase. She recalled how in warm weather, water flowed from the basin at the top into the pool at the base. The trickle would spray onto passersby, annoying office workers and delighting children. At the moment, though, the fountain was dry. One of the three classical figures that flanked the vase stood across from Anna. The nude female looked downward demurely and cradled the globe in her left arm. She represented The Stars, one of the three allegorical figures called The Arts of Ocean Navigation, along with The Sea and The Wind—Anna knew this, because she'd looked it up after discovering the spot a long time ago. But much of the carving perplexed her. Why didn't The Stars look up? Why a globe and not a star—or a baby? What was Henry Bacon thinking when he designed it? Why did the women have to be naked? Anna could relate. Having just been put on leave for unknown reasons, she felt exposed too. Who had taken her picture at the gala?

Anna stared a while longer. She forgot about her own predicament and got back to Evy. What about Evy's friends? Where were they? None of the assistants at the Bank had called back. None of the people Anna had found on social media with the same or similar name seemed to be the right Evy Poole.

Wanting to vent, she called Sasha. As the phone rang, a flock of pigeons swooped in. Cooing, they swooshed over to a young mother and her toddler, who were feeding them bread crumbs. Other people in the park were going about the usual—eating, talking, playing chess, sleeping, riding scooters. One guy was standing under a tree and singing. Sasha's voice mail at the Bank picked up, so she dialed his cell.

Sasha answered on the first ring, explaining he was working at his condo on California Street in nearby Kalorama Heights. He was hurrying to finish a project. Making it quick, she asked if he could do lunch. He needed a little time, but suggested the Greek Place, half way between them, a plan to which Anna gladly agreed.

Anna killed some time at a used bookstore, then went to the café a little early. Feeling ravenous, she ordered a gyro platter, took her tray out the back door and scored the only empty table left on the deck. The warmish DC weather had propelled people outside. Two twenty-something women and a scrawny man wearing headphones were pecking at laptops at the tables next to her. She looked down the alley—parking spots and garbage cans. She ate a fry and watched a rat sniffing the air in the alley. Most normal days, she would have been disgusted, but today she didn't care. She took another bite.

Anna had finished the fries and most of her gyro, when Sasha finally arrived carrying a Greek salad with extra feta and a lamb kebab.

"Anna, darling," he said, pointing at her stitches and placing his tray on the table. "I'm relieved. Your injury doesn't look that bad."

"Thanks," she replied, standing up and swapping air kisses with him on both cheeks. "I hope you don't mind I started."

"Of course not," he said, sitting across from her. "The plot thickens."

"You heard what's going on?"

"I saw the *DC Mirror*, if that's what you're wondering," he said. "I hope it was worth it. How much did you get?"

"Very funny," Anna said.

"Let me guess. The newspaper is totally behind you. The editorial board released a statement refuting all that nonsense."

"Yeah, right. A couple of big shots from New York kicked me out. I even had to hand over my laptop."

"Bloody hell," Sasha said, taking a bite of his lamb. "Does that mean you can't proceed?"

"Depends. I still have all my research, which I back up obsessively—lost some important material once, never do that again. Of course, they don't own public information."

"You backed it all up?"

"Nor do they own my thinking process," she continued. "But it's the principle that drives me nuts. They threw me under the bus."

"You're fired?"

"Not exactly. Tanner seems to have staved that off. I'm on leave."

"Is that good?"

"It's good. But it still pisses me off."

"So, what you're saying is that you weren't in the venture with Channarong?"

"Of course not. If you have to ask that question, why are we even talking?"

"Just checking. You know, trust but verify."

Anna made a face.

"What's your next step?"

"Analyzing these documents, talking to the idiot who wrote that story, this Jordan Green guy, and following up with his other sources. Who would do this? It's all messed up. Meanwhile, I have to keep on top of the Channarong story, and Evy, and figure out how it fits together."

"You don't think the *Mirror* story about you has anything to do with Channarong, do you?"

"How could it not? All hell broke loose after I started covering this story."

"How's your colleague?"

"Raven? Fine. Her wrist is sprained—something with the airbag. She can still type, though."

"Maybe you should drop the story."

"Gotta love that English sarcasm."

"I'm quite serious." Sasha finished his bite of salad and put down his fork. "It's plainly dangerous. I thought you put danger behind you when you left Moscow. You don't earn enough to put up with this."

"I'm glad you're concerned with my welfare, Sasha. But this is my job. It's what I get paid for, even if not much."

"Risking your life for a newspaper article!"

"Where have you been, Sasha?" Anna snapped. "Journalists risk their lives for the truth all the time."

"Maybe, but you might be the last man—woman, person—standing."

"Not at all. The bureau is full of people with a profound respect for the truth. Just not those in charge of my future, apparently."

"Like finding the truth is even possible. The truth is elusive, my dear—a moving target."

"Sasha, you're supposed to be helping me."

"Face it: Your job is interesting. You get to travel and meet important people. But you also need to survive. And right now, you need a reboot and a living wage. This is a sign, Anna! There's a PR position opening up at the Bank—perfect for ex-journalists. No risk to your person."

Anna held up her hand to speak her mind, but thought better of it. "I'll think about it, Sasha," she said instead. "Let me know about the post, sure. I'll check it out. Maybe you're right. I'll consider it. But, meanwhile, I need to figure out who Evy's friends were and what other people think happened. Can you keep your ears peeled for me? Help me get around the gatekeepers? I haven't heard back from Jennifer Reynolds."

"You're pursuing the investigation, even if the paper screws you over?"

"Of course. But don't look so worried—you're white as a sheet. I'll be fine."

"Given the risks, it's not worth it, Anna," he said. "I mean, why?"

"You know why, Sasha," she said. "People need to know the truth."

Chapter 28

Washington, DC – Friday, Feb. 21, 5:00 p.m. EST

Anna flinched when she heard a knock on the door of her apartment. Her place was on the 9th floor—whoever it was had bypassed security. She got up and looked through the peephole. It was blocked.

Before she had time to consider the options, however, she heard a deep, "Surprise!"

"Viktor!" she cried out as she opened the door. She rushed at him, draped her hands around his neck, looked into his dark eyes and stretched up to kiss him. "What are you doing here?"

"I was worried about you!" he said, caressing her face and gazing down at her stitches. "But you look gorgeous!"

"Thanks!" She took a good look at him. His curly dark brown hair, cut in a low fade, looked especially sexy with the five-o'clock shadow he had acquired during the trip. She also appreciated his choice of navy ski jacket, indigo jeans and Italian black leather oxfords. "You don't look so bad yourself! Come in!" She guided his wheeled suitcase inside for him. "How did you pull this off?"

"Magic." He stared at her and smiled. "Well, truth be told, it was a logistical nightmare."

"That bad?"

"Kind of, but I made it, as you can see. I dropped everything as soon as you told me about the accident yesterday morning."

"I missed you," she said.

"I took a week off. Are you surprised?"

"Totally—it's awesome!"

Viktor gestured around the room with his hand. "Great neighborhood, NoMa. Great building. I see there's a pool on the roof and a gym on the ground floor—with windows. Nice."

"I knew you'd say that." She grinned.

Viktor approached Anna and pulled her close. He put his arms around her waist and they kissed.

Acutely aware of the heat of his body, she looked at him again and smiled.

He moved his hands slowly up to her shoulders, then cupped her head in his hands and brushed his fingers through her hair. She reached around his back.

"You smell like cinnamon," he said. "And flowers."

She laughed. "You smell like Dulles taxi air freshener. And mints."

"I missed you so much," he said, holding her.

"I can't believe you're here," she said, grasping his hand and pulling him into her bedroom.

He stared at her, as she unbuttoned his shirt, swept her hands over his muscular chest and pushed him backward onto the bed. Straddling his body, she leaned down and kissed him. He flipped her over, brushing his hand along the inside of her thigh, and their lips met again. Then they tore off the rest of their clothes and quenched the desire they'd held at bay for weeks.

Afterward, she lay on her stomach, used her crossed arms as a pillow and stared at him. Viktor rolled toward her, placing his leg over her side, kissing the back of her neck. He drank her in, memorizing the scent of her skin.

"Now I will keep you here forever," he whispered into her ear.

He balanced on his side and lightly ran his finger from the nape of her neck down to the tip of her spine. She shivered.

"Or, I could make you some dinner," he said.

"Terrific," she said, admiring his six pack as he pulled on his boxers. "See what you can scrounge up."

Anna put on her robe and followed him into the kitchen.

"So, tell me. What's going on?" Viktor asked her, as he surveyed the food in her cabinets and refrigerator. "People in the office are saying you're on leave."

"Right, you made me forget about that for a while, but yeah, I'm on leave," she said, finally cooled down about it. "It's stupid, but I guess you heard. I had to 'take one for the team.' Higher ups in New York demanded it—all that BS." She offered him pinot noir, a case of which she had just received from friends who owned a vineyard in California—former journalists on to a second act. She poured herself some too. "Who told you?"

"Everybody's talking about it. You know how texts travel faster than wildfire."

"I was hoping I could keep it on the down-low."

"Nice try."

"They're being rash."

"Look, I know you are innocent, but they have to investigate—rule out plagiarism, lies, conflicts of interest. People need to be held accountable. Those jerks drag us all down. Remember that guy at the magazine in New York? The one who made up his sources?"

"It makes me sick. You know that."

"It will all come out in the wash."

"I'm glad you're confident about that," Anna said. "My concern is they won't try very hard. They don't have the financial incentive to investigate on my behalf. If I go away, the problem goes away—for them."

"Well, what are we going to do about it?"

"We?"

"You don't think I'm here to visit the Smithsonian, do you?"

"You don't need to waste your time on little old me," said Anna, smiling at him.

Viktor took out onions, green peppers, mushrooms and ginger root from the fridge. "I see you haven't totally abandoned your kitchen."

"If you work too hard, how are you going to have the energy to take care of me? That ginger is ancient."

"I always have energy for you, Anna. Besides, cooking isn't work."

She sat on a stool at the kitchen peninsula, as he put rice in the steamer and began to chop the vegetables.

"So, what have you found out since we talked?" he asked.

"You mean about Channarong?"

"No. I mean about you—the fake news about you."

"That's just it. There's more than one story now, and I'm convinced they're connected."

"I would agree. So you want to start with Channarong, then?"

"No word from his immediate family—wife Grace, daughter, son," she said. "All of them have been impossible to reach. They hired a publicist to field the inquiries, which are pouring in from around the world, and right now, they don't have anything to add to the official World Bank statement."

"People say his wife was having an affair with Senator Caleb," he said.

"You heard that too? All the way in Moscow?"

"I contacted a couple people en route. It's an open secret in DC, I guess."

Anna squinted at him. "You don't have to do my work for me."

"Come on. Maybe we can dig up someone in Caleb's office who knows something about Channarong."

"Well, my guess is everybody over there will keep mum."

"The quieter they are, the better for the Senator, true," Viktor said, returning to the fridge. He took some boneless chicken out, unwrapped it and cut it into chunks. "But maybe someone is pissed about it—and would want to spill."

"Maybe you're right. I could pursue the Senator's staff more. I've been calling around and sending emails to all kinds of people, trying to hit up relevant groups—friends, neighbors, colleagues. Nobody has been forthcoming. I even stopped by the loading dock of the Bank on my way home."

"The loading dock?"

"Somebody in maintenance or security might talk. Also, this wasn't in the official news release, but Tanner said his police contact told him a 'cleaning lady' found the body.".

"Did you get lucky?"

She shook her head. "People acted like I had the plague. But I did get one woman to take my business card. I had written my private cell number on the back. She promised to pass it on."

"I can picture you lurking around the loading dock, trying to strike up conversation."

"You know I love that stuff," she said, clenching her left fist.

"Better than nothing, I suppose."

"I also tried to track down the real estate agent who supposedly showed the suite to Channarong. This Jeanne somebody."

"And let me guess."

Anna nodded.

"She's fake," he said.

"Indeed. The real estate agency exists, and the suite exists, but I couldn't find such a person. Suffice to say I am confident no one else can either."

"Figures. Were the other sources fictional too?"

"No, actually," Anna told him.

"No?" Viktor said.

"In fact, I spoke to both of them this afternoon. They were angry and ready to blab."

Chapter 29

Washington, DC – Friday, Feb. 21, 6:30 p.m. EST

Anna beamed at Viktor, who was dumbfounded that any of the supposed sources in the *Mirror* story were real people.

Blinking and shaking his head in disbelief, Viktor added the chopped vegetables, ginger and oil to the sauté pan. "Jesus. That's amazing. What did they say?"

"The guy Walker Maslow was especially fed up," Anna explained. "He said the *Mirror* story was full of misquotes, and he'd never do an interview again, since we write whatever we want anyway."

"Great." Viktor slapped his hand on the counter. "Glad to hear Green is out there holding up the highest journalistic standards!"

"In both cases, the sources' qualifying statements were taken out of context and twisted."

"Specifics?" he asked, seasoning the sizzling vegetables with salt and pepper.

"Well, Rose Gibson—the former colleague—said she did say what happened to Channarong's son was sad, but she also told Green that

Channarong had handled it well, and the son was on the road to recovery, thanks to an excellent rehab in Virginia."

"Of course, Green never wrote about that part."

"Right. And Maslow said Green asked leading questions, like 'If Channarong left the Bank, could he have avoided personnel conflicts and earned more money?'"

"Jesus," Viktor repeated, shaking his head.

"Maslow said she shoehorned his replies into a 'pre-cooked' story."

"Wait, she?"

"Jordan Green is a 'she'. Maslow told me."

"What else do you know about her?"

"Not much. Maslow got the impression she's young, but I couldn't find her bio, not even on the *Mirror*'s website or 'about us' page or staff directory. Of course, I called the bureau and left messages—both for her and the bureau chief—but I don't know who her unnamed sources were, or if they exist. As you can imagine, Green never talked to me—or even tried to. I doubt she talked to Canter Wang either. I have a couple of calls in to her too."

"Check this out," said Viktor, who had been searching the web on his phone while keeping an eye on the vegetables. "When I was in college, the *Mirror* used to exploit its college interns pretty badly—you know, under the guise of training. So, I searched 'Jordan Green journalism,' and I found this person," he said, showing a picture to Anna. "See—a female Jordan Green at Prince George's Community College in Maryland. Her internet profile says she aspires to become a writer. It looks like she graduated from high school last year. I could be wrong, but I bet that's her."

"It would explain the botch job. Someone probably fed her the whole thing. Thanks."

"No sweat. Look, her email address is on her profile."

"I could shoot her an email right now."

"And say what? That she's a shitty journalist?"

"No!" Anna laughed. "I could say...I read her story, and want to talk to her about it. That's all. Go from there."

"Give it a shot."

Anna threw the email together and sent it. "Interesting," she said. "Her vacation responder is on. It says she'll be out of the country for a few weeks, checking her email sporadically."

"Weird time of year for a college student to be away. Hope she's in better shape than Evy."

"Ugh," Anna said.

"What about an editor or somebody else at the *Mirror*?"

"Sometimes, *Mirror* people show up at Karl's, you know, that beer garden I told you about, where all the Hill people go. Maybe my friend Mel knows someone."

"Does she still work on the Hill?"

Anna nodded. "She's now the foreign affairs L.A. for Senator Bakerton. Covers defense, homeland security and intelligence. Same as us really, except she writes talking points, reports and briefing papers solely for him."

"Cool job. Good for her," he said. "What about other people at the Bank?"

"The whole place is on lockdown, following orders from the mothership. Radio silence."

"Even Channarong's assistant?" Viktor asked.

"Especially her. Her name is Sara Reedman. I left her a bunch of messages too. Rumor had it they were having an affair."

"What? Who?"

"Channarong and his assistant, Reedman," Anna replied. "And yet, I find that hard to believe," Anna continued. "It doesn't fit."

"Since when has that stopped anybody?"

"It is so, like, twenty years ago," she said. "At this point, it's surprising any old dog would make a move on an assistant. Wasn't he worried he'd be accused of harassment? And why would she want that kind of relationship? Anyway, Sara took some time off, at least according to the head of media relations. But that makes sense, right? It's understandable. All I can do is hope she will consider my plea and give me a call."

"Dinner is ready," Viktor said, frowning at a series of text messages that had popped up on his phone. "I'll deal with these afterward."

Chapter 30

Washington, DC – Friday, Feb. 21, 8:30 p.m. EST

Just as Anna and Viktor were finishing dinner, Viktor's phone rang. "Hang on, I should take this," he told Anna as he walked into the bedroom. "I've been ignoring these texts for too long."

Anna shrugged and carried her wine glass to the couch. She picked up her friend's new book about the Chesapeake foodshed, which was on the coffee table, and leafed through it, but her mind wandered to Channarong and Evy. With so little information from the police, she kept thinking about the deaths, searching for patterns or clues.

When Viktor reemerged, she asked, "What was that all about?"

"That was Raven."

"Raven? My colleague?" Anna asked.

"Yes. Our colleague. She's still in Miami—staying with family."

"Why did she call you?"

"She wanted to talk about the accident."

"With you?"

"Maybe she didn't want to bother you. She knows I'm your boyfriend."

"OK, that's a little weird."

"And she doesn't think her uncle is behind the accident."

"Oh?"

"I get what she's saying," Viktor said.

"What? She's obviously conflicted. He's her uncle," Anna replied.

"I don't know."

"You are going along with that?"

"With what?"

"The theory that Torenmaas wasn't involved?"

"They're family."

"How could he not be involved?"

"I trust her judgment."

"What are you even talking about, Viktor? Why would you trust her judgment?"

Viktor looked at Anna for a moment before replying. "She's sharp. She's a fellow journalist. Not unlike you."

"Not unlike me?"

"And she is the one who got you the interview, after all."

"But what was she doing down there? Isn't it a bit of a coincidence she was on the same plane?"

"Didn't she say it was a funeral?"

"Likely story," Anna said, scrunching up her nose, as if a foul smell had wafted through the apartment. "You believe her? You barely know her."

"Uh," he said. "That's not exactly right."

"She's a colleague, Viktor."

"No, I mean, I know her a bit better than that."

"What do you mean, you know her?"

"It's ancient history, Anna."

"Viktor. We have been together for four years, and you knew I was transferring to DC where she was working, and you never mentioned Raven was your ex-girlfriend?" Anna stood up.

"Anna, come here," he said, walking toward her.

"And you know how I feel about her! You know she gets under my skin! She's some special kind of weird rival—no matter where I go, she pops up. How could you have never said anything?"

"You are overreacting."

"Don't ever tell me I'm overreacting," she said, pushing him back and circling around him. "What a dumb guy-thing to say." She went into the bathroom.

"Come on, Anna. I didn't tell you about it, because she doesn't matter to me, not like that."

"Listen to yourself, Viktor," she said through the door.

"Hey, I dated Raven for a year or so—after college, way before you and I met in Moscow—and I know her family a little. But it wasn't a big deal."

"A year or so? Why did you break up?"

"I don't know."

"You don't know!?"

"Bad match? We were young and stupid? I don't know! It didn't work out. You've had other boyfriends too. I'm sure you haven't told me about all of them."

"But I don't talk to them at our office all the time, either! That's a bit different."

"I don't talk to her all the time. Only once in a while."

"Viktor, it's not the same thing. I see this woman! Every day! And she knew about me. The least you could have done was tip me off about her!"

"When you put it that way, it sounds bad, Anna. But it didn't matter to me, because Raven is just a friend."

"It matters to me." Anna went into the bedroom and collected Viktor's clothes and suitcase. "You're going to have to stay somewhere else. If you're going to keep secrets like this, I don't know if we can be together."

"Anna, we had such a nice evening. I came all the way over here from Moscow for you, not Raven. I want to help you figure this mess out."

"I'll figure it out by myself," she said, rolling his suitcase to the door. "Here," she said, handing Viktor his clothes. "Put these back on, and go help Raven."

"Anna, this is ridiculous."

"You need to stay somewhere else right now."

He reached to hug her but she pushed him away. "Viktor, really," she said, opening the door to her apartment and holding it ajar. "Don't touch me. If you're so close to Raven, go stay at her place."

"Anna, I don't have anything going on with Raven." Viktor put his clothes back on and stood there.

"Go," she said. "Go."

"I'll call you in the morning," Viktor said, backing out of the apartment.

Anna let the door go, and it slammed with a bang.

Chapter 31

Koh Samui, Thailand – Friday, Feb. 21, 10:00 a.m. local time; and Miami – Thurs., Feb. 20, 10:00 p.m. EST

Sitting on the couch in the living room of his private villa on Koh Samui, Jesse clenched his teeth and called Jimmy Lin again—his fourth attempt in so many hours. As he did so, he looked outside. The wide-open sliding doors created the effect of a picture frame. Joanna was reading her daily devotions on a lounge beside a sea-green infinity pool. A glass of ice water stood beside her on a little bamboo table. She wore a wide-brimmed sun hat and yellow sundress. Behind her, the palm trees swayed in the breeze, and beyond them, the Gulf of Thailand stretched out toward the coasts of Cambodia and Vietnam.

Jesse softened for a moment at the sight of her. He felt glad he had not disappointed her in Bangkok—accompanying her on the floating market tour and making their flight the following day to the beach on time. During their plane ride south, Jesse had divulged everything Ko had said—

regardless of Ko's desire for privacy. Joanna was a shrewd observer, and he wanted her opinion.

"Keng is a wild card," she had warned.

He knew Joanna was right. They were all risk takers, but Keng had always stood a little closer to the edge. Whatever apprehensions Jesse had repressed about Keng nagged at him now.

All knotted up, Jesse listened to Lin's phone ringing and ringing—without even a kick into voicemail. What if neither Lin, nor Keng was reliable? If Lin would answer the damn phone, maybe at least one problem could be cleared up. The line went dead.

He dialed again. The temperature outside was a pleasant 78 degrees, but Jesse's head was heating up, as if he were in a sauna. He wiped his fingers across the front of his neck to gauge how much he was sweating. His hand was dripping. The phone kept ringing.

"Hello!" Lin answered.

"Finally!" Jesse shouted, drying his hand on the white upholstery. "Where the hell have you been?!"

"What's that supposed to mean?" Lin yelled back.

"Ko tracked me down in Bangkok a few days ago. Channarong and that girl are dead. And you vanish!"

"I've been busy taking care of everything. Unusual circumstances call for special stealth. You understand."

"No, I don't understand at all," Jesse growled. "Do not go dark on me! Ever! You are not the only middleman in this world!"

"No, but I am the best."

"You arrogant little cocksucker!"

Lin laughed. "Rest assured the wait was worth it. I've been working for you this whole time. I didn't call, because I didn't trust the phone lines. But I just got this new end-to-end encryption tech—no back doors. We're totally secure. Now, what can I do for you?"

"Tell me what the hell is going on—because Ko set off alarm bells!"

"Forget about him, and don't worry about Channarong or the girl. Those deaths are outside our purview."

"That is not Ko's position. He is concerned, and he was not happy about informing Keng. I tried to reassure him. It would do us no good if he loses his head, but his concerns are my concerns, Jimmy. Ko and I go way back."

"I know your history, Jesse," said Lin, stretching out his words. "Your father was the minister in their village. You grew up there. You were like brothers. I get it."

"But do you?" demanded Jesse, incensed. "Get it?" Jesse's childhood memories flooded his mind. Tropical snakes and storms, later the Vietnam War. He heard his father reassuring him. "God will take care of us," and, "Pray for peace," he used to say. Jesse recalled that many people—in Vietnam, Thailand, Cambodia, the United States, and elsewhere—did pray. Yet they didn't get peace. They got more war and death and displacement. These things did not reveal God's mercy to Jesse, so he decided to pray for something else. Jesse prayed for strength.

"I get it," Lin said snidely with a sigh.

Jesse was not satisfied. "Do you have any idea how their people suffered?"

"Yes. Centuries of invaders. Burmese, Khmer, Chinese, Japanese, British. Do we count Americans?"

"Their chance is now! Ko and Keng have a chance to break free now. They must not lose this opportunity!"

"Calm down. I, too, have long-standing contacts. I, too, know when to heed warnings. And I repeat: These deaths in DC change nothing for our deal."

"I told Ko we're well-insulated, and it must remain that way."

"Look, I don't want to get dragged through US courts for export control violations. That's why I hand-picked this Dutchman. He's the best man in the cargo business."

"That's the whole damn reason I involved you," Jesse interrupted. "We need to keep up appearances."

"As you have told me before, this is not your average every-day semiautomatic pistol shipment. We are not dealing with a simple delivery from your home factory there stateside to your American collectors. I get that. A little creativity must be involved."

"Shit!" Jesse said. "A lot of creativity! The supplementation must be managed very carefully!"

"Yes, I understand."

"You sarcastic asshole!" Jesse replied. "You must guarantee invisibility!"

"Look, this will work out. You are the best on the supply side. You know all the other manufacturers and dealers—black markets too—used, repurposed, diverted. Even ghost weapons. And you have a reputation to uphold, I know. But that's the point. I am the best on the ground in-country. I want this as much as you do. We need each other."

"Everything must arrive in pristine condition."

"The utmost care."

"Rifles, grenade launchers, detonators, every single item! Shipped invisibly and cleanly!"

"I assure you, as I have assured Ko: There are no weak links in our chain."

"You better be right," said Jesse, nodding as his double chin opened and closed. "I am depending on you to get this shipment all the way to Myanmar."

"It's exactly as we planned."

"Ko and Keng are like brothers to me. And God wants my brothers to be free."

"No worries, Jesse," Lin said. "God is on your side."

Chapter 32

Chiang Mai – Saturday, Feb. 22, 10 a.m. local time (10:00 p.m. EST on Friday, Feb. 21 in DC)

Ko awoke to one of Keng's guards yelling, "Out!" He blinked and his body tensed up. Two men were waving semiautomatic pistols at him, signaling to leave Keng's "guest house." Ko jumped to his feet and followed the first man out the side door and along Charoen Rajd Road. The other guard followed.

Sweating in the mid-morning sun, Ko contemplated an escape, but decided against it. Keng's hulking men might shoot him. The lead man took the foot bridge west over the Ping into the main part of town. Half way across, Ko looked back. Cafés, galleries and trees lined the riverbank behind him. A delivery truck had parked along the side of one of the restaurants, and men were unloading crates.

Once on the other side, they pushed through the crowds in the fruit market to Ratchawong Road, which ran north. Double-parked in a side alley, a car awaited them. They took the 20-minute ride to Huay Tung Tao Lake at the foot of Doi Suthep, where the driver dropped them off at the main parking lot for the mountain preserve. The shorter of the two guards pointed to a structure in the distance, and Ko went off alone.

Ko had heard that more and more tourists had discovered the lake, a reservoir built to ensure Chiang Mai's water supply, but he saw mostly locals, fishing and biking. He approached a row of floating bamboo platforms with open sides and thatched roofs, which were set up for lounging. He ambled toward the one at the far end. A faded sign indicated the "Circle Trail," where one could take a shower under a waterfall. Technically correct, he knew. But you'd best bring a machete and spider repellent. Did the tourists know about the leeches? Did Keng meet people here often?

Inside the floating bungalow, Ko sat at the table. Its pink tablecloth flapped in the breeze. A wave of vertigo came and went as the strange body chemistry of jet lag still coursed through his veins. The shirt and pants that Keng had furnished him were clean but ill-fitting, and he was exhausted. Though he remained physically unharmed, he had slept poorly for the two nights that Keng had him holed up. He had asked himself endless questions. What had people found out about Nou's death? Since when have I been in the dark? What pieces is Keng leaving out? Why didn't he tell me? Ko tapped his fingers on his knees.

Hearing voices and footfall, Ko looked up. Keng was walking toward him followed by three waitresses carrying platters of food and beer. Another two men in training pants and track jackets followed.

"Cousin!" Keng announced when he got down to the platform. "Glad you found it," he said, patting Ko on the back.

"Yes," Ko said. "Your men brought me here."

"Let's eat," Keng said, motioning for the women to place everything on the table.

Ko's eyes lit up. Several whole fried fish on a bed of greens looked up at him. The aroma of garlic and spices made Ko's mouth water. The women also served spicy pork with basil, catfish salad, water mimosa with red chili peppers in oyster sauce, and different kinds of rice—plain white, blue and sticky.

"You are hungry?" Keng asked.

"Some of our childhood favorites. I am humbled," Ko said, scrambling to comprehend his cousin's mercurial ways. Why was Keng being gracious?

"Nothing less for my good cousin," Keng said, sitting down and telling the women to serve the food and pour the beer. "While you have been enjoying my guest house, I have been in touch with my CIA facilitator at the Bank."

Ko's mouth went dry. "What 'facilitator'?"

"You didn't think I was operating in a vacuum, did you? The facilitator has been watching over your shoulder."

"No. I mean, I don't know," Ko said. "Are you talking about Jesse?"

"No!" Keng laughed, as one of the women placed the plates down. "Jesse, our old friend, is an entrepreneur. In his business, he knows how to make deals with the CIA, and he has coordinated some of our purchases, but," he said, pausing and leaning back, spreading his arms upward. "No. He is not the facilitator. We have high-level support. High-level. The important thing now is that the facilitator has conveyed that you are in the clear."

"That's a relief," Ko said, looking askance. What was Keng talking about? How could Keng doubt me? We are family!

"Let us drink to victory!" Keng said.

"To victory!" Ko said, affecting his best poker face.

Keng resumed the conversation. "One cannot be too careful."

"Are you saying the CIA is assisting you, and they have someone at the Bank?" asked Ko, too upset to eat.

"Sometimes you are like the son, and I the father," Keng said. A stilted laugh emerged as he chewed a piece of catfish with his mouth open. "All that university has expanded your mind here, and shrunk it there," he went on, pointing to his skull.

Ko looked at the floor, not out of deference, but because he was afraid Keng would read the disgust in his eyes. *Now I see. It is you who is betraying me. What facilitator?*

"Of course, I have been dealing with the CIA," Keng continued. "How else would all of this planning, this groundwork, have been possible? What did you think?"

"I thought we agreed to keep the circle tight. Bring the one hacker into the fold, that's it. I thought we were arming our brothers and sisters to the north so they can free themselves of Burmese shackles," he said, more loudly than he had ever dared to speak to Keng. "And I thought we were striving for the full implementation of the Panglong Agreement, after more than 70 years of waiting!"

"Ahh, Cousin Ko! That is important, yes. But we can't bring back the past. We must adapt. We have accomplished feats others called impossible—unifying the militias in Shan and Kachin states, halting the 'armed conflicts,' 'ethnic clashes,' and 'skirmishes.' Next we will take back the rights to our timberlands, pipelines and mines—the gold, iron, jade, sapphires and rubies! But to do this, we had to embrace modifications."

Ko frowned at him. "Are we no longer talking about secession?"

"Something even better! The NNT will be an autonomous region under the umbrella of Thailand! Did you ever imagine that, Cousin Ko!? We will be one, all the way from the peak of Hkakabo Razi southward across the historic Burma Road, all along the Chinese border, past Chiang Rai and down the Mekong."

"Annexation?"

"Rearrangement. Let us call it 'inclusion'."

Ko stared at Keng for a moment before speaking. "You are a powerful leader, Cousin. You have always—."

Keng cut him off. "That's right, I am a powerful leader!" he bellowed. "But I could not bring these people together all by myself!"

"I thought you—."

"Money and arms," Keng interrupted. "With the money, I pacify the war lords and militia leaders. And with the arms, I secure the territory. Both of these things have been pouring in here thanks to the Americans—and your assistance at the Bank."

"My assistance?" Ko said. His mind reeled. "It seems I played a smaller role than I thought. You said yourself that someone was watching over my shoulder."

"Let us say you were partners. The facilitator couldn't have done it without you, my dear cousin. You are the economist. You two needed each other."

"But you have been keeping secrets from me all these years."

"How else could I succeed?"

"Why tell me now?" asked Ko, reminded of the fine distinction between freedom fighter and terrorist, between visionary and lunatic.

"It is time. You will have an important place in the new government."

"Me? Is this why Channarong is dead? Did you silence him?"

"Cousin Ko, that is a serious accusation. It's interesting that you thought I might organize such a thing. But you would be mistaken. And if I didn't respect you greatly, I wouldn't tolerate your wicked tongue."

"Then who did it?"

"He was weak. He took care of himself. That is all." Keng waved his hand, as if swatting a fly.

Ko flinched. What was Keng really saying? "You really think this is possible? This inclusion?"

"Why not? Do you want to count beans in that small office in Washington forever?" Keng sneered.

"I don't know," said Ko, as neutrally as possible.

"Look at Crimea! Russia took it back! Nobody did anything."

Ko stared at the pork. His food was getting cold. Keng was out of his league, the plan outlandish.

"Cousin Ko. Tell me your concerns!" Keng said, continuing to eat heartily.

"Keng, I don't know."

"I want to know your advice."

"Forgive me, Keng, but I doubt you want my advice."

"If you see a problem, you must tell me now," insisted Keng, leaning forward on the table. "Your analysis is of great value."

Ko felt trapped between two equally bad options. Should I risk Keng's wrath by telling him what I think, or risk the whole operation because I don't, he wondered. "Alright," Ko said. "Autonomy, or even secession, is not the same as adding territory to Thailand. Other countries will oppose this—especially the military in Myanmar."

"Ackh," Keng scoffed. "The military in Myanmar is a paper tiger! The generals try to look strong, but they're no match for the NNT. Besides, the Rohingya crisis down in Rakhine is like a stone around the neck of a dying man. Our operation will be a blow to the central government in Naypyidaw, but there is nothing they can do. They will be forced to accept it."

"You can't say the same about China. Don't you think China will defend its pipeline? After all, it runs from Kyaukphyu on the coast all the way past Mandalay and across the mountains to Kunming—and you know they need that shortcut for their Saudi oil. They'll fight to avoid the Straits of Malacca! And what about Chinese hopes for the Myitsone Dam, which is supposed to power Yunnan Province? The plan has been delayed, but I don't believe the Chinese leadership has given up on that. Or what about the railway that will bring Chinese passengers from the western provinces all the way to the Bay of Bengal? Some of the warlords are in the pockets of the Chinese. These people benefit from the current anarchy. Face it,

China has been quietly planting seeds throughout Myanmar. They are not going to walk away."

Keng's eyes flashed. "Beijing will not be pleased. But they will not stop us either. They are distracted—protests in Tibet, Xinjiang, Hong Kong, Taiwan, incidents in the South China Sea, the nuclear challenge of North Korea. And this Silk Road initiative! What conceit! Sure, they try to buy off the local warlords, but these men are smart enough to play both sides. The Chinese are spreading themselves thinner and thinner. Besides, they underestimate us. The Chinese have left their precious pipeline vulnerable. With the arms and equipment we now have distributed— along the borders and at strategic locations—the Chinese must agree to our terms or risk the entire thing—which they will not do."

"And what will those terms be?"

"A handsome payment. The pipeline, the power plants, the railroad, the dam, the river—the Chinese are welcome to use them all. But now they are our—what do they call it?—cash cows."

"Who will be running all this?"

"Me, of course! I will be Governor."

Ko was speechless.

"I can see you are contemplating the future, Cousin Ko," Keng said. "Let me repeat that I will need you here at home."

"You don't need me anymore, Keng."

"But I do! You are my right-hand man. You will have a prominent role. Vice Governor, State Finance Minister, Special Adviser, whatever you choose. When I get to the national level, I will need you close by my side."

"You really believe this can happen—an expanded Thailand? With such glory for the New Northern Territories?"

"It is happening already," Keng said. "The factions are committed— they are fed up with decades of war and Chinese meddling. Plans are in place—border patrol and security for the pipeline already exist; arms and tanks are in position; hackers, cyberexperts are online. There will be guards along the rivers—all the way from the Chindwin and Irawaddy to the Mekong. The police, media, and transport hubs, gasoline, food and water—we have plans to secure them all. We will even distribute baht and assist the return of our refugees from China. And don't forget, we have the support of our facilitator. The final phase is imminent."

"Your plans are thorough. Yet, what about Bangkok? What if the leadership changes?"

"It will. One must expect that. But I have contacts all around, and no matter who is in power, this plan is a plus for Thailand. The NNT will declare itself a part of Thailand, and what's a good neighbor to do? Bangkok will gain financially and geostrategically. They will accept the proposal as a way to lessen tensions. Done!"

"With all due respect, Keng, what happens when people find out about the CIA involvement?"

"They won't, but even if they did. Nothing," he said, shrugging. "The US and Thailand are great allies. China, the UK, France, Russia, even Ukraine all know that—which is why they desperately chase weapons contracts here to push the Americans out. Thailand already purchases millions in arms and military equipment from US sources each year. There are joint military operations. Look, ever since the OSS worked with us during World War II, we have found common ground with the Americans. You know Thailand was a staging area for the Americans during the Vietnam War. This is nothing new."

"The other powers might care if they find out the CIA has been using the World Bank like an ATM," he said.

"No one will. The Facilitator has taken care of that. We make it look like we finance our operation with the drug trade. No one would doubt it. Now, eat, cousin, eat!"

Chapter 33

College Park, MD – Sat., Feb. 22, 10:00 a.m. EST

At the College Park Hotel & Suites, Anna spotted Viktor sitting in a reading nook in the corner of the cavernous lobby beyond a glitzy bar area. He was staring down at his phone and scrolling. He still hadn't shaved, and she thought the stubble made him look particularly attractive. She reminded herself to pretend she didn't—the meeting needed to remain strictly professional.

He looked up, caught her eye and smiled.

"Hey," she mouthed as she walked toward him.

Viktor stood up and nodded, but he didn't touch her. "Anna, I'm glad you agreed to meet, and I...."

"Viktor," she interrupted. "Look, I'm still upset about whatever is going on with Raven. I only agreed to meet you this morning, because you said it was urgent, and you have to go back to Moscow."

"Nothing is going on."

"You weren't being honest with me."

"I left some things out, but I didn't intend to...."

"You'll have to leave that conversation for later, Viktor. Here's the thing. I'm in College Park as a favor to my friend, the one who teaches journalism up here at UMD. I'm supposed to do a lecture about foreign correspondence for her students this morning—despite the circumstances, she said I should still come. So I don't have a lot of time now, but that's why I told you to meet up here in the burbs. What couldn't you tell me on the phone?"

"Have a seat. And I'll get straight to the point."

She perched at the edge of a couch.

Viktor returned to his chair. "Jordan Green's mailbox was full. You couldn't leave a message, remember?"

"Mm-hmm."

"I have a friend at the *Mirror*—in IT—and I had tried to reach him as soon as I heard about this mess. Well, he got back to me last night. Turns out he remembers Green, set up her laptop and phone. He didn't want to give out her number—but he contacted her and gave her mine."

"Great," Anna stated flatly.

"Yeah. Because this morning, at the crack of dawn, she called me back."

"Oh?"

"And she wants to help. She said she became disillusioned working at the *Mirror*. The standards they were using—or weren't using—ran counter to everything she was being taught at college."

"What can you expect from the *Mirror*?"

"I know, but she said it was a rude awakening that they didn't care. They published unsubstantiated stories, made false claims, whipped people into a frenzy—all to sell papers. So, after the fiasco with your story, she quit."

"Wow. Where'd she go?"

"I don't know. She's out of town, said she's scared."

"She admitted to making that story up about me?"

"She didn't make it up."

"You've lost me."

"Her editor fed her the story and the angle. Apparently, he told her he had the sources pinned down, and that she should trust him. He told her which quotes to use, said she didn't need to worry about confirmation, substantiation or fact-checking. He was worrying about it for both of them."

"Which was pretty much not at all."

"Right. Also, she knew who fed the story to her editor, and you're never going to believe this, but it was Steven Brown, the communications director in Senator Caleb's office!"

"Holy," Anna exhaled in a whoosh. "Given Grace Channarong's involvement with the Senator, that would be an interesting coincidence. But why would he want to discredit me? Does that help her in some way?"

"I don't know. You need to figure out more about this guy."

"Interesting," she said, pausing, then raising her eyebrows in a quick "huh" motion. "Wow. Thanks. Really, thanks a lot." She smiled at him and stood up. "But I should go."

"Wait," he said, approaching her. "You know, this hotel is great—off the beaten path, yet near downtown and the metro. Surprisingly upscale, yet uncrowded," he added, moving closer. "The only problem is we don't have a room," he whispered in her ear.

"No, Viktor," she said, flustered at the warmth of his breath on her neck. "We need to sort things out."

He took her hand. "Let's sort them out now."

Her face flushed, and she felt her insides melting, but she did not relent. She pulled her hand back. "This isn't the right time."

Viktor withdrew but kept his gaze on Anna. "You are amazing. You are smart and funny and clever. You have chutzpah. You are strong and gorgeous."

Anna gave him her fed-up look.

"And I don't want to lose you, Anna."

She rolled her eyes. "What am I going to do with you, Viktor?"

"Come on, Anna, don't walk away."

She hesitated. "You want to escort me to my friend's office on campus?"

"That's not what I was hoping for. But I'll take it," he said.

Outside the hotel, they crossed Baltimore Avenue near a mowed field where students were playing Frisbee. Walking across the dry winter grass, Anna glanced at Viktor and thought about their relationship. Their chemistry was great, but sometimes there was also negative tension. Even before her move to DC, it had been rising. A competitive element had always been present—they had been working for rival companies, after all. But six months ago, when the *Daily Journal* had poached her from the wire service, the strain had intensified. Officially they were encouraged to cooperate, but the paper also demanded scoops, which pitted them against one another. Now, with his connection to Raven, it was all worse. It was like being on the high school soccer team when the coaches said to pass the ball for the good of the team, but the only girl who got any credit was the one who made the goal.

Then Anna's eye caught the mammoth new building next to the university's main gate, and it prompted her to wonder who paid what for what. "So, is this Steven Brown flying solo, or is the Senator in on it?" she asked without expecting an answer. "And did he do it for himself, or did someone pay him to smear me?"

"I can check that out, if you want," Viktor said.

"If you can figure out what's going on with Brown, I admit that would be helpful."

Viktor nodded.

They approached a traffic circle and followed the flow of students past concrete construction barriers, and around and up the hill toward the student union.

"I should have driven out here," Viktor said. "It would have been much easier."

"No. Walking is good. And the campus is pretty."

"College Park is hardly Paris," Viktor scoffed. "Up here, a bunch of boxy academic buildings and work zones. Down there, a patch of chain restaurants and tattoo parlors. Frat row. Decorative cabbages."

"You're such a snob," she said, flashing her dynamite smile. "There's a meadow, a church on a hill, and innovative architecture."

"I'll try to be more appreciative. There's certainly a lot of construction."

They continued up the hill, navigating the pylons and wire fencing.

After another block, Viktor added, "Hey, if you don't want me in your apartment right now, that's fine. But you have to let me help you get your job back. It's stupid if we don't work together this week."

"Where did you stay last night?"

"That hotel down on K Street by the office—you know, by the steak place."

"I see."

"We can talk about Raven, or whatever you want. Working together, we would be more efficient in the investigation."

"We'd be more efficient, would we?" She laughed.

"Look, with or without me, I know you're going to untangle this web. It's how you are. You'll get to the bottom of it."

"Thanks." She smiled at him.

As they passed the student union, people came from all directions, zigzagging across the road, while a dump truck in reverse beeped its shrill, rhythmic warning.

"The J-School is coming up," Anna yelled above the din, as she noted a silver SUV with Virginia tags slowing down on their left.

A pasty balding guy was at the wheel, while a similarly pallid woman with a brown-blond bob and bangs rode shotgun. An empty baby seat filled the middle of the back. The woman zipped down the window and smiled. More students flooded the crosswalk. It appeared classes were changing.

Jostled by someone's backpack, Anna smiled back. Nice periwinkle blue scarf, she thought. Anna opened her mouth to ask the woman if they needed directions, but she caught her breath. The long barrel of a silencer, balanced on the door frame, was pointed right at her! She wanted to scream some kind of warning—students were everywhere! But before she had time to blink, the gun went off—thunk, thunk! Anna felt something bump into her, her leg buckled, and she collapsed on the cold ground.

Yelling in fear, students ran helter-skelter like startled mice, as the car melted into campus as anonymously as it had come.

Anna felt stiff as panic rose in her body and her left leg burned. Where was Viktor? Her head throbbed. She reached her right hand up to check her stitches, which seemed to be intact. She reached down. Blood was seeping through her pants on the left side. A man in a black trench coat and a bucket hat crossed her field of vision, and a siren blared.

"Viktor?" she called. On her left, he was lying on his stomach. He didn't answer. "Viktor!" Anna's head throbbed harder. She leaned over and placed her right hand by Viktor's ear. He was breathing. "Viktor, don't worry. I'm here," she said, stunned and unsure.

Police cars raced up, sirens wailing, followed by two ambulances. The man in the bucket hat told Anna she would be alright, as one EMT looked at her leg and another examined Viktor.

Consciously forcing herself to pay attention to detail, something that usually came naturally, Anna surveyed the scene. Bystanders were staring. A woman with a bike was crying. "Did anyone see the car or the shooter?" Anna asked the EMT.

"I don't know, mam," the EMT said.

"Where are we going? Which hospital?" Anna asked.

"Dispatch will let us know."

Anna realized Viktor was being strapped onto a stretcher. They were taking him away! Anna reached for him, but the EMT held her back. "Where are they taking him?"

"One step at a time," the EMT said. "Let us do our job. Both of you need to get into an ambulance."

Chapter 34

Washington, DC – Sat., Feb. 22, 8:00 p.m. EST

When Mel arrived at Karl's, she scoured the crowd for Anna, who had called muttering. Mel didn't understand, but it was clear Anna was at Karl's, so Mel backed out of her dinner with Saloma and went over. Karl's was crowded. Under different circumstances, the atmosphere would have been perfect—clear night, not too cold, good music, energetic crowd. But Anna was in a crisis, and she was nowhere to be seen.

Mel strode toward the back and found Anna wearing a coat, slumped over a picnic table near a space heater. Her left arm was tucked in toward her body, right arm spread out in front of her, face planted on the table. Mel gently touched her forearm, and Anna jumped like she'd been hit with a cattle prod.

"Hey! I'm sorry," Mel said. "It's me." Anna's make-up was smudged, her clothes disheveled.

"Mel," Anna said, blinking.

"You look awful," Mel told her.

"Get me a drink. Something with vodka."

"How about some water," she said, pouring her a glass from a pitcher that stood in front of her. "Didn't they give you pain killers?"

"What difference does it make? Everything is all screwed up," she slurred.

"I couldn't tell what you were talking about on the phone."

"Viktor's in the hospital." She hailed a waiter. "Two vodka martinis with olives."

"In Moscow?" Mel said.

"Mel. Were you listening at all?"

"I'm sorry, Anna. You weren't making much sense."

Anna pulled herself together and told Mel about Viktor's arrival, their meeting in College Park and the walk to the journalism school.

When the waiter returned, Mel paid for the drinks and pushed them to the side. She poured more water. "But, wait. I don't get it. Were you shot—or not?" Mel asked.

"Yes, but the bullet just grazed my thigh," said Anna, sobering up. "People were swarming around, so I guess the shooter got spooked, or I moved unexpectedly, or I don't know. Someone bumped into me, I think."

"And Viktor?"

"Viktor fell and got knocked out. It totally freaked me out. I had no idea what was wrong with him."

"Then he wasn't shot?"

"No. He hit his head—maybe on a metal post or a cement barrier or who knows. He has a huge goose egg and stitches, and he might have a concussion, so they kept him for observation. The medical team urged me to go home. At first, I said no, but Viktor was awake at that point, and he kept saying he didn't want me to be so uncomfortable. So I went home, and I showered and changed and tried to rest, but I couldn't. Then I called you, but you didn't answer, and I didn't want to be alone. And here I am."

Mel wanted to talk strategy—how to find the shooter and the link to Anna, how to untangle the mess with the *Mirror* and revoke the firing.

Instead, she said, "Should we be worried? How bad could the concussion be?"

"They'll know more in a few days."

"It's not your fault."

"Isn't it?" Anna asked, gulping her martini. "He wouldn't even be in DC if it wasn't for me."

"Come on, Anna. I knew guilt was rolling around in your head. It's typical Anna. But he's a big boy. Have you heard any more from the authorities about Channarong, Evy, or the accident in Miami?"

"Nothing."

"What about the police in College Park? Did you talk to them?"

"Of course. I called them from the hospital."

"Well?"

"The public affairs person said the working theory is a gang stunt," she said.

"What the hell! A 'gang stunt' by a couple *in an SUV with a baby seat*?"

"They said it wasn't targeted."

"*Not targeted*? Do they know about your investigation of Channarong? Or what happened in Miami?"

"They don't really care. Miami is far away, and Channarong's death has officially been ruled a suicide. It can't be related."

"That's messed up," Mel said, shaking her head. "You should get a gun."

Anna groaned.

"I'm serious. Get a pistol. The firearms safety course is online. The background check would be a piece of cake for you. And, in your line of work, you'll have a great argument for concealed carry."

"I'm not getting a gun, Mel," she said. "If I have to defend myself, well, that's what the Krav Maga is for."

"You still do that? I thought you quit after college."

"No, *you* quit!" Anna said. "When you entered the Army, you forgot all about it, but *I* still needed it. And you know, it turns out it goes way beyond that basic self-defense stuff. It's full-on hand-to-hand combat. Not that I would initiate, of course, but it's interesting to know. There's a great studio near my place."

"OK," Mel said, nodding. "You won't use a pistol, but you'd kill a guy with your bare hands. Cool."

Anna let out a chuckle. It felt like old times for a minute. "But there's something else," Anna added, ruefully.

"What?"

"Viktor and I had a fight."

"Oh no, Anna," Mel said. "Before or after the shooting?"

"Before."

"About what?"

"He used to date my colleague Raven, and he kept it a secret."

"Yikes."

"But that's not even the point. The thing is, after this shooting, after the hospital, I felt bad about everything, and I had this stupid idea to call Raven and tell her what happened to Viktor. It's dumb, I guess, but I thought she should know."

"Uh oh."

"I called her at her parents' house. When I was in Miami, she had given me the number, said I could reach her there, just in case. Anyway, her mother answered. She was cordial, so I extended my sympathies for their loss. But get this," Anna said, pausing. "Her mother said, 'What loss?'"

"What do you mean?"

"Raven lied about her reason for being in Miami. There was no family funeral."

Chapter 35

Chiang Mai – Sunday, Feb. 23, 5:30 p.m. local time (5:30 a.m. EST in DC)

As the sun began to cast its enchanting evening shadows, Raven gazed up at the pagoda of Wat Chedi Luang. The temple was by all accounts one of the most impressive in Chiang Mai, no matter that it was a partial ruin. Steep steps led up a multi-storied square base. Oversized stone-carved elephants stood at attention facing outward, guarding the temple's interior, and seven-headed Naga serpents curled up the staircases. Four Buddha statues faced each direction—north, south, east, west.

Out of the corner of her eye, Raven detected movement near her feet. A honey-colored dog about the size of a small retriever ambled over and began scratching at the raked dirt. Then he circled and plopped down. She wanted to pet him, but remembered a stick-figure sign at the compound's entrance of a dog biting a person.

Instead she strolled over to an area under a tree, where sayings in Thai and English had been written on little placards and hung in the branches. She read, "Be deep in something," "All kinds of liberty are bliss," and "If you train your mind well, happiness will surely come." But what was the meaning of "well"? The air was hot, and a breeze swept her hair. Three monks in burnt-orange robes walked down the lane. She wondered about their lives, and if they would ever come any closer to the truth than she would. What was their day like? Who did their laundry? Where did they sleep? She read another placard. "Loving kindness cements the people of the world."

"Raven?" a man said.

She turned around.

"Raven," he repeated, reaching out to her. "I'm Theo's friend, Ice."

He was taller than she had expected. Over six feet, for sure. He was also younger. In fact, Uncle Theo had never said how old Alex Ice was. She had assumed he was old. But this man was around 30, maybe 35, and muscular. He wore black leather bracelets on one wrist, a maroon T-shirt, jeans and fashionable sneakers. His high cheekbones and low ponytail accentuated a striking silhouette.

"Mr. Ice," she replied, reaching out to shake his hand. "Thank you for meeting me."

"Oh, please, no 'Mr.,'" he said, laughing and shaking back. "Just Ice."

"Ice? What about Alex?"

"Alex, that's what your uncle says. He doesn't like calling me Ice, but Ice is what everyone else calls me. My father came up with it when I was born. It's not my last name."

"Excuse me," she said, flustered.

"It's OK. Westerners always wonder about Thai nicknames."

"Oh. Awkward. Sorry."

"Forget it. I hope you like the Old City," he added, spreading his arms out wide.

"How could you not love it? The moat and ancient walls, enchanting cafés, all these tropical plants, the lights and lanterns—it's like a dream."

"Chedi Luang is the center of the universe—according to traditional thought. I always bring my visitors here."

"Of all the temples here, this one is the most amazing."

"Yes, it's more than six hundred years old. The pagoda, or stupa, here at Wat Chedi Luang once housed the Emerald Buddha, the most important Buddhist relic in existence," he said. "As you can see, it's being restored."

"I read in a travel guide that the reconstruction is controversial, though. Some argue there aren't enough Lanna style elements."

Ice laughed.

"Why are you laughing?"

"Thai people tend to err on the polite side, you know, avoid difficult topics. You, on the other hand, brought up the controversy inside of two minutes."

"I'm sorry," she said, gritting her teeth. "I guess I wanted to show I did my homework."

"No worries. I got you. I studied Fine Arts here at Chiang Mai University, but I also studied in the States."

"Oh, where?"

"Iowa, the arts workshop. I earned an MFA in print-making there."

"Uncle Theo didn't tell me. That helps to explain your perfect English."

"Thank you for the compliment. Now, let me ask, did you know this temple hosts 'monk chats'?"

Raven shook her head.

"If you need guidance, or perspective, you can meet with a monk, ask anything you want and learn about Buddhism. They do it every day."

"I probably could use some of that."

He observed her but didn't reply. He showed her the famous pavilion with the 30-foot reclining Buddha, and they roamed around the grounds.

As they reached the exit, he pointed upward. "See this tree that towers over the entire complex?"

She nodded.

"It's a dipterocarp. It protects us. If it ever falls, it will bode ill."

Raven didn't know what to say. Trees don't last forever. How could the end of its life portend bad times? She noticed Ice watching her Western wheels spinning.

He did not try to explain.

The exit gate deposited them onto a packed sidewalk. Tourists milled about as vendors unpacked their trucks for the Sunday Walking Street market. Raven and Ice browsed for a while, and then Ice suggested dinner. She agreed, and he showed her to an unmarked door in a century-old building on Rachadamnoen Road, the main east-west artery in the Old City.

"My friend established this place," Ice told her as they ascended a dark staircase. "Northern Thai cuisine. People called him crazy, because he refused to hang a sign, but now it's very popular."

A beautiful woman welcomed Ice as soon as they emerged into bright light on the second floor. The sister of the chef, she had known Ice since childhood. Ice introduced Raven to her, and she told them to make themselves at home.

"Let's go to the veranda," said Ice, guiding Raven to a table along the railing. "This is the best seat in the house. I would like you to have it. The staff will bring out each dish, as it becomes ready."

"Thank you," she said, pleased with her view onto the bustling pedestrian zone, now glowing in the setting sun. "That sounds wonderful."

"Would you like some Thai beer?" he asked. "Or do you prefer wine?"

"Thai beer is great," she said. "Thanks."

"Good. I already ordered it," he said, as a waiter placed a couple of bottles down on the table. Holding his bottle up and smiling at Raven, Ice added, "Cheers!"

She did the same, and they drank. "Great beer," she said.

"Thanks." He leaned back. "So, what do you want to know?"

"Well, my uncle sent me here to discuss some things...about your project."

"It's reassuring to hear he's still interested."

"What do you mean 'still'?"

"Now that Nou has died, the project is in jeopardy. He was our biggest cheerleader."

"You heard about Nou's death?"

"How could I miss it? He was a giant around here."

"Because of the Bank?"

"Oh no! The Bank doesn't work here anymore. We are 'developed enough'," he said using air quotes. "And it's true that in some ways things are looking up. Tourism is a big draw, exports are more diversified and higher value-added, the middle class is growing. But we need economic development that is environmentally sustainable and that 'lifts all boats,' as Nou used to say. The lives of the poor must be improved and the middle class expanded. Nou's work here was entirely private. He funded cultural and environmental projects, and he leveraged his influence to draw in other players, you know, bring in more money."

"Like my uncle?"

"Exactly."

"He gave me a general sense of your work, but can you flesh it out for me?"

"By all means—I want to link the art museum to local community centers, boosting traditional crafts and tourism. Both of these things would generate income in rural areas. It's not complicated. Many of these puzzle pieces exist already. The Thai government and other groups are helping now, but they aren't linked in the way that I envision. My contribution would be to bring it all together, and spread it around."

"My uncle and Nou were benefactors. Were there others?"

"They were among a group of 10. Some of the money is already in the pipeline, but we were about to launch a new initiative—and, you know, a new financial commitment. With Nou gone, I could cover the difference with a bit more from each of the others. I was hoping this meeting would help me with that."

"We're talking about this art project only? Nothing else?"

"Why? Do you have another idea?"

"No," she said, embarrassed. "I wondered if there were any ideas besides the community art thing."

"There are probably thousands of other ideas, but this is the only one I'm working on right now. Would you like another beer?"

Raven accepted, and as Ice signaled to the waiter to bring two more, she asked Ice for a rough history of the city and its extensive art scene. He gladly obliged.

When the waiter returned with the beer, he also brought an appetizer of chili relish and rice balls, while another waiter placed soup on the table.

"It's *khao soi*," Ice explained. "Creamy coconut noodle soup with chicken—a big Chiang Mai thing."

"What a treat!" Raven exclaimed. "Authentic local food. You'll have to try Cuban food some time."

"Deal," he said.

Soon after, more colorful platters were placed on the table: house-made *naem*, a fermented pork sausage wrapped in banana leaves, *sai oua*, a grilled sausage with lemongrass and galangal, as well as chicken in a yellow curry sauce, and a sampling of mushrooms, sliced vegetables, fresh herbs and chili dips.

Almost forgetting why she had come to Chiang Mai, Raven tried them all. She could easily tell why the region was so famous for its cuisine—all the delicious flavor combinations. When she couldn't eat another bite, Ice insisted on paying and excused himself to settle up.

Content, Raven sat back and mulled over her host. He talked a good talk. He was polite and smart and fit. Why hadn't she expected that? From the street below, she caught snippets of many different languages. The breeze seemed to blow words up like leaves—*ausgezeichnet, harasho, merci, ka.*

She gazed over the railing and marveled at the throng. The world's curious shuffled along, taking in the atmosphere, eating street food and window shopping, all the while infusing rubles and yuan and yen and euros and dollars into the Thai economy. An endless rotation of humanity, so many different types of people, yet all on some sort of quest—everyone seeking something—pleasure, thrills, absolution, meaning. She wondered how effective their wanderings would be. How many of them would attend a monk chat?

Across the street from the restaurant, a foot massage parlor with lawn chairs in an alley was conducting a brisk business. Next door, people had formed a line outside a tour operator arranging elephant sanctuary visits, hiking and rafting trips, cave tours. The store after that sold jewelry.

Raven was contemplating buying an elephant pendant for her niece, when she saw a woman with platinum-blond hair—that natural, Nordic color—pass the shop. Her hair stuck out. But that wasn't all. She looked familiar. As Raven asked herself where she had seen the woman before, Ice returned, and his athletic walk distracted her.

"What?" he said to her.

"What?" she said. Under those loose-fitting clothes, you're hiding a pretty damn good physique, she said to herself.

"You were staring."

"No, I wasn't!" she protested. "But you know what?" she added, diverting the conversation. "I saw this woman outside—down on the street—who looks like someone I know in DC. It's probably a coincidence, but I'd like to run and see if it's her."

"No problem. Let's go," he said. "We're all set."

"Thank you," she said, as they descended the stairs. "The food was amazing."

"Yes," he said. "I'm glad you like it. My friend is a talented chef."

Downstairs, Raven feared she'd lost the woman, but after a good scouring of the crowd, she glimpsed the hair a couple of blocks away. Raven signaled to Ice, and they bumped through the crowd. They left Rachadamnoen and went north away from the market.

About to reach shouting distance, Raven's halted. "Oh my God. Stay back."

"What?" Ice asked. "You're acting weird, even for an American."

"It is her. See that woman with the white blond hair in the short red skirt? She's with a guy, and I know him too. I wonder what they're doing."

"The same as everybody else? Enjoying an awesome, luxurious, inexpensive holiday. This is Chiang Mai."

"Maybe you're right."

"You want to keep following them?"

"Don't you have something else to do tonight, Ice?"

"I could go to my studio," he said, putting his palms up and down as if comparing the weight of two things. "But adventure is good for art."

"For the sake of your art, then," Raven said. "Let's go."

Chapter 36

Chiang Mai – Sunday, Feb. 23, 8:00 p.m. local time (8:00 a.m. EST in DC)

Realizing their quarry was getting into a tuk tuk, Ice rushed over to hire another one. Speaking to the driver in Thai, he signaled Raven to get in. "I told him to trail the other tuk tuk, and stay hidden," he explained.

"Perfect," she said, grabbing the metal frame. No seat belt! No doors! She held on as they bumped up and down, and the wind slapped her face. It didn't take long before they left the alleys of the Old City and were racing along the four-lane ring road, keeping up with the cars. "Is this safe?" Raven asked.

"Depends," Ice said. "Thailand has the highest accident rate in the world, but don't worry. You're not here very often."

Raven made a face and shrugged. Too late now! Her hair flew in the wind.

They swerved around a corner, took an exit and followed the other tuk tuk down a country lane, an access road to the Ping Chiang Mai Spa. A steady stream of taxis and tuk tuks filtered through, picking up and dropping off guests along a path lined with palms and fountains. The woman and her partner got out. The man put his arm around her as they walked inside.

Raven and Ice settled up and disembarked. They followed the couple inside to a lounge and chose a table well-placed to observe, though the light was dim. Ice ordered more Thai beer, and they talked about Ice's time in the States while keeping watch. When a third person joined the couple, Raven took a moment to focus. She gasped.

"You know who he is?" Ice asked.

"Would you mind hanging out here for five minutes while I go make a phone call?"

"No problem," Ice said, leaning back and drinking his beer. "I'll wait right here. Thai bodyguard and artist, at your service."

Raven smiled. It was funny and not funny. Maybe I need a bodyguard—I have a bad feeling about that trio, she thought.

Slinking out, Raven returned to the lobby. Opposite the main entrance lay an archway and beyond it a sprawling swimming pool shaped organically, like a lake. It glowed from beneath, its lamps illuminating the surrounding tropical plants. She crossed a bamboo bridge and found a bench in the shadows beneath a banana tree, leaned down and called Anna, who would be in the middle of her day.

"Shit," she said. "Shit. Shit. Shit," she mumbled. Where are you, Anna? "Pick up!" she exclaimed out loud again. Anna's phone went to voicemail.

"Anna, I've got to talk to you! I'm sorry! Don't be mad. I know you think I'm in Miami, but I'm in Chiang Mai with that artist friend of my uncle, Alex Ice. I mean Ice. Anyway, something weird happened. We were at dinner, and I spotted this blond woman who looked familiar. Finally, I realized I saw her at Nou's Starlight gala. And now she's here. And guess who she's with? That hot finance guy from the Bank, Sasha something. They're together. I mean, together together. You know? And it gets even weirder, Anna. I followed them, and they're in a lounge at this five-star spa place, the Ping Chiang Mai, meeting with another guy from the Bank. His name is Ko. All three of them were at that gala! This can't be a coincidence. I'll call Tanner later. Now, I've gotta run! Call me when you can."

When she hung up, Ice was approaching. He crossed the bamboo bridge and stood before her. "Hey. They're leaving. I ordered a taxi. Do you want to follow them?"

"Oh my God. This is crazy. What should we do?"

"Better decide fast." He cocked his head, shrugged and held his hands up—the universal what-are-you-going-to-do pose.

"Are you up for this?"

"Why not? It's way more interesting than my usual routine," he said, waving her over.

They hurried back to the lobby in time to see Sasha, Ko and the woman getting into their taxi.

Ice spoke with a bellhop and turned to Raven. "That's ours," he said, pointing. "Get in!"

Chapter 37

Washington, DC – Sun., Feb. 23, 10:00 a.m. EST

Anna woke up late and headed straight for her programmable coffee machine, which had finished brewing a pot right on time—several hours earlier. She poured a lukewarm cup. The wound on her leg ached, and her head wound felt tender. She longed to play a game of racquetball to let off steam, but her body was in no condition.

She checked her voicemail. There were only a few messages. Besides the usual scams, Tanner had left one saying the investigation was still pending. Another had come in from Raven. As soon as Anna heard the intro, though—"Anna, I've got to talk to you! I'm sorry! Don't be mad."—she hung up. Whatever Raven had to say could wait.

Facing the accumulation of emails, notifications and texts was harder, but she quickly assessed most of it was junk. One bright spot—her cousin had sent baby pictures on a family group text, to which she replied with heart emojis. One other text from an unknown number jumped out. "This is Elle Mann. I have info about Nou for you. Meet me today at 11 at the corner where you saw Mayhem," it said.

Shoot, Anna thought. How could this person, Elle, know about that? Could this be one of Evy's friends? Is that how she got my number? What time is now? Am I too late already?

Deciding to run for it, Anna downed the coffee. She shot a quick email to Tanner telling him she received his message and was eager to get back to work, threw on her clothes, and ordered a ride. By 10:45, Anna was standing at the corner. At 11, doubt seeped in. And at 11:15, she was about to leave when a woman wearing yoga pants, a mint green sweatshirt and a plain black cap bumped into her. "This way," she said, passing Anna.

More annoyed than intrigued by the sneaking around, Anna trailed her. After several blocks, yoga woman entered the National Portrait Gallery. Anna followed her through two sets of doors past a security guard, the info desk and a couple of elderly docents to the Kogod Courtyard, a four-story concourse the size of a football field. Constructed of glass and steel arcs, the roof appeared to undulate like waves, lending the wide-open space an eerie calm.

The woman sat down at a café table tucked in a corner of concourse. The playful screeches of a couple of elementary-age kids echoed as they ran around and their drooping parents attempted to rein them in. Besides the family and the two women, no one else was there—the place had opened a mere ten minutes before.

"Hey," Anna said as she sat across from yoga woman. "Nice to, meet you, uh...Elle?"

"Hi," yoga woman said, exhaling audibly. "I know this routine seems ridiculous, but things are not normal. This was Evy's idea."

Anna's neck tightened. "Evy?"

"She was my best friend," she added, pulling her cap down on her face. "I'm Sara Reedman."

"Ah," Anna whispered. "So, you got my messages?"

"I already knew who you were."

"You did?"

"Remember that night when you went to see 'Mayhem' with your friend Mel?"

"Of course."

"We were there."

"What do you mean? 'We'?"

"Evy and I. We followed you there—remember you walked over from the bureau?"

"Why?"

"She wanted to meet you in person, on her terms," she said, wringing her hands.

"Why the stunt with the phone? Why didn't she just ask me then and there?"

"I don't know. She was totally stressed out. She was trying to be extra careful, I guess. She said people were following her—which seemed a little wacky to me at the time. There was no way to get your cell number. I guess the office routes people to the voicemail on the old landline, right?"

Anna frowned. "Were you at the Egyptian with her too?"

"No, after she got your number, she told me to head out—I had other plans originally. So I left. Of course, I had no idea what was going to happen." Sara looked at the ground.

"I'm sorry," Anna said, remembering now that Mel had said the klutzy woman who turned out to be Evy was with a woman.

"Yeah, me too," Sara said, finally making eye contact.

"Why did you decide to contact me? Aren't you supposed to keep it zipped?"

"I was thinking about everything you said in your messages—that I could talk to you on background, that you wanted to get to the truth, yada yada. The thing is, Evy told me to get in touch with you, if anything happened."

"Me? Why me?"

"She did her research. She said you were the best. So I'm trusting her judgment."

"Maybe her judgment wasn't that good, after all," Anna said. "I'm sorry. That was dumb," she added a moment later.

"It doesn't matter. Her judgment was flawed. It's true," Sara said, wincing. "But you are what I have left."

"OK. Thanks, I guess."

"Her boyfriend Giovanni wanted her to talk to a journalist in New York, Bob something, or David. I don't remember his last name."

"Did she?"

"No. That's the point."

"What do you mean?"

"Evy had her own mind," Sara said, hands trembling. "I told you, she thought you were the best. She wanted to talk to you—for a bunch of reasons, like, you are a woman, you cover international finance, you are here in DC. Plus, you have a great reputation."

Anna nodded and pursed her lips. Is this woman playing me? "Thanks. And who do you think this Giovanni is?"

"Listen, we might not have a lot of time, so," said Sara, surveying the giant indoor space. "So, yeah, Evy was dating—and working with—this guy Giovanni Salazar. He told her their mutual friend Charles de Jeanbourg recommended her."

"For what?" Anna recalled the diary entry that the tech had found, in which Evy had rejected Giovanni. She couldn't forget Evy's statement, "Fuck the CIA." Would Sara's story line up?

"That's what I'm explaining to you. They both know—knew—Charles de Jeanbourg. Like, Evy went to grad school with Charles, and Giovanni and Charles both work for the CIA, and I want to find out more about them, especially Charles. You can help me with that."

"More CIA?"

"What do you mean?"

187

"Have you ever heard of J.D. Smith—he works at the Bank—or Steven Brown?"

"No, why?"

"Forget it. Sorry. You're saying they worked for the CIA?"

"Yes."

"And, wait, which graduate school did Charles and Evy attend?"

"It was an international affairs degree thing in New York."

"OK."

"So, Giovanni approached Evy in Bangkok," Sara continued. "It was, like, more than a year ago. While she was there, she had to attend an American Embassy function. Giovanni said Charles told him about her, that she would be perfect. She let him take her to dinner. That led to more dinners and you know, more. They saw each other here, in Bangkok and other places—I don't know all where. He paid for her flights and stuff, and he convinced her to listen to his proposal, some kind of part-time contract. At first, she told him she'd think about it—that's what she told me—and he told her to keep it to herself—but she blabbed it to me. I told her to forget those freaks, who think they can go around commandeering anybody they want. Like, I urged her to drop it. She never wanted to do that kind of work. But she was into Giovanni, and she said the gig would help her pay off her school loans."

"You're saying she took the job?"

"Yeah, she thought it would be fine, at least at first."

"At first?"

"Yeah, but something got weird, and right before she died, she was freaked out and said someone tried to push her onto the metro tracks."

Anna made a face.

"I know. I questioned it too. But she tried to contact Giovanni and talk to him about it, and he wasn't reachable. She was upset, and she asked me to help her find out more about his background."

"Did you?"

"Not yet, but I tried. I sent an email to Charles. He didn't answer."

"I suppose the metro story is plausible, considering what happened to me and Viktor yesterday," she said.

"What do you mean? Who's Viktor?"

"Viktor," Anna said, suddenly reluctant to worry Sara even more. "He's my boyfriend. We were attacked yesterday—but we'll be fine."

"You were attacked?" Sara hissed. "Oh my God." She wrung her hands.

"It's OK. He's at the hospital—only for tests. And I have stitches in my leg. That's it. We'll be OK."

"Oh my God," Sara repeated. "Evy was right. We have to hide."

"Hide?"

"What do you think this charade is for? Evy told me to keep a low profile. I'm lucky I took the cat-sitting gig."

"Cat-sitting?"

"I'm not staying at my place. I took a cat-sitting job up in Spring Valley." Sara crossed her arms and hugged herself.

"Hey, I'm sorry you're wrapped up in this," Anna said, giving Sara a sincere look of regret. "Let's get back to Evy. Did she tell you what this Giovanni wanted her to do?"

Sara was shivering but continued. "They wanted to reveal some scandal in our division, clean up the Bank, or something."

"You told her not to?"

Sara nodded.

"Why? Were you protecting the ED?"

"What do you mean by that?" Sara snapped.

"Nothing," Anna said. "I'm sorry. I heard some gossip, that's all."

"What? What did you hear?"

"There's a version of this story in which you were dating Channarong," Anna told her matter-of-factly.

"Are you kidding me?" Sara said, shaking her head. "The gossip mill at the Bank is so ridiculous. Who dreams this stuff up?"

"So you weren't with him?"

"Of course not!"

"OK, I apologize. I had to ask," Anna said. "Did anyone else know what Evy was doing?"

"I have no idea who knew what. The Bank has all kinds of experts and their assistants on regions and sectors—there are country managers, external relations people, finance types, editors, employees directly in the President's office—like 10,000 people worldwide."

"But Evy was going to expose somebody in your department?"

"I think so."

"Well, that does narrow it down a little. I've reviewed the directory, but the hierarchy isn't exactly crystal clear in there. Can you help me out?"

"OK, sure," she said, looking at the ceiling. "Nou was one of 25 Executive Directors, you know EDs. His division, South East Asia, handled 11 countries, including Vietnam, Myanmar, Thailand and the Lao PDR. He had an 'alternate,' that is, a second-in-command, and a bunch of advisers and assistants who specialize in work on those countries."

Anna nodded. "And you had how many advisers?"

"Seven. Well, four 'senior advisers,' and three 'advisers.' Venny Kumar, Ko Maung Mai, Bo Pham and Judy Beekley were senior advisers. There were also James Cowherd, Ellen Tallmin and Rosalie Rocke. On the program assistant front, we have, I mean had, four: Evy and me, Ingrid Jonsson and Brad Bell."

"Did you ever notice anything strange about anybody in your office?"

"No," she said. "Honestly, no. I didn't."

"What about Nou?"

"What about him? Nou was an amazing person. He was kind and brilliant, and he never touched me. He didn't look at me in that way, or make gross jokes. I want to finish my PhD in econ, and he was helping me revamp my dissertation. That's it. He was like a good dad. That's part of what I wanted to tell you. I'm here for Evy, but I'm here for him too."

"Why would he hang himself?"

"No idea. I can't understand it at all," Sara said, standing up. "But as far as I'm concerned, that dude Giovanni is responsible," she added, looking all around again, as if a monster might charge out. "You need to find Giovanni—and Charles," she said, and then she fled.

Chapter 38

Chiang Mai – Sunday, Feb. 23, 10:00 p.m. local time (10:00 a.m. EST in DC)

Raven and Ice took off in the taxi, trailing Sasha, the blond woman and Ko. In the dark, they raced down back roads past industrial sites and scrubland. As they came to the Nimmanhaemin area on the west side of the city near the university, signs advertised bars and restaurants, lights twinkled, and the traffic thickened. At the fifth traffic light, Ko jumped out, leaving his companions in the taxi.

"And now?" Ice said.

Raven hesitated, wondering what to do. "Follow the couple!" she announced. "In the car!"

Ice directed the driver to continue down the avenue and pointed out the back window of the taxi. "Ko went toward Zen 67. See? Famous place," he said.

"Famous?"

"Hottest club in Chiang Mai, at least for tourists—they have a special show."

"Great. Well, I hope he has a great time—and that I didn't pick the wrong people to follow."

At the next light, Raven tried to take it all in. Revelers swarmed the crossing as they waited. Trendy restaurants, many with outdoor patios, dotted the avenue. Art galleries and specialty boutiques filled the spaces between the restaurants—bikes, foreign language books, a custom tailor. Bolts of silk fabric behind a mannequin displaying a stunning haute couture dress called to Raven. Food trucks, many of them retrofitted camper vans, parked half-way onto sidewalks, surrounded by snacking partiers.

Ice took out some baht and handed the money to the driver. "They're getting out," he observed. They emerged from the taxi only three blocks from Zen 67, but the atmosphere was markedly quieter.

"I can see them down that lane," she said, nodding.

As Ice and Raven followed, he put his arm around her. She didn't object. Her nerves were jangled and she felt a chill. His muscular shoulders reassured her.

"I'm used to chasing stories, but not like this. It feels like a TV show," she said.

"You're sure to figure it out soon. The heroine always does."

Raven tilted her head in doubt. The car accident and all the headlines about Nou and Evy raced through her mind, and she wrestled with a "that's-never-gonna-happen" message. But as they walked along, her sleuthing instincts resumed. "Hey, check it out," she said, pointing at a French-style mansion with a Mansard roofline. "They went in there." The large oblong leaves of banana trees framed the front door, and a row of European sports cars stood at the valet station. "Oh," she added. "See that gold plate next to the doorbell?"

Ice nodded.

"It says 'The Embassy.' I read about that place online. Very exclusive. We'll never get in."

"We'll see," he said. "Follow me."

They approached the entrance, where a line had formed. Maybe 20 people were waiting. Ice ignored them, walked up to the plush burgundy rope, and said a few words to the bouncer. In an instant, the man opened the door and ushered them inside.

"Nice move," she said over the techno music.

"No problem. See, I'm a great local guide," he whispered into her ear. "Come on." Ice took Raven's hand, and led her through the rooms.

The building had been somebody's home once—parlors, stairwells, hallways, little rooms that might have been servants' quarters—but the throbbing music and cigarette smoke erased any trace of the family who once lived there. Dancers pulsed up and down in a room called Salon Z— but there was no sign of anyone Raven recognized. She tugged on Ice's hand. She pushed through the crowd toward the bar. "Over there," she said. "They have drinks. I'll get some too, if you keep an eye out."

He nodded.

Raven returned with two martinis and handed one to Ice. She nodded at him. "Thank you for your help."

"Cheers," he replied, sampling the drink. "They don't know you?"

"I hope not. I recognize them, but that's my job—saw them recently at a big event. They wouldn't have any reason to remember me, but they could, theoretically."

"Follow me," Ice said, taking Raven's hand.

Raven let Ice lead her again, circling to a position nearer Sasha and the woman, but still out of sight.

The woman was leaning back, looking up at Sasha, who pressed his left hand against the wall next to the woman's head. His right hand carried a rocks glass full of clear liquor, neat. He stared down at her as he talked. She smiled at him and laughed. Then he lowered his left hand, passing it slowly over her breast, downward along the counters of her body and under her little red skirt. She looked to the side. Then abruptly, he stopped, chugged the drink, dropped the glass and grabbed her with both hands on the shoulders. He kissed her hard on the mouth.

Raven winced and turned away. Wow. They're in it together, thick as thieves, whatever "it" was, she thought. When Raven looked back, the woman was holding Sasha's hand, leading him deeper into the club.

Raven and Ice inched through the crowd too, observing as the couple sat down on a couch in a lounge area.

"It's too loud in here," Ice said. "You'll never hear anything."

"Maybe not," Raven said, unlocking her phone, clicking an app and holding the device up to show Ice. "But this is a recording app for press conferences and interviews, and it works even if there's interference or background noise."

"Want me to place it?"

"That would be awesome. You can casually 'forget' the phone on that ledge behind their heads."

"I see you have some moves too," Ice said, taking the phone. He proceeded slowly, pretending to talk on the phone and survey the dance floor. When he finished his martini, he rested the glass on the ledge, where he simultaneously left the black phone, which blended in to the décor, and returned to Raven.

"Perfect," Raven said. "Now we wait."

"How about I get you another drink?"

"OK."

When Ice came back, he and Raven sipped their drinks while monitoring the other couple on the couch.

Sasha shifted positions, resting his hand on the woman's neck for a moment, then leaning toward her again.

"They should get a room," Ice said.

"Glad you can find humor in this," Raven replied.

"Hey, I'm up for following them all night, but how about you fill me in on what's really going on here?" Ice asked.

"Wait," Raven said. "Look."

The woman had stopped kissing Sasha, and they were on the move.

Leaving their drinks half-full, Raven and Ice scrambled to keep up. Raven grabbed her phone off the ledge on the way out. Once again, Sasha and his girlfriend took off in a tuk tuk. Once again, Raven and Ice followed suit.

Bouncing down the lane, Raven replayed the conversation they had recorded. It was barely audible over the engine. She held it up to her ear. At first, the blather bored her. But by the time the tuk tuk was speeding down the main drag, Raven received her reward:

> "Hard to believe Evy is dead," the woman said.
>
> "Collateral damage. Ko is the one who will regret it," Sasha said. "It looks bad for him, doesn't it? He can't squirm out of it."
>
> "He'll go down with Channarong—he is the biggest idiot," she said. "But you, Sasha, are a genius."
>
> "Thank you, Ingrid," he said.

Their conversation paused. Raven waited. The woman's name was Ingrid? Perhaps the lull was because he was kissing her? Then Ingrid resumed talking.

> "Poor Sara. She better watch her step," Ingrid said.

Raven heard Sasha reply, but she couldn't make out his words. Her mouth dried out, as if she were at the dentist and it was stuffed with cotton. Poor Sara? Suddenly, she could hear Sasha again.

> "Ingrid, I couldn't do it without you," Sasha said. "I need you."

"Oh my God," Raven said, shutting the recording off. "I have to send an email. Can you watch where they're going? Make sure the driver follows them?" Raven asked Ice.

"No problem," he said.

Raven typed an email to Anna: "URGENT: Sara Reedman is in danger. I overheard Sasha and the blond woman (Ingrid) talking. He said Ko will 'regret it.' She said it 'looks bad for' Ko, and Ko will 'go down with Channarong.' She called Nou 'the biggest idiot.' Did Ko and/or Nou kill Evy? Ko was with them earlier. More soon."

Chapter 39

Washington, DC – Sun., Feb. 23, 12:15 p.m. EST

Anna darted after Sara, who dashed through the Portrait Gallery foyer, barreled out the north door and flew down the museum steps. "Wait, Sara!" she called. At first, Anna stayed on her heels. Limping slightly, she wove around some loiterers, crossed G and ran up 9th. She was on her trail—until she wasn't. Sara was nowhere to be seen. What next? Was Sara telling the truth? Did Giovanni kill Evy?

Anna kept walking up 9th and took a left at the Carnegie Library onto Massachusetts. Along the way, she called Viktor at the hospital—no answer. She passed block after block of hotels and condos. At Scott Circle, she headed north again on 16th, where the condos ended and row houses lined the streets. Traffic was minimal—it was Sunday. People were sauntering along, laughing and holding coffee cups. The atmosphere felt oddly normal.

When she crossed U, 16th began a sharp incline. The thought of a taxi entered her mind. The doctors had told her to take it easy, but the calming effect of the walk seemed to outweigh the discomfort in her leg. She kept going. The Italian gardens of Malcolm X Park emerged as she ascended the hill. At the top, she turned around and looked—the city sprawled out below her like a rolled-out map. It was spectacular. She reversed again and continued. Beaux Arts mansions lined the strip. She passed little plaques announcing the foreign representations—the embassies of Lithuania, Cuba and Poland, the Cultural Center of the Embassy of Spain, the Mexican Cultural Institute.

At Columbia Road, she checked the time. She'd been walking for about an hour. A new place she'd heard about—an historic church, abandoned for decades, and now a hotel—lay only a few blocks away. She headed over. The lobby still screamed of church foyer, but the enormous square-shaped two-story sanctuary had been transformed. No stained glass here. The midday sun beamed from clear windows in the vaulted ceiling. Plush couches, tables, and chairs dotted the space, flanked by bars on either side. Waiters were delivering brunch drinks and tapas. Nearly a dozen dogs lounged on the couches, not under them. Anna laughed. Canine companions in a DC restaurant! What loophole was this?

Anna found a table and ordered a beer—mimosas weren't her thing. She wanted to call the New York grad school where Evy and Charles had gone, but it was Sunday. Otherwise, she had two main leads: the ex-NSC guy Garrett Zarribe, who might be a horse's ass, like Mel said, but still able to produce dirt on Charles de Jeanbourg and Giovanni Salazar; or Steven Brown, the communications director in Senator Caleb's office, who supposedly fed the lies about her to the *Mirror*. She wondered what she could say to Brown. Hey, I heard you're a CIA plant. What are you really up to? And what the heck do you have against me?

She picked Garrett Zarribe. His number at the think tank was easy enough to find on the internet. Waiting for her beer, Anna dialed the phone.

"Mr. Zarribe, this is Anna Jones," she said on voicemail. "I hope you remember me. Rick Nadyam was your son's roommate in boarding school—and Rick was my boyfriend back in college, you know, freshman year. I was with him the other week, when we ran into you at Karl's. I don't know if you've followed the story in the news, but I'm on leave from the *Daily Journal* due to some BS about a business deal. The story is a lie, 'fake news' as they say, and I need help. Please call me back!" She hung up. How many days would it take for a horse's ass to call back?

The waiter brought the beer and Anna took a swig. Then the phone rang—caller ID indicated it was Garrett Zarribe. "Maybe I'm the horse's ass," she said out loud. She answered the phone. "Mr. Zarribe? Is that you already?"

"I'm not the only one working on a Sunday?"

"Hardly. But, then again, I'm working to save my own sinking ship. I gather you're putting in time for the think tank."

"Oh, no. The scrambling to keep oneself afloat never ends. I've got a fellowship application due Monday. Got to keep up with the foundations. Need a change of pace from the war games projects for the military contractors, you know? Not ready to be put out to pasture."

"Thanks for calling. I didn't expect it. I wasn't sure you'd remember me."

"Oh, ye of little faith. Of course, I remember you. Not often I get to meet my son's friends. Yes, learned of your predicament in the news. How can I be of service?"

"I am hoping you can help me figure a few things out. But first, I'm afraid I have to ask if you would be discreet about this?"

"Cross my heart and hope to die. Scout's honor."

"OK, then. Here goes." Anna told Garrett Zarribe everything, except for the part about Sara Reedman. "So, it seems like Evy was on to something at the Bank. She was planning to tell me about it, but apparently someone wanted her to keep quiet."

"Heavy load, Anna. My role is?"

"Sniff around? Talk to your contacts in the intelligence community and your ex-NSC pals, whomever, and see if anyone knows these guys

Charles de Jeanbourg and Giovanni Salazar? Nose around about Steven Brown and the guy at the World Bank, J.D. Smith, too? They're all rumored to have ties to the CIA. It doesn't add up, Mr. Zarribe."

"OK, no problem. Back to you by COB," he said. "Over and out."

Chapter 40

Washington, DC – Sun., Feb. 23, 5:00 p.m. EST

Anna was purchasing a latte for a late afternoon pick-me-up on her way to visit Viktor, when Zarribe called back.

"Mr. Zarribe?" Anna answered as she handed a five to the cashier.

"I don't have much, Anna, but it's not for lack of trying," Zarribe said.

"Oh," Anna replied, disappointed. She made a fist with her left hand and held it close to her chest. With her right, she pushed her bag's shoulder strap back and then grabbed her latte, giving a quick smile and nod to the barista. "Thanks, anyway," she told Zarribe.

"But I do have a little," he added.

"Oh!" she repeated, this time enthusiastically. She stood near the door of the shop to listen.

"Charles de Jeanbourg is smart as a whip and doesn't suffer fools," Zarribe began. "He's a linguist who conducts research. That is, I confirmed he's officially a CIA analyst, don't know his expertise. Didn't hear anything CIA about the other three: Smith, Brown or Salazar. None of my agency contacts had anything on them."

"That's it?"

"Yup. But think of it this way: A dearth of information can also be useful."

"How so?"

"It means one of two things. They are either under serious cover, or they really don't have anything to do with the CIA."

"And what is your best guess?"

"Called around, as you asked. Talked to some security-military folks, and some people who are not in the intelligence community. Asked about these clowns. From what I heard, if I had to guess? I don't buy it that Brown is somehow a mole for the CIA. In the Senate? Come on! Paranoia is ubiquitous these days, but that doesn't pass the smell test. Spying on the Senator would be a waste of time and money. Besides, he couldn't do both jobs at once."

"OK," she said.

"Regarding Smith—the CIA might place a computer nerd over at the Bank, somebody to monitor communications—or one might imagine there are foreign intelligence operatives working undercover as Bank types. Maybe such persons are supposed to keep eyes on the Bank. Just thinking out loud here. But, Smith, nah, I don't see it. My contacts over at the Bank say that guy goes home and plays computer games. He could be a hacker, but he doesn't have the people skills to be in traditional intelligence. And he doesn't blend in."

"What about Salazar?"

"Now Salazar is another story. Real mystery man. Slick. Well-travelled. Multilingual. He was in Bangkok when he met Evy, from what you told me, right? Follow that lead."

"Thanks, Mr. Zarribe. This has been helpful. I appreciate all your time."

"There's one more thing," he said. "I'd find out where these CIA stories are coming from."

"OK. Got it. Thanks again."

"Let me know if you need anything else," Zarribe said.

Anna called Viktor again. No one answered. She sent him a text saying she was planning to stop by, and ordered a car. No sooner had she stepped outside when her phone rang again. The caller ID read "unknown name," which hardly ever happened anymore. She had to laugh at the irony—since the telemarketers and scammers hijacked other people's real names and numbers, the tell-tale "unknown name" was someone important.

She picked up the phone but said nothing, still half-expecting a computerized voice threatening her about her IRS delinquency.

"Anna Jones?" a man said into the void.

"Yes," she said.

"We don't know each other, but my name may ring a bell. I'm Charles de Jeanbourg."

Chapter 41

Chiang Mai – Monday, Feb. 24, 5:00 a.m. local time (5:00 p.m. EST on Sunday, Feb. 23 in DC)

Sasha and Ingrid staggered down the hall and tumbled into their room, as Raven and Ice watched from the stairwell.

As soon as their door slammed, Raven whispered, "Now what?"

Ice held the stairwell door open for Raven, and they both stepped into the hall. "It's almost dawn," Ice said. "You need sleep too. Have you heard anything from your people yet?"

"Nothing. I'm sorry I wasted your time."

"It wasn't wasted," he said, allowing his glance to linger at her. "You tracked them here. And, for me, it's been a pleasure getting to know the niece of Theo van Torenmaas. How about we split up? You check in here and sleep for a few hours. Meanwhile, I'll watch their door. Then you come back and switch with me, and I'll rest in your room. If they leave, we follow together."

"That's an amazing offer," she said, stifling a yawn. "Wow. I'm embarrassed to take you up on it, but I'm about to collapse."

"I'm a night owl—and I don't have jet lag."

"Come with me to reception? These two aren't going anywhere in the next 15 minutes."

"Sure."

"You know, in case I run into any snags."

"Right." He smiled at her. "We can go this way," he added, calling the elevator.

They stepped in. As the doors closed, an arm thrust into the elevator. The doors bounced and retreated. Raven pushed "door open." She looked up, and her knees went weak.

"Shut the hell up. Push 'door close' and '7'," the man said, pointing a pistol, waving it back and forth at both of them.

"Ko," she whispered. Shaking, she pushed "7." Ice moved closer to her, standing almost in front of her.

"You fool," Ko said to Ice. "Do something stupid, and I'll get two for the price of one. What a bargain."

Ice stood taller but said nothing. Raven broke out in a cold sweat.

On the 7th floor, Ko ushered them out. "Down the hall, second door on the left. Be quiet."

Raven and Ice walked. Ko kept the gun pointed at them, swiped a key card and signaled them to enter. Ko commanded them to sit on the end of the bed. He arranged the desk chair in order to sit and direct the gun at them.

"You won't shoot us here," Raven said. "Someone will hear it."

"And you would never get away," Ice told him. "Raven is a foreigner. The police will never let this drop. You are the one who better not do anything stupid."

"Both of you, shut up," Ko hissed.

"No! We will not shut up!" Raven yelled. "You killed Evy! You killed Nou! And now you're going to kill us," she shrieked. "And probably Sasha and Ingrid too!"

"Preposterous!" Ko said.

"We saw you with them tonight," Raven said. "We heard them talking!"

"Shut up, I told you," Ko said, staring at Raven. "You think you know what's going on, but you don't. I've been following you since Zen 67. You don't know anything." Ko grimaced.

Ice took Ko's moment of distraction to leap. He grabbed Ko's pistol with one hand and punched his nose with the other. Ko tumbled off his chair. His gun clunked on the ground. Ice then punched Ko hard in the stomach and neck, but Ko fought back like the tough street boy he had once been.

Grabbing a bedside lamp, Raven yanked the cord out of the socket. Before she had a chance to strike, however, Ice lay moaning, doubled over on the floor holding his ribs, mouth bloodied, while Ko was upright again, pistol in hand.

Disheveled and sweating, Ko grabbed Raven by the arm and shoved her into the desk chair next to Ice, who remained on the floor. "Sit!" he yelled at her. "Or you will be the one with the lamp on your head—or the cord around your neck!" He reoriented the pistol at her. "And, you!" he commanded to Ice, "Stay! Or I will shoot her." Once more he turned to Raven. "Tell me what you heard Sasha say about me!"

Raven's hands trembled. Her arm ached where Ko had grabbed it. "He said you killed Evy," she stammered. "It seemed like Sara was next."

"He told Ingrid I killed Evy?" Ko barked.

"He said you wouldn't be able to squirm out of it."

Ko hesitated. "Why would I kill the girls?"

"I don't know," she replied, careful not to reveal her thoughts.

"And Ingrid? Did she say anything?" Ko said, backing up.

"I don't know!" she said, thinking back for a crumb that might satisfy Ko. "Not really. She lavished compliments on him, said he was 'brilliant'."

"Sasha? Brilliant? Ha!" Ko spit out. "That lying little prick," he choked. "He's setting me up. Don't you see? Listen to me! Both of you," commanded Ko, waving his gun back and forth again. "Go back to your art center," he told Ice, who was now sitting up, leaning against the wall.

"Forget you were ever here," Ko said, suddenly swiveling toward Raven and adding with great disgust, "And you! This story isn't worth it." Then, in one quick swoop, Ko shoved his pistol inside his jacket and bolted.

Chapter 42

Washington, DC – Sun., Feb. 23, 6:00 p.m. EST

Anna wasn't exactly surprised when Charles de Jeanbourg called her—she was used to sources aiming to spin a story, and plenty of people called journalists all the time telling bald face lies hoping to mold reality. She was, however, taken aback that he contacted her so soon.

"Well, Mr. de Jeanbourg, you are quick," she said.

"You have been asking around about me," he said. "I'd like to talk."

"And why is that?"

"I'll tell you when we meet."

"I bet you will."

"How about now? At Union Station."

"Right now?"

"Yes."

She paused. The car was on its way anyway. Viktor would understand. "Give me fifteen minutes."

"There's a Belgian coffee shop near the entrance on the west side. Do you know it?"

"Of course."

"I'll meet you there."

"How will I find you?"

"Buy two cups of coffee, sit down and *I'll find you*," he said, and hung up.

Anna opened the ride share app and entered a new destination. Within a few minutes, she was on her way. Once more, she tried to reach Viktor, to no avail. She left a message.

When they reached the semicircle in front of Union Station, traffic was piled up. Despite his efforts to follow the navigation system and get in the correct lane, the driver missed his turn-off. Anna told him to stop, but he overshot the main entrance to the station. She stepped out a block further down Massachusetts Avenue than necessary.

"No worries," she told the driver. "Have a great night."

She walked the block back toward Senate Park. The crosswalks and lanes in front of Union Station were as convoluted as ever. What failure of urban planning had caused this tangle of roads, and why did it perpetuate? Was Charles de Jeanbourg already there?

At the café, she bought the two coffees, sat down and waited. Various single men stared zombie-like at their electronic devices. Nobody made eye contact with her, not even the undesirable variety. Anna was about to dial Viktor again, when a thirty-something man wearing black sunglasses landed in the chair across from her.

"Sorry to keep you waiting," he said, removing the sunglasses.

She took him in: hair—brown, trim cut, contrasting with shaggy beard; skin—basic pale, no obvious tattoos; eyes—blue; features—average, handsome in a nondescript way, like that actor who's in every movie but whose name you forget, Paul something; clothes—tapered rust-colored jeans, pointy black leather oxfords, black belt, grey long-sleeved collared shirt, nice but not too expensive. "It's fine," she said, wondering what path led this hipster to the CIA. "I was surprised you came to me, though, and so soon."

"Mm-hmm," he said, handing her his wallet and showing her his driver's license and ID cards. "Here. And tell me how you heard about me."

"Let's get straight to it, then. No idle chitchat? Don't you want your coffee?" Anna pushed one cup closer to him.

"Thank you," Charles said. He took a sip, making a slurping sound.

Anna reviewed the contents of his wallet. The ID cards looked realistic. But what if they were fake? How would she know? She shrugged and handed them back. "To answer your question," she said. "I spoke to Sara Reedman, Evy's friend."

"I see," he said. "She told you about me?"

"Yes."

"Where is she?"

"None of your business," Anna said. "Now, Sara told me that Evy said you guys went to grad school together."

"That much is public knowledge."

"Drop the attitude, de Jeanbourg," she said.

"It's de Jeanbourg, soft 'j,' like 'zh.' The ending sounds like 'pour' not 'iceberg'."

"Fine, de Jeanbourg," she said, re-pronouncing his name. "But you are the one who told Salazar to contact Evy. You sang her praises to him, and that's why he asked her to do the gig for the Agency."

"What did she say about Salazar?"

"You must know more about him than I do. He's your boy. Sara told me Evy liked him. She said he was a flirt, smooth but funny. In short, Salazar offered Evy your gig and she took it. He knew which buttons to push, right? What the heck, Charles! Evy got killed because you drew her into this CIA nonsense without knowing what she was doing."

"It's not what you think."

"It never is."

"I can't speak freely. Clearances, leaks, you know, everything has to stay locked down, and I can't jeopardize anything. But I wanted to hear your account."

"Oh, great. Now you have my version of what Sara said that Evy said that Salazar said. Glad I could help you out with that. You don't want to jeopardize anything? Nou and Evy are dead! I'm out of work. Viktor is in the hospital. Sara is afraid of her own shadow. And you can't tell me anything? Where are we supposed to go from here, Charles?"

"Look. Evy was my friend too. I'm doing the best I can. But...there are many layers."

"Like a cake," Anna said, rolling her eyes and getting up. "Good day to you too."

"Wait. I do have one thing for you."

"By all means. Spit it out."

"This may come as a surprise. But here it is: Giovanni Salazar does not have anything to do with the Agency."

"What?"

"That name is most likely an alias. We don't know his identity, and he is not one of ours."

"What?" Anna repeated.

"The man is unknown to us."

"Which means that Evy was not working for the CIA?"

"Yes," he said. "I mean, no. She wasn't. At first, my colleagues thought she was a traitor. But I knew she didn't have the constitution for that—and besides, she wasn't anti-American. She was always telling people how the U.S. had its shortcomings, but it was the best country in the world. Finally, after checking her out, my colleagues backed off. Now they agree that she thought she was working for the CIA. It's just that she wasn't."

"Then who was she working for?"

"Exactly," he said.

SOURCE OF DECEIT

"You're not going to tell me?"
"Jones, I'm afraid I have to go."

Chapter 43

Washington, DC – Sun., Feb. 23, 7:30 p.m. EST

Disgusted at de Jeanbourg's disappearing act, Anna was sitting on her couch, eating a piece of pizza and plotting her next move, when the phone rang. Caller ID showed who it was, but she didn't answer. The phone warbled again. She took a bite of the pizza and looked at the phone. It rang the third time. She stared at the display. When it sang its little song for the fourth and last round, she grabbed it after all.

"Raven," she said, putting the pizza down. "Hey."

"Oh my God, Anna! Thank God! I'm so glad I caught you. Didn't you get my messages?"

"No," she said flatly. "I didn't."

"I need to tell you what's been happening!"

Anna's phone vibrated again. She had been expecting Mel. "Hold on a minute, Raven. I have to take this."

"Wait!" Raven said.

Anna switched to the other call.

"Hi. I'm downstairs," Mel said.

"See you in a minute." Anna called the doorman and asked to let Mel in. Then she went back to Raven.

"Anna!" Raven yelled. "It's urgent!"

"I had to let my friend Mel in, and..."

"Listen to me!" Raven interrupted. "I'm in Chiang Mai. With my uncle's contact, remember? And that guy Sasha is here too. He and Ko are involved!"

"Where?" Anna said.

"Chiang Mai."

"Involved with what?"

"Evy's death. Sasha and Ko."

"Sasha who works at the Bank? What are you talking about? I just had lunch with him a couple days ago."

"Well, he's here now!"

Anna frowned. "Why should I listen to you anyway? You've been talking to Viktor behind my back!"

"Oh, forget that, Anna!" she implored. "The thing with Viktor was a long time ago."

"A long time ago? Really?" Anna demanded. "You've been lying to me since I got to DC."

"What do you mean?"

"Look, Raven, you can stop the charade. It's not just about Viktor. You and your uncle are up to something. I know there was no family funeral in Miami."

"OK! You're right. I lied!" Raven paused. "And I may have been a little jealous of your relationship with Viktor. And that may have made me a little—unwelcoming. But my uncle and I are not up to anything. Tanner sent me to follow you."

Anna felt like she'd been slapped.

"Ask him about it!"

Anna's stomach turned. Would Tanner do that? He might.

"He did it as back-up," said Raven, reading Anna's mind. "He thought the shock of Evy's death, after your history—you know, the shootings in Moscow, Viktor and all—might stress you out. What if you have PTSD or something?"

"I don't have PTSD, Raven. That's absurd."

"Well, I don't know. He was protecting you, Anna!"

"More like he was protecting the paper," Anna said as she heard a knock on the door. "Hang on a minute," she said, putting Raven on hold, trying to grasp the implications of Raven's assertions. She let Mel in and pointed at the fridge. "I'm back," she told Raven, as Mel walked over to the refrigerator, took out a bottle of beer.

"Thank God," Raven said. "I was afraid you would hang up. Please. Listen! It makes sense. Tanner has to protect the paper first."

Anna hurried to assess Raven's argument. Had she really been sent in as back-up? It was not so far-fetched. But what did that say about Torenmaas and the accident? And Raven? "I don't have PTSD," Anna said once more.

"OK. Fine. We can talk about the personal side later, but right now, please listen to me! I'm telling the truth. Tanner sent me here too, and now I have some pretty insane pieces of the puzzle. This is not about my uncle, and Sasha is not in DC! I need you to listen to me."

Anna sighed hard. "OK, I'm listening."

Raven explained everything that happened as she followed Sasha, Ingrid and Ko.

"Raven, this is surreal," Anna replied. "Sasha and Ko are there? Sasha is with Ingrid? And Ko threatened to shoot you!? It's really crazy."

"That's what I've been trying to get through to you!"

"I've known Sasha for years, and he never mentioned Ingrid. It's hard to get my head around it. Are Sasha and Ko in league with one another, or not?"

"Whatever went on before, seems like not anymore."

Looking at Anna, Mel turned her hand in circles.

"Raven, I'm putting this call on speaker—my friend Mel is here," Anna said. "I've known her forever, and she works on the Hill—she might lend some perspective, alright?"

"Sure," Raven replied.

Mel nodded, continuing to nurse her beer, as she listened attentively.

"What did your uncle say?" Anna asked.

"My uncle?" Raven asked.

"Didn't you ask him what Sasha and Ko are doing there?"

"Why? He wouldn't know them. He's just funding the project with Ice."

"Rather a large coincidence that they are all there now, right after he sent you too, isn't it?"

"Not really. I don't know. Why would he tell us to come here and inspect his operation, if he had anything to hide? I thought you would have an answer. Does any of this fit with your Bank research?"

"Raven, you need to call your uncle."

"Fine, I'll call him. But he's not going to know anything about Ko and Sasha. Now, can we move on?"

"If you agree to call him, and really press him on this, I'll share what I found out."

"Finally," Raven said. "Deal."

"I've been analyzing the information Evy left on her phone. Also, Tanner assigned a couple of people to help slice and dice the data, and he sent stringers to check out the projects on the ground. Putting it all together, I realized we were on to something."

"But I thought you were persona non grata over there," Mel interjected.

"Tanner is keeping me in the loop," Anna said.

"That's surprisingly cool," Mel said.

"It's not altruism," Anna added. "He's covering his own butt—he knows the editors in New York are wrong, and he doesn't want the paper to lose the real story."

"So what did you find out?" Raven said.

"A lot of the projects have been starved of financing," Anna said.

"How starved?" Raven asked.

"None of them was running full capacity—far from it. Potemkin Villages. Millions and millions of US dollars are being diverted," Anna said.

"The projects are fake?" Raven asked.

"Not fake," Anna said. "But not exactly real, either. I think they're fronts."

"But what does this have to do with the dude Giovanni Salazar?" Mel asked. "And what Jeanbourg told you at Union Station?"

"What stuff?" Raven interrupted.

"Basically, Evy thought she had a side gig with the CIA through Salazar—to help expose some sort of corruption—but it seems he didn't actually work there."

"Whoa," Raven whispered. "So who was he working for? And why would he care about exposing corruption at the Bank?"

"Yeah, why publicize it?" Mel added. "What could he gain from that?"

"I don't know," Anna said. "Also, I don't see the link to Channarong. Or Sasha. Yet."

"Maybe Salazar was blackmailing somebody," Raven said. "Sasha, Channarong, somebody else? Like if they didn't comply, he would have this information leaked?"

"Raven, maybe this is too dangerous for you," Anna said.

"I'll be fine. If I don't keep up with Sasha, we'll lose him, and besides, I want to help my uncle. It'll be better for everybody, if we figure out what's really going on here. Ice can help me, and I'll keep you updated. Now, I've got to jump," Raven said, hanging up.

Anna shook her head.

Mel walked over to the fridge and grabbed another beer. She raised her eyebrows at Anna. "Beer?"

"No thanks," Anna said.

"We need to warn Sara," said Anna, picking up her phone. "I can't believe that man—having Raven shadow me." She shook her head. "Speak of the devil. Check this out. He just sent a text, says to call him right away."

Chapter 44

**Bangkok – Monday, Feb. 24, 7:30 a.m. local time
(7:30 p.m. EST on Sunday, Feb. 23 in DC)**

Despite the warm breeze, Mr. Gold shuddered as he waited on bench number twenty-three near the lake in King Rama IX Botanical Garden. Morning joggers trotted down the sandy paths. The spire of the park's central pavilion glimmered in the distance, and by all accounts the weather was perfect. Nevertheless, Mr. Gold broke out in a cold sweat. He lowered the brim on his baseball hat and stared at the pages of his book, a history of the U.S. Federal Reserve, but he couldn't concentrate. Recent events reverberated inside his head—and no matter what he did, he could not cast Giovanni Salazar out.

Eventually, Mr. Diamond came jogging toward him in purple athletic shorts and a UCSB T-shirt. Nearly 80, his body was grizzled and gaunt, but also surprisingly spry. He sported a greasy, white-grey comb-over.

"Mr. Gold! What a coincidence!" Mr. Diamond said, popping up and down in front of the bench. "If I can make it around this park, you can too," he taunted. "What are you doing?"

"Excuse me, Mr. Diamond. I apologize, but I am a bit under the weather today. Maybe the flu," Mr. Gold replied. "Or I would have. Now, you are in great shape. You look so young."

"Thank you," he said, sitting down. "Beautiful morning. Swan boats are nice for the children."

"Yes, wonderful," Mr. Gold affirmed, according to the code.

"Now," Mr. Diamond said, fixing his piercing black eyes on the boats. "We must discuss your failure. You have made a serious error in judgment."

"If you would permit me to say so, Mr. Diamond, I still believe in Mr. Salazar," Mr. Gold interjected. "Mr. Salazar will complete the mission. I have dispatched him to Washington to salvage the operation, and he is approaching Ms. Poole's friend to finish the job."

"I am not talking about Mr. Salazar. I am referring to the rogue agent. You did not anticipate his action against Ms. Poole."

"No, I did not anticipate that," Mr. Gold said, biting his lip. His insides seethed, and he employed all his energy to appear placid. His inner dialogue screamed: I didn't anticipate that! But neither did anybody else, apparently! How was I supposed to know? Weren't you bigshots supposed to take care of that? Weren't you monitoring every last shred of data? It wasn't my fault. "I'm terribly sorry, Mr. Diamond," he offered in an even tone. "But I've done everything you asked me to do, and I remain your loyal servant." I can't believe I'm the scapegoat! How will this affect my family? What can I do but grovel?

"Your development of Mr. Salazar was too slow. In turn, Ms. Poole was allowed to take too much time. This gave the rogue agent a chance to discover her intentions," he said, shrugging. "Unfortunately, your failure has landed us in this precarious position. She is dead, and the rogue agent is pulling the strings. It is unacceptable."

"It is unacceptable," Mr. Gold repeated.

"We cannot allow this to develop any further," Mr. Diamond said, facing his underling directly. "Your Mr. Salazar has two days to rectify this situation, and the exposé must be published right away." Mr. Diamond looked back at the swan boats.

"I understand," Mr. Gold stated. "Right away."

"Otherwise, we institute Plan B. It is a much less desirable way to put an end to this, Mr. Gold. The risk of exposure is high. Keeping a low profile is a far superior method. However, a direct intervention may become necessary. For both of our sakes, Mr. Gold, Mr. Salazar better come through, or more than your reputation will be on the line."

Mr. Gold nodded, sweat pouring down his temples.

Mr. Diamond stood up and with a bony hand he slapped Mr. Gold on his shoulder, American style. "Take it easy," he said and jogged off.

Chapter 45

Washington, DC – Sun., Feb. 23, 7:50 p.m. EST

Tanner, it's me," Anna said, calling her boss back as requested. She put the phone on speaker again, so Mel could hear everything. Now, it was Anna's turn to bark. "I can't believe you...."

"Not now, Jones. Listen!" Tanner said, as if they had already been in a conversation. "Remember, somebody tried to call Evy after she died? The number tracks back to a company based in Bangkok called Cutting Edge Forex."

"How did you find that out?" she asked.

"I have my contacts here and there, Jones. I've been working in DC for three decades. It's one of the only benefits of being old," Tanner said.

"Thailand again," Anna said, agitated. "But Tanner, now you listen! I have to ask you this. It's important."

"Alright, Jones," Tanner acknowledged. "Settle down. I hear you. Fire away."

"Did you send Raven to Miami to follow me?"

"You would've done the same thing, if you were in my position," he replied without missing a beat. "Someday, you probably will be, you know. Anyway, that's beside the point."

"But all this time, I wasn't sure if I could trust her. I even thought she might be sabotaging me!"

"Look, you're new in my bureau. You might have needed back-up—or babysitting. How could I know? Besides, I was aware Raven was Torenmaas' niece. Nice connection, right? Get over it, Jones. Move on. This story is hot, and you can't be in two places at once. Understood?"

"OK," she said with a sigh. "Truce."

"So Raven wants to stick around Chiang Mai, and I've got the local hire checking out Cutting Edge Forex. What's your next move?"

"Get in touch with Sara ASAP, then focus on Evy, find out who she was working for and what Sasha had to do with it."

"Sounds good. Go ahead and warn Sara. Move on to Evy and Sasha. He's Russian, right? What does that say about him? Call me when you have something." Tanner hung up.

Anna turned to Mel. That was abrupt, she thought. "'Sasha's Russian, right? What does that say about him?'," Anna repeated, mocking Tanner.

"What?" Mel asked.

"I mean, Sasha has a Russian background, sure. But so does Viktor—partly anyway. Viktor's mother was German but his father was Russian. And so? 'What does that say about him?' What?! Just because he's ethnically Russian, is that supposed to mean he's running to aid the Kremlin?"

"I don't know what he thinks."

"Well, what is that supposed to mean?"

"It depends, right?"

"On what?" said Anna, exasperated.

Mel didn't reply at first. Considering her answer carefully, she finally said, "A lot of things. Family, beliefs, circumstances. Tanner is just saying you should dredge Sasha's background for clues."

"Slippery slope, that."

"True," Mel agreed. "And yet—how many times have you told me your mom's father was born in Georgia—and I know, the country, not the state—right? But his family fled to Poland when the Soviets took over at some point."

"1921," Anna said.

"And that his first wife died? Which was the reason he immigrated here before World War II?"

"1934. He was already 39, and he had to start all over again."

"OK, so that's when he found your grandmother, also from the Georgian émigré community. And that's why you ended up learning Georgian and Russian, right?" Mel lowered her chin and raised her eyes at Anna, as if she had on reading glasses.

Anna sat there.

"We all have our roots," Mel continued, shrugging. "It's bad to generalize, obviously, but they affect us. Why don't you tell me about Sasha? Details. It might help you recall something relevant."

Anna gave Mel a knowing glance, a kind of capitulation. She sat back and looked at the ceiling. "He's a poor loser," she began. "We used to play tennis—he's the type that throws his racket. He's older than I am—maybe ten years? And, yes, he does have Russian background. His education was in England, though—hence the accent—and he's American by citizenship. At least that's what I thought."

"OK," she said. "Well, what about his extended family?"

"Don't know much more than that."

"Alright, so what else? How did you meet?"

"I was living in New York—he worked in finance." Anna paused to remember. "We had a mutual friend, Valeria—studying art history. She's the one who introduced us. She was always wearing bows in her hair, and knee-length poofy skirts, a 1950s look." Anna chuckled at the memory. "Anyway, I lost track of her, but he and I kept in touch. When I was posted in Moscow, he'd call when he was in town, and now that I moved back here, we've hung out a few times."

"And back then, what was he like?"

"A bit of a smart aleck, but also amusing. He's always been fit—he used to go running a lot, still does. He had great clothes, you know, bespoke suits, and expensive taste in food, wine, restaurants. Also, he's always been the player type, flirting—with everyone, me and everyone else," Anna laughed. "Once we were standing on the subway platform, and he actually leaned toward me and said, 'You know, if I weren't dating Jules, you're the type of girl I'd ask out'."

Brow furrowed, Mel looked at Anna questioningly.

"No. Never. I laughed in his face. Too arrogant to make a good boyfriend. Besides, not my type—too blonde."

"So why would he be involved in this? To support his lifestyle?"

"No, that can't be it. His family has money."

"You sure?"

"Not 100%, but I am pretty sure," Anna said. "I'm just so mad at myself. I can't believe I didn't see this coming. I knew he could be a jerk to his girlfriends, but this, I didn't expect."

"So what else is there? Revenge?"

"Love? Jealousy? Thirst for power?"

"What about ideology?"

"I just don't buy it that he has any kind of 'loyalty' to Mother Russia," Anna said, shaking her head. "What am I missing?"

Chapter 46

Chiang Mai – Monday, Feb. 24, 11:00 a.m. local time (11:00 p.m. EST on Sunday, Feb. 23 in DC)

Peeking out the door of a laundry vestibule, Raven watched Ingrid and Sasha leave their hotel room. She had her new friend Ice to thank for the excellent lookout point. After Ko had accosted them and abruptly let them go, Raven's nerves were beyond frayed. More desperate than ever for some rest, she went through with the plan to book a room and crash for a couple of hours. Meanwhile, Ice gave a bonus to the housekeeping manager so he could use the spot for observation. Only a half hour ago, Raven had switched places with Ice. Now, she texted him, "On the move."

Ingrid gave the impression of the perfect social media darling. She wore strappy beige sandals and a metallic gold bikini, clearly visible through her sheer white cover-up dress. With its double slit and deep V-neck, the flowing garment accentuated her legs. Ingrid's platinum blond hair was piled up in a messy bun, and she was carrying a large woven bag with short tortoiseshell handles looped over one arm. Sasha's navy-blue bathing-suit shorts, white polo shirt and loafers suggested Nantucket. Together, they made quite an attractive pair.

Strolling down the hallway, putting their heads together and laughing, they seemed carefree, as if they were indeed on vacation. Sasha draped his arm around Ingrid's neck, resting it on her shoulder. She reached her hand up to hold his, as they joked about the night's exploits and their hunger.

Raven trailed at a safe distance. She followed them to the pool, where they settled into lounge chairs along the main deck and signaled for the waiter. Questions ricocheted in Raven's mind. What were they really doing? How could they relax so well amid their deal-making? How dangerous were they?

Raven texted her new location to Ice, who appeared within minutes. She pointed discreetly to the other couple.

"Want me to eavesdrop?" he asked her. "Or set up your phone again?"

"Great idea," she said, tapping on the screen. "Here, take it, but this time, we'll use it as a listening device. It's quiet here—I'll be able to hear."

"You've got all kinds of super spyware, don't you?"

"It's a normal app, widely available," said Raven without sarcasm, as she took a second phone out of her bag. "That primary phone transmits, and this secondary one receives. The primary will pick up everything in the surrounding area. Easy. Data gets saved in the cloud. I'll go to the lobby and listen. OK?"

"OK. Whew," Ice said. "Glad you're not suspicious of me."

Raven cringed. What did he mean?

"Off I go with my two phones," he said.

"Wait. Take off your shirt."

Ice raised his brows.

"If you're going to sit by the pool, you need to look the part," she said. Rummaging around in her bag, she took out some sunblock and handed it to him. "Here. Give me your shirt and pick up one of those big pool towels in that rack."

Standing before her, Ice removed his shirt, revealing a large chest tattoo—an elaborate, geometric eight-pointed star that Raven recognized as a Buddhist symbol. "Better?" he asked.

Raven shot him a flirtatious look and reached for his shirt. Surprised how distracted he made her, she worried she was blushing and pushed her private thoughts to the back of her mind. "Better," she said, tucking the shirt in her bag. "Thanks."

He went on his mission, while she found a comfortable chair by a fountain in the lobby. She knew Ice had accomplished his task because she could hear Sasha and Ingrid clear as a bell—they were talking about food. She put the phone on speaker and rested it on the table. Then she put her hair in a ponytail, took a spy novel out of her bag and pretended to read while she listened. When a waiter cruised by, Raven billed an ice tea to her room.

After a while, Ice texted, "They're eating 'tropical' fruit, 'American-style' pad Thai and sparkling water."

She sent him an alien emoji.

"Save me," he wrote.

"Not yet. LOL."

The conversation between Sasha and Ingrid lagged. Guests strolled by, and Raven passed the time by imagining their lives. Who were they? What were they doing? Where were they from? Her eyes felt heavy, but she knew the situation could morph in an instant. She couldn't afford to doze off. "Any action at the pool?" she texted Ice.

"1 pregnant woman managing a toddler on deck, husband on phone. 1 woman swimming laps. S sleeping. I reading. 8 lounging," Ice wrote.

All of a sudden, Raven heard what she was waiting for.

> Sasha: "I need a drink."
> Ingrid: "Calm down. I'll hail the waiter."

Ice texted, "S woke up."

No kidding, Raven said to herself. Sasha was complaining the service should be faster. Abruptly, music blasted.

A text message from Ice popped up. "Teenagers!"

All Raven could do was wait. After an anxious minute, the music stopped and the voices of Sasha and Ingrid reemerged. When they did, Raven swore she heard Sasha say "Evy." She grabbed the phone, raised the volume again and held it to her ear.

> Sasha: "I told you she was stupid. Did she think she could do it without being detected? So naïve. That woman had no idea what was at stake."
>
> Ingrid: "Be thankful for her foolishness, Sasha. That's why we found out—and took care of it. But my question is this: Why don't your colleagues know what's at stake? Why won't they stand up? Why are they willing to forfeit their power?"
>
> Sasha: "You know that line of thinking started before your father died. There are too many restrictions now. There's neither enough on-the-ground intelligence, nor enough data collection. That's where you and I come in."
>
> Ingrid: "When my father was there, the place still had guts. They would never have let China go unchecked like these people do now."
>
> Sasha: "I know. Drained of people, resources and political support. Our enemies sit back and laugh. We zero in on the radical Muslims—and forget Russia and China also seek to mow us down."
>
> Ingrid: "I never forgot. You never forgot. How could we, when the Communists stole everything from our families?"

Raven gasped. I know the history, she thought. Cuba was like that. My family was torn apart too—poverty, injustice, dictatorship and corruption leading to revolution. Then Communism heaped on more misery—expropriation, extrajudicial killings, new forms of repression, corruption festering all over again. So Sasha and Ingrid hated Communism, but now what were they doing? Had they gone too far? Heart racing, Raven stared at her book and listened like her life depended on it.

> Sasha: "Precisely why it was imperative we took on this fight. *We* remember the mission. *We* are guaranteeing the future of America, and we are safeguarding democracy around the world. People will thank us!"

Raven suddenly felt blazing hot. She prayed the recording would be solid.

> Ingrid: "I know. We must remain vigilant. The Russians and their cybercrimes and election games, that's one thing, but this 'Belt and Road' strategy of China is something else. Overt and yet invisible. Blanketing these countries with Chinese investment, Chinese lending, Chinese products, Chinese tourists, Chinese everything! Why don't more people see what that does? A stealth invasion. A quiet infiltration of the entire world! It's outrageous. It sickens me. And if you don't do something about it, I will!"
> Sasha: "My, my. When your father told me you were seeking employment, he didn't tell me you were prone to insubordination. Rest assured, darling. I am at least as vigilant as you are. These people who think China will cooperate and share are fools! This is not a sand box. If we don't crush China, China will crush us!"

Ingrid: "Exactly. Use Chinese rules. Play their game."
Sasha: "Right you are! And you deserve some credit too, Ingrid. I must say, you are not only a stunning woman, but one brilliant hacker. Smith and Ko won't know what hit them! What magic! Thank you, darling."

Raven heard the conversation go dead. Was it over? A text from Ice illuminated her phone: "PDA." She made a disgusted face and waited. A woman's voice broke the silence.

Ingrid: "This will be the turning point, Sasha."
Sasha: "Yes. The Thai buffer zone will push China back. With one front protected, we can move on."
Ingrid: "America will be better off, the CIA will reclaim its glory, and you'll be back in."
Sasha: "I've had enough sun. Let's go to the room. We have a little time before our next meeting."

Raven lost the conversation and assumed they had walked away.

Before she had a chance to worry about it, Ice sent her a text: "On their tail."

"Thx. I'll meet you," she typed with jittery hands. Shocked by the scale of their scheming, she took a couple of seconds to think of what else to do. Then she shot off a message to both Anna and Tanner: "URGENT: OMG!!! Uploaded audio files of S&K to OfficeBox. Explosive! MUST LISTEN! S&K on the move again. Gotta run. Will keep you posted."

Chapter 47

Miami – Monday, Feb. 24, 12:30 a.m. EST

Jimmy Lin drove to Torenmaas' place—he owed him that now. When Lin arrived at the security booth, he gave his name, made his case, and waited for the guards to check with the boss. Lin stared at a lizard hopping up, swirling around the trunk of a palm tree in the beam of a floodlight. He wasn't sure what Torenmaas' reaction to his late-night visit would be. Perhaps he would still be pissed and not want to meet. Or perhaps the post-midnight time would trigger his curiosity.

The gates lurched open and the guard waved him through. No more discussion. Satisfied, Lin parked and walked up the path. Hendrik, waiting at the front door as if it were noon, showed him in. They filed past the vase on the antique Javanese table to a windowless office off the center hallway.

A portrait of Torenmaas' late wife hung on the wall. An antique clock ticked. Lin barely had a chance to get a good look at the painting, before Torenmaas popped in.

"Jimmy. Unusual timing."

"True," Lin said with a nod. "True."

"Make yourself comfortable," Torenmaas said. "I suppose this is important?"

Lin sat down in a leather arm chair. "Look. I owe you an apology."

"Is that so?" Torenmaas said, sitting across from him.

"I thought you were being overcautious. Maybe age was causing cold feet. But after Raven had the accident, I did what you said. I asked my people to dig around. And it seems your hunches were right."

"Go on," Torenmaas said.

"Our seller, Jesse Martin, is as clever as they come. The man can navigate the most treacherous waters, and he bothers to spend on the best legal counsel. You know his reputation is rock solid, both as an arms dealer and a manufacturer. There's nothing new there. So I moved on. The lead buyer is Martin's childhood friend, this guy Ko, the economist at the World Bank. Nerdy professor type. Remember, they grew up in the same village—Martin was a missionary kid. Martin's choice to get into gunmaking is intriguing, given his Christian upbringing, but that's another topic."

"And."

"And Ko works with his cousin Keng, as you know. While Ko is the globe-trotting front man, Keng is the military commander—the stereotypical rebel leader. Ko and Keng were partners, and I'd heard Keng wanted to work with us. Still, not complicated. We too have a reputation—and he wanted the best. All the financials reflect this—as I've shown you," Lin said.

"So?" Torenmaas said.

"So here's the problem: Keng is also working with a guy named Sasha Bolokov. It seems he is the one who pushed for me—and you. And Bolokov works at the World Bank."

A wave of concern passed over Torenmaas' face. "The missing piece. A whole new factor. This Sasha guy."

"Yes, it's the first I hear of his involvement. In fact, I'd never heard of him at all. I thought we were working with the rebel cousin duo, Ko and Keng, and I thought they knew my name through Jesse. If I had known Mr. Bolokov was hovering in the background, I might not have been involved."

Torenmaas harrumphed. "Fuck. I told you something was off. If he is the source of the mystery money, whose coffers is he pillaging? And what else is he doing?"

"I have the same questions. Look, we could have guessed rebels placed these orders—if we thought about it. Not that we did. But now that we're probing, I'm hearing talk of unusual activity both at the port in Bangkok and north of Chiang Mai—all kinds of 'chatter' about action in Kachin and Shan states near Yunnan—you know along the border of Myanmar and China. Some are even reporting unusual patrols along the Mekong down toward Laos."

"I don't give a shit about their border disputes, Jimmy. And I don't care who buys arms and weapons systems from or through Jesse Martin. I just care if they pay me for my services, and if I remain undetected. I need to keep my profile low, and now we don't even know who our business partners really are. This is a God-damned cluster fuck!" Torenmaas shouted, punching his fist in the air.

"I hate to say it," Lin replied. "But you were right. The buyer's financing was suspect. There are players we don't understand. And they are not protecting our interests."

"You are apologizing."

"Listen. There's something else too. Raven's journalist friend thought you were behind their accident, right? And you thought it was me. But I knew it wasn't either of us, so I hired an investigator to look into the truck."

"The truck?"

"The truck that hit them. My investigator knows a guy over at the precinct, right? So we got the police report. Raven and her friend called in information about the plate, vehicle color and markings. The police got tied up in red tape, but my friend was less restrained by legal requirements. He didn't need more than five minutes to track down the registered owner."

"What did the owner say?"

"I went over to see this joker myself, and I asked him who hired him. You also won't be surprised to know that he would not tell me—at first. But I did a little convincing, you know, and he changed his mind pretty quickly. He realized how badly he wanted to help me after all, you know? Right?" Lin said. "Now guess what name he gave me?"

"Tell me, Jimmy."

"Bolokov," Lin said.

"Huh," Torenmaas puffed. "Looks like I owe you an apology too, Jimmy."

"Consider us even. What do you want to do?"

"Extract ourselves immediately," Torenmaas said.

"Agreed. Abort the deal. I'll set that in motion as soon as we're done here."

"Fine. Do it as quickly as you can—and by the way, where is this asshole right now?"

"In Chiang Mai, with Keng and Ko. Why?"

"Fuck!" Torenmaas said. "Raven is there. She's meeting with the artist I'm promoting. She doesn't know anything about our work with Ko and Jesse—nor does he—and I wanted to keep it that way."

"How about this?" Lin said. "I'll have a chat with one of my friends in the Thai military."

"Good idea, Jimmy, my old friend," Torenmaas said, his eyes twinkling. "They might like to hear about Mr. Bolokov's activities."

Chapter 48

Chiang Mai – Mon., Feb. 24, 4:00 p.m. local time (4:00 a.m. EST in DC)

Raven and Ice sat in the back of a tuk tuk on the shoulder of a two-lane road outside of Chiang Mai. The driver, who didn't understand English, leaned forward and drooped his arms over the steering wheel as if he might collapse. He stared into the distance, awaiting instructions.

"Thank God you noticed Sasha and Ingrid leaving," Raven said. "Or I would have lost them. I wish we could follow them into this place. What is it? An elephant sanctuary?"

"Could be. All the sign indicates is a private estate," Ice said.

"This must be the meeting they were talking about."

"Let's watch from over there," Ice said, pointing to agricultural land on the opposite side. "It'll be a better vantage point and more hidden than the back of a tuk tuk—scrub brush, fence posts, shed. Come on," he said, as he paid the driver.

"Fine, but I better not see any spiders—or snakes," Raven replied, getting out.

"Can't promise you that," Ice said, as the driver took off.

They jumped over a ditch, walked under the trees lining the road, and headed for the shed. On one side, the dirt of a recently tilled field lay open and exposed; on the other, rows of bushy plants stretched into the distance. A wooden bench stood in the shade of the shed. They sat down, leaning their backs on the wall.

Raven did a double take at the bushy plants.

"Strawberries," Ice said. "We're famous for it up here. Did you see all the people at the airport carrying boxes of strawberries back to Bangkok?"

She nodded, but she hadn't noticed. "What's next?"

"Act natural," he said.

"I'm more of a city person. Besides, aren't we trespassing?"

"Nobody is here," he said, gesturing outward with both arms. "If anybody comes, I'll tell them my American girlfriend couldn't take the heat."

Raven mustered a smile. "I haven't told you everything," she said.

"No kidding."

"I work for the *Daily Journal*."

"Oh, that, I knew that," he said, laughing. "Torenmaas told me his niece was coming, so I looked you up on the internet."

"You checked me out ahead of time?"

"Obviously."

Raven laughed. "Fair enough. But I didn't tell you that my colleague was assigned to investigate Channarong's death. The truth is that I didn't just come here to check on you and my uncle's charity. I also came to snoop around."

"Also obvious," he said. "Good thing you work for a newspaper and not an espionage service!"

Embarrassed, Raven looked at the ground. She hadn't realized she was so transparent.

Ice continued, "Don't feel bad. It's good you have nothing to hide, and that you're bad at hiding. I like that about you. It's also clear this guy Sasha is cavorting with that woman Ingrid, and they are playing games. They are full of themselves. He thinks she's his minion, but she's smarter than he realizes. Yet it doesn't matter which one of them is on top, because both of them are fools. I don't need a deck of tarot cards to tell me that."

"You're pretty observant," she offered with a side-eye glance.

"They have 'business'," he said using air quotes, "with the tall guy Ko and his local friend, here in this villa or whatever is in there," he continued. "What I don't get is the connection between these people and Channarong—and your uncle."

"My uncle?" Raven asked. "No. He doesn't have anything to do with these people."

Ice wondered how much he should protest that idea, but before he had a chance to reply, an unusual noise resounded in the distance.

"What's that?" Raven asked. "Do you hear rumbling?"

"Thai military," he said, raising his eyebrows and pointing to a convoy racing down the road. "Check it out. Interesting. Some kind of domestic response operation," he announced like a commentator.

Raven squinted in the sun and gaped at the line of military vehicles fast approaching.

The first one, a light tank, screeched around the corner into the compound's main entrance and without stopping rammed the gate. In a bout of thunder, the gate lay like road kill on the shoulder. Dust whipped around. An armored car came to a halt at the security booth.

"Oh my God!" she whispered.

Three uniformed men jumped out—two of them attacking the guards, grabbing, cuffing and restraining them on the ground at gunpoint. Another officer took control of the booth. Most of the other vehicles played follow-the-leader pursuing whatever was down the road.

"Keep your head down," Ice said. He spoke softly, but it was a command. "Try to fit in," he said and grabbed a rake that had been leaning against the shed. "And put your phone away—don't draw attention."

Raven hadn't seen Ice like this. He had slipped into the skin of a much more serious person. She bent over her knees and tied her sneakers. How could she possibly fit in? From her hunched position, she steadied her phone on the bench and attempted to take a video.

"Some kind of raid," Ice said, reading her thoughts. "It's going to get interesting." He grabbed a bin on the ground, kneeled over a row of plants and began to pick fruit, carefully placing each handful of strawberries into the bin, all the while observing the entrance. "It's OK. Play along."

Though the sun was on the wane, the heat baked her. Sweat soaked the back of her shirt, and a mosquito buzzed in her ear. Reluctant to encounter spiders or rotting fruit, she tied and untied her shoes, stealing glances at the road. From time to time, she verified her phone was still working. Another mosquito or ten attacked her ankle. She slapped and swiped, as her inner voice yelled at her to pay attention to the raid. Focus on the convoy, not the bugs! She thought back—at least three light tanks and two armored personnel carriers had passed. There were also several trucks. Local police had joined in—five cars now stood guard at the entrance. As for the soldiers, there had been three or four per vehicle, perhaps 20 vehicles, thus 60 or 80 people.

The dust died down. The air held the calm of the eye of the hurricane. Raven consciously inhaled and exhaled, long slow breaths.

An explosion blew through the silence of the farmland. Then another! The popping of semiautomatic gunfire took over.

Ice picked up his bin and walked to the shed. "We need to get out of sight," he said, trying the door handle. "We're in luck. It's open," he said. "In here."

Raven followed him inside. The heat was stifling. Light streamed in between the wall boards. Bins and pails stood stacked in one corner. Two hoes, two shovels and a rake hung on the wall. Otherwise, the shed was empty. The cracks between the wall boards were large enough for them to view the entrance of the compound. "What are they up to?" she asked.

"Could be illegal trade—timber, exotic animals, heroin, meth, even humans. Happens too often, I'm afraid. The military tend to get involved when it comes to drugs. But still, the scale of this is surprising."

More gunfire erupted. "Let's sneak in," said Raven, pointing across the street.

"Go in that compound, now?" he said. "No way. I've been following your lead until now, but that's crazy. I'm not doing it, and neither are you. We'd die. Certain death. No joke."

Taken aback by his reticence, Raven stayed put.

They both pressed their faces against the shed wall, staring through the cracks.

Out of nowhere, a car shot out of the estate toward the security booth, swerving and kicking up a cloud of dust. Raven and Ice were not the only ones to notice. The police at the entrance opened fire on the raging vehicle barreling toward them. Bullets sprayed the windshield, hood and tires of the car.

Raven gasped and instinctively crouched as a stray bullet hit the roof of the shed with a thwack. Her heart pounded. For a split second, she and Ice made eye contact. Realizing they were both unscathed, they immediately darted their eyes back to the unfolding pandemonium just in time to see the car veer off the driveway and crash into a tree.

For a moment, the scene was eerily quiet. Then the shouts of two officers broke the silence. They inched toward the car with weapons poised.

"They're commanding the people in the car to drop their weapons and freeze," Ice explained.

"A mad dash to escape?" Raven asked. "Playing dead?"

Ice shrugged.

One of the officers approached the driver's side. The window had shattered—small pieces of blueish glass littered the ground. Peering inside, the officer thrust her hand through the empty frame and under the airbag. She repeatedly attempted to open the door, but it remained stuck, too mangled to budge. As she retreated, the second officer shouted commands toward the passenger side. Again, there was no response. He grabbed the handle and attempted to open the other car door. At first nothing happened, but then all of a sudden, the door swung open and a body tumbled out, landing in a heap. No screaming. No moaning. Only a heap.

"Oh my God!" Raven exclaimed. "Look who it is!"

Chapter 49

Greenbelt, MD – Monday, Feb. 24, 6:30 a.m. EST

Thanks for coming with me," Anna said, as Mel barreled north up Rhode Island Avenue toward Maryland. "And for driving in this crappy weather." The windshield wipers on Mel's new electric car throbbed. Shaw's turn-of-the-century row houses shone in the sleet and headlights.

"No problem," Mel said. "The crack of dawn is my time. Did this bozo say why he wanted to meet way out there—at the scenic Greenbelt metro station, the proverbial end of the line? It's a bit far from Langley."

"He mumbled something about commuter camouflage and NSA proximity."

"Oh, right. Now we know where to discover spooks at clandestine meetings."

"It's not every day a CIA hack wants to be a source. This guy's got an agenda, and I'm going to figure out what it is." Anna's phone blipped. "It's Raven," she said, clicking on the most recent message. As she read it, her face hardened.

Mel glanced right and noticed the stony countenance. "And?"

Anna exhaled in a whoosh. "Oh. My. God. Holy crap."

"You're fogging up the windshield. What!"

"Sasha and Ingrid. Raven says they're dead."

"Both of them?"

"Yes. Her text says: 'Sasha and Ingrid are dead. Car accident. Uploaded new audio and video.'"

"What does that mean for your story?"

"I don't know. That's the only text she sent." Anna made a face as she opened her email and OfficeBox, and tried to access the files Raven sent. "This stuff won't download here. Bad service, or maybe the files are too big. I've got to see this ASAP—but we can't go back now."

"That's fucked up," Mel said. "I mean, that Sasha's dead. Weird to think he's your friend—but I can't say I'm sorry."

"Was," Anna said, biting her lip. "Was my friend. Or wasn't, ever, actually. He was one messed-up dude."

"A 'messed-up dude'? How about two-faced, deceptive, manipulative mother fucker!?"

"Yeah, that," Anna said, shaking her head and staring out the window.

Mel's maps application occasionally broke the silence. Following the robotic voice, Mel crossed Eastern Avenue into Maryland and kept going through Mt. Rainier and Hyattsville. They turned east, crossed the railroad tracks and wound their way up Kenilworth, which provided some open road. Anna remained lost in thought, and Mel didn't press her.

When Mel pulled into the fire lane at the Greenbelt metro station, Anna kicked back into gear. "I'll scan the crowd," she said.

"Are you sure we're in the right place?" Mel asked

"I'm sure."

"Are you still thinking about Sasha?"

"No," Anna snapped.

"OK, then,"

After a moment, Anna replied. "I feel stupid for trusting him, of course. I can't believe I didn't see through all that flirtatious crap, his stupid charm. All that background information he was supposedly imparting to me, his dear friend. He must have set that in motion years ago. And I had no idea—but right now, I don't have time to dwell on my gullibility. I have to look for de Jeanbourg. He has a brown hipster beard."

They caught glimpses beneath scarves, hoods and the occasional umbrella. The windshield wipers pulsed, keeping the light sleet and a few snow flurries at bay.

"You think he'll drive?" Mel asked.

"Who knows," Anna said. "If he does, what's most inconspicuous? Basic four-door?"

"Dingy old minivan?"

"Maybe he rides the metro. And there he is—at 2 o'clock. Navy blue beanie, open blue-and-white golf umbrella. Brown beard. See?"

"Here we go," said Mel. She pulled toward de Jeanbourg and lowered the window. "I believe I'm your ride, sir," she said, unlocking.

"Right," he said, shaking his umbrella off, then getting into the back.

"Let me introduce you two. Mel Allen, Charles de Jeanbourg, Charles, Mel," Anna said, waving her hand back and forth.

"Allen," he said.

"Which way, John-bird?" Mel asked.

"It's de Jeanbourg—soft 'j,' the ending sounds like 'pour' not 'iceberg'." Anna smirked.

"Staying here is fine," he said. "Sorry I'm late. There've been developments."

"No kidding," Anna said. "What's this about Sasha and Ingrid?"

"You heard already? Social media is bad for us law enforcement types," de Jeanbourg said. "Rabble's always a step ahead."

"Should I take that as confirmation? Or an insult?" Anna asked.

De Jeanbourg shrugged and tipped his head, holding his hands outward and open.

"And if I'm the rabble, why do you want to talk to me so badly?" she continued. "Again?"

"Don't get your pretty feathers all ruffled, Jones. The truth will set you free, or me in this case, and my employer. That's the reason I want to talk to you. I want you to know the truth. I'm screwed if you don't."

"I thought you were screwed if I do," she said, ignoring his obnoxious bird comparison. "I doubt your bosses will like it, if you reveal CIA secrets."

"Now, now. What makes you think I'd do that? I'm going to steer clear of CIA secrets. I'm going to tell you everything that's not CIA. Nothing classified, secret or top secret. Not even confidential. And all of it on deep background. Got it? No video. No audio. You can't quote me. Understood?"

"What a surprise. Deep background. Information seeping in, like osmosis."

The precipitation trickled to a stop, and the wipers fell silent.

"It's not that you can't use the information," de Jeanbourg said. "After our little conversation here, I'm sure you'll be able to secure the story with other quotable sources. You'll know where to look. Double and triple check everything. Please! Be my guest! Corroborate! Get other people on the record and pin it down," he said, leaning forward. "Thank me later."

"Let's get on with it," Anna said.

"There's one problem," de Jeanbourg said.

"Now what?" Anna asked.

"Your friend, here. She needs to step out."

"But you're the one who said you didn't care if she drove me out here."

"I didn't care about the drive. But I do care if she listens to our little talk," de Jeanbourg said. "She has to go."

"But why? She already knows what you look like," Anna said, chuckling. "Your cover's already blown."

"I don't have a cover, Jones. I'm an analyst. I'm out in the open. Everyone knows where I work," he said. "But it's my policy. I want to speak to you, the journalist, alone."

"This is silly, de Jeanbourg. Your policy?" Anna asked. "Where's she supposed to go? There's nothing here. And it's freezing outside."

Mel cut in, "It's fine, Anna. I don't care what Da Jerk-Bird has to say. I can wait inside the station. No problem. Text me when you're done." Mel stepped out. "One thing, though," she said, holding the door open. "Anna, take the driver's seat, in case you need to dump this pseudo-hipster and get outta here."

Anna smiled. She got out and walked around to the driver's side. "Thanks," she told Mel. "Really." Anna sat down behind the wheel and slammed the door shut as Mel marched into the station.

Before Anna had a chance to ask a question, de Jeanbourg said, "Mock me and my policies, if you want to, Jones. But I'll say it again: I'm a great source."

Chapter 50

Greenbelt, MD – Monday, Feb. 24, 7:00 a.m. EST

Anna shifted to face de Jeanbourg in the back seat. He looked smug. "OK, so what?" she asked.

"I'll get straight to the point," de Jeanbourg said. "It was Sasha."

"That's your big truth?" Anna said, squinting, jostling her head and pursing her lips in a what-are-you-talking-about way. "I already know that Sasha was full of crap, de Jeanbourg. In fact, he was a full-blown two-faced, deceptive, manipulative mother fucker."

"Beautiful description, but did you know he used to be with us?"

"Why should I believe that?"

"I'll lay it out for you as simply as I can, Jones," he said. "Sasha was at the World Bank for close to a decade. We used to have a relationship with him. His international finance posts provided good cover. He could travel freely. He could access certain funds." He paused. "So far, so good?"

She shrugged.

"However. Sasha lost his way, let us say. And the agency cut him off."

"The CIA fired him?" Anna asked.

"More or less. Exactly. We didn't have a relationship with him at that point."

"You're saying he went rogue—he was a rogue CIA agent?"

"He worked for himself," de Jeanbourg repeated. "Exactly."

Anna caught de Jeanbourg baring his teeth, lips curled, like a dog about to growl. He snapped his mouth shut. Was he conscious of it? Would he stop repeating "exactly"?

Sitting straight up, de Jeanbourg continued: "Bolokov and his hacker girlfriend were playing games with Bank funds, and Bolokov financed container loads of arms to Keng, all in the name of the United States—except, it wasn't."

Glancing out over the steering wheel and back to de Jeanbourg, Anna crossed her arms over her chest. "But why? He was already wealthy," Anna said. She was kicking herself. Why had she trusted Sasha? "Why would he steal money and deal arms? All he cares—cared—about was having a good time."

"There's where you're wrong, Jones. Sasha kept his ideological fervor well-hidden beneath his English boarding school veneer. But he was an American patriot, down to the bone—his hatred for Communists ran deep—and it extended to China. He wanted China in a chokehold."

"So, he sold arms to rebels on China's border, just like that?"

"Of course not," de Jeanbourg said. "Sasha's connection to Keng goes back to when Sasha was on the CIA payroll. He's been orchestrating arms imports, small and large—guns, tanks, rocket launchers, weapons systems, drones, software, what have you, for years."

"And Sasha, Ko and Keng were working together?"

"Ko was working with Keng, yes. But old Ko was ignorant of certain dimensions—he didn't know Sasha was dealing with Keng, and at first he didn't know Sasha was with Ingrid either."

"And Ingrid, a hacker? How did that work?"

"She was a cybersecurity expert. Ko gave the go-ahead to hire her in their division, but Ingrid was Sasha's plant, and she was a strong partner—background in math and econ. She carried her own weight, possessed her own motivations. In fact, her father was once head of clandestine services at the Agency. Growing up, she witnessed China on the rise and Daddy on the decline—and she didn't like it. She felt the CIA's warnings weren't being heeded, and America's interests were threatened. She didn't want to wait until it was too late—until China has the whole continent buttoned down."

"You convey a lot of details, Jeanbourg, about an operation that the CIA knew nothing about," Anna said.

De Jeanbourg puckered his lips.

"Let me guess," Anna said. "The CIA turned a blind eye to Ko's weapons deals, because it behooved the US to do so. Presiding over a key buffer area encompassing the old Burma Road, controlling the resources and trade routes, isn't bad, is it? What a nice zone of American influence!"

"We are proud supporters of self-determination," de Jeanbourg said. "At times."

"Weren't you worried about wrecking the Bank?"

"The Bank will be fine," de Jeanbourg replied.

"It didn't bother you that you used Sasha? He was doing it for himself, and yet he wasn't. You said yourself he was acting in the name of the United States. You knew. You let him. And you don't care about him at all."

"That makes us sound bad, Jones. He was under no delusions. He knew we cut him loose. He continued doing his thing, because he wanted to. He was unfettered. He was rich. We didn't stop him. That's all. Meanwhile, my agency is limited—we face hurdles. Things like Congress, the Constitution, international law. We can't go around giving arms to rebels!"

"Or embezzling funds designated for the world's poor. So that's it?" Anna asked. "Sasha and Ingrid conspired to embezzle funds and sell arms to rebels, and now they're dead, and that's that?"

"Exactly."

"Don't you think there are a few missing pieces left, de Jeanbourg?"

"Like what?"

"Like why are Nou Channarong and Evy Poole dead, and why is someone trying to kill me and Viktor?"

"Oh, come on Jones. You're smart. Isn't it obvious now?"

"Spell it out for me, de Jeanbourg."

"Until now, Sasha hadn't gotten caught for a reason. He was cunning, and he and Ingrid—and even Ko—were fastidious. They had tracking and surveillance and security in place to protect themselves. Therefore, when Evy was fishing around and talking to Sara about it, Sasha and Ingrid detected something was up. They pursued it and realized she was planning to leak the scheme."

"What are you saying?" Anna asked.

"I repeat: It was Sasha. Sasha had Evy eliminated. He hired someone to shut her up."

"How could you know that?"

"American intelligence isn't completely useless, Ms. Jones," de Jeanbourg said. "It's not all turf wars, you know. The US intelligence community includes 16 agencies, or 17, if you include the ODNI, which oversees them. And here's a news flash: We do cooperate. The MPD is playing its part too," he said, indignantly.

"Isn't that impressive."

"Journalists don't care for sharing information with the police. You think it's a conflict of interest. But you people aren't the only ones investigating these deaths."

"Hold on," Anna said, raising her hands in protest. "There's a reason why journalists and members of law enforcement and the military don't intertwine their work."

"Spare me," de Jeanbourg said. "Save the ethical discussion for another day."

"How do I know it wasn't you?"

"Who?"

"Maybe the CIA had her killed."

"We didn't," he said.

"But how do I know? I mean, for sure?" she asked. "It seems to me that you would have had just as much motivation to kill her as Sasha. And maybe you're glad she's dead too."

"We didn't have her killed, and I'm not glad she's dead," de Jeanbourg said. "Sasha went off the rails. He took things too far."

"I don't know." Anna rolled her eyes. "Why are you even telling me this?"

"I told you why—because I want you to know that none of this has anything to do with the CIA. The truth will set us free, remember? The CIA is not involved."

"So you're saying you can't be seen supporting rebel groups on the Chinese border, and you don't want to have anything to do with embezzlement and money laundering at the World Bank."

"Exactly."

Anna frowned. "And, you want me to write this story and say you have nothing to do with it."

"Again, we *don't* have anything to do with it."

"But what about Channarong? What really happened to him? And why would Evy snoop around?"

"Sorry, Jones," de Jeanbourg said. "You'll have to do some of the work on your own."

Anna was about to tell him off, but Charles' phone beeped.

"Excellent!" he announced. "I received clearance from public affairs for you to use a few nuggets on the record. When you write the story, you can say this: 'World Bank employee Sasha Bolokov was not affiliated with the CIA. The CIA has no involvement in the trafficking of arms to the rebels in Myanmar, or the embezzlement or misuse of World Bank funds, according to a spokesperson for the Agency'."

"Great, de Jeanbourg. Great. I'll write that down," Anna said, shaking her head in disgust.

De Jeanbourg further stared at his phone. "There's more," he said. "You may also state: 'The CIA acknowledges with regret that Bolokov claimed to be a CIA officer. The Agency, however, cannot be held responsible for individuals with mental health challenges who experience delusions of grandeur or conjure up notions of working in the intelligence community'."

"Or embezzle millions from the World Bank or conduct illegal arms deals on behalf of the CIA?" Anna replied.

"Jones," de Jeanbourg said. "I'm forwarding these quotes to you via email," de Jeanbourg said. "I want you to have them word-for-word."

"Very generous of you," Anna said facetiously.

"Also, a caveat," he said as he stepped out of the car. "After Bolokov put a contract out on Evy Poole, he added you and Sara Reedman to the list." Before the door slammed shut, he added, "But don't worry. We're in touch with the FBI. An investigation is ongoing. And we've got your backs."

Chapter 51

Washington, DC – Mon., Feb. 24, 9:00 a.m. EST

Sara reviewed the security-system keypad, verifying the windows and doors of the widow's house were closed. She pushed "arm," and ensured the heavy front door locked behind her. Hurrying toward the Spring Valley Plaza on Massachusetts, passing mansion after mansion, she tried to get her mind off her troubles by considering which home she would buy, if she had enough money. She remembered Evy had said you couldn't pay her to live in Spring Valley, with all its cigar-smoking lobbyists and golf-clubbing politicals. But the villas with trimmed bushes, hundred-year oaks and three-car garages pleased Sara. Evy didn't know about the owners' circumstances or charity work, she thought. Damn! Evy's in my head again. Evy!

When Sara reached the main road, just north of American University, she stopped on the corner by a doctor's office, waiting for the light to change. She looked forward to the Café de Nimes, anything to avoid being alone, all the more so since she wasn't going to the office. Her mouth watered in anticipation of her daily brioche and café au lait, especially after her sleepless night.

She crossed Massachusetts and traversed the parking lot. The sleigh bells on the door jingled as she entered. The familiar sound and the warm, coffee-scented air offered her a sense of relief. A few other customers had already settled in. Engrossed in their laptops, they paused now and then to eat and sip. Things were normal.

The owner Jean Claude, face frosted in grey stubble, greeted her with a *"Bonjour, Mademoiselle!"*

"The usual," she said, smiling at him.

"You are late today," said Jean Claude. "Working too hard?"

"Stressed out, I guess," Sara replied. "Things have been...busy."

"Oh! Perhaps it is that new French boyfriend who is distracting you?" he asked.

Sara stiffened. "What boyfriend?"

Jean Claude made puppy-dog eyes. "I didn't mean to embarrass you, *Mademoiselle.*"

"It's OK, Jean Claude," she said. "But, please, who are you talking about?"

"Alors," he said. "A man came in here yesterday evening looking for you. Tallish. Dark hair. Polite. Charming. And French!" he said. "He wanted to know if you had been in lately."

"Did he know my name?"

"But of course!" Jean Claude said. "That's how I knew he was looking for you!"

"I don't understand," she said.

"He said he was an old friend, told me your colleague...ah, what's her name? She told him he could find you here," he said.

Weird, Sara thought. Bad weird. Should I leave now? Hide? Exit through the back?

"Evy!" Jean Claude shouted. "That's the name. He said Evy told him to find you here."

Oh no. Evy. "What did you tell him?"

"Nothing. I don't know you." He shook his head and smiled.

"Thank you, Jean Claude. I appreciate your covering for me. Is the café au lait ready? I've gotta run."

"Yes, *mademoiselle*! Here," he said, offering the drink in a to-go cup and brioche in a bag. "Pay me tomorrow. I have kept you talking," he added.

"Great. Thanks," Sara said, bounding out the door. She had to think fast. Where to go? The Spring Valley house seemed too isolated, her apartment on the Hill too dangerous. What would Evy do? Maybe duck into the furniture store across the street and pretend to shop? Too early— not open. Evy would call someone. Evy would tell Anna.

Sara took out her phone, which she had set on mute to reduce anxiety. When she unlocked it, she was surprised to find two missed calls from Anna. There were no voicemail messages, but she had sent four texts. At 7:41 a.m. Anna said, "We have to talk ASAP!!!" Another text came at 8:00 a.m. "Need to bring you up to speed." At 8:15 a.m. she wrote, "Call me right away!" Finally, at 9:00 a.m., only about 20 minutes prior, she had texted, "Where are you???"

Panicking, Sara continued along 49th and dialed Anna as she took the usual path toward the metro. Her voicemail picked up. "Anna! You're asking me where I am, but where are you? I'm freaking out! You've got to help me. I don't know what to do. I was at my coffee place, Café de Nimes, and I found out this guy had been there looking for me. What if it's someone trying to kill me? Like someone killed Evy? What if they want to kill me too! Call me!" Sara hung up and sent a text. "Freaking out!!!"

Sara speed-walked northward on 49th, right again on Albemarle toward the A.U. Tenleytown station. Maybe I can wander around the Healthy Foods Market or the Galleria, where there's safety in numbers, she thought.

Reaching the corner of 48th, she glanced right. A dark-haired man was approaching from the south. The sight of him gave her a start—knee-length camel-hair coat, black slacks, nice shoes, and a beige-black-red plaid scarf. Attractive face. Expensive-looking. She noticed him noticing her, so she picked up her pace.

"Sara, please!" he yelled.

Sara's stomach turned at the sound of her name, but she started running as fast as she could toward Wisconsin. Panting, she berated herself for not going to the gym more often. Should I ditch my bag? She glanced behind again and saw the man catching up. She prayed she wouldn't slip on the ice.

"Sara, I need to speak with you!" the man yelled. "Please," he repeated, gaining ground.

She kept running, kept panting. Bang on a door? Escape into a backyard? Push a garbage can in his path? Flag down a driver? But the man was grabbing her coat, and Sara stumbled.

"Sara, I'm Evy's friend, Giovanni Salazar. I need to speak with you. I won't hurt you. Please!"

She slowed to catch her breath, but kept going. "Don't touch me!" she yelled.

"Can we sit in that café back there? Or somewhere up ahead?"

"You are not her friend! Some friend! Evy is dead!"

"That's why you have to talk to me," he pleaded. "You are in danger, and I can help you."

Sara trembled. "You! Help me? You got her killed! Or did you kill her yourself?" she screeched, instantly regretting it. What if he is the killer? How stupid can I be? Still, what if he is telling the truth?

"You are right," he said, holding both hands upward in front of him, like he wanted to give someone a hug. "It is my fault that she died. But I didn't kill her. Please, listen to me. That's why I have to help you—it's all I have left."

Standing still now, Sara stared at the man. He had tears in his eyes. Was he acting? What would Evy do? Frozen with fear, Sara deliberated, and the man stood there. He did not grab or lunge. "Walk toward the café!" Sara spit out. "And stay ahead of me!"

He skulked like a beaten dog.

When he was several paces ahead, Sara followed. "How do you know who I am? And how the hell did you know I was at that café?"

"Evy told me!" he shouted toward the emptiness in front of him. "She showed me pictures! She said you were cat sitting in Spring Valley, and if I needed to find you, you liked a French place with good brioche up on Massachusetts. It wasn't that hard to find."

"Go! And shut up," she stammered, unable to remember what she had and hadn't told Evy.

Sara took out her phone to contact Anna again. She texted, "URGENT: Meet me at Café de Nimes NOWWWWW!" Then she typed in 911. She didn't hit "call," but she held the phone out in front of her, in case.

Chapter 52

Washington, DC – Mon., Feb. 24, 9:45 a.m. EST

When Sara and Giovanni arrived outside Café de Nimes, Giovanni looked at her for guidance.

"Go," was all she said. He understood, and she followed him inside.

Jean Claude's face lit up at the sight of her. "Ah, *Mademoiselle!*" he said. "Your Frenchman has found you!"

"Yes, Jean Claude," she said, mustering a smile. "Two more café au laits, please."

"Right away, *Mademoiselle!*" Jean Claude said.

Sara pointed to a booth in the back. Giovanni went ahead. They draped their coats over the seats and sat facing one another.

"Hang on," Sara said. She looked at her phone, but had trouble unlocking it. Her fingerprint wouldn't register. Trying to use her password, she kept hitting the wrong keys. What about this man? What the hell did he want? Finally gaining access to her phone, she checked her texts. Anna had replied. Thank God. She's on her way.

Giovanni leaned in and whispered, "Your life is in danger."

"Is that a threat?"

"No!" he said in a louder whisper. "I came to warn you."

"That doesn't help Evy!"

"No, but I could help you. Listen to me...please."

Sara tried to calm herself down. "Hold on," she said. "You've got to slow down. You're freaking me out. I can't even think. Shut up for a minute."

He remained quiet.

Jean Claude startled Sara with the delivery of two giant mugs of café au lait. "Ça va?"

"Ça va," she replied, deadpan. "Everything's fine."

Jean Claude let his glance linger on Giovanni, like a protective father inspecting his daughter's new boyfriend. He tipped his chin up momentarily. "If you need anything else, don't hesitate to ask," he said before returning to the register.

Sara clung to her warm mug. She concentrated on the heart that Jean Claude had formed in the milky foam.

Giovanni leaned forward again and said, "I loved Evy. I really loved her."

"So? So the hell what!?" she hissed. "What does it matter now, if you loved Evy?" Sara got up.

"Stay!" he said too loudly. He reached out to grab her arm but refrained.

Other customers turned to look.

"There's something else," he said. "Please don't go."

Sara sat back down. "Hey, I've got to go to the bathroom," she said, jumping up again and walking away this time.

"Please come back," Giovanni begged.

"I have to go to the restroom," she repeated.

Sara went to the bathroom, peed and washed her hands. She checked her phone and realized Anna had sent updates. The latest text was, "2 blocks away."

Sara texted again, "Come to the bathroom."

When Anna entered the women's room, Sara blurted, "Thank you so much for coming!" Then she sobbed. "I," she gasped. "I. Got. So. Scared."

Anna gave her a hug. "It's OK," Anna said, leaving out what de Jeanbourg had said about the killer after them. "Anyone would be scared," she added, trying to assess whether they were safe at the café. "What has Giovanni said so far?"

Sara managed to recap the conversation, concluding with, "And he keeps babbling about how he loved Evy."

"You think he's still out there?" Anna asked.

"I don't see why he wouldn't be," she said. "He wanted to talk to me."

"OK. So, assuming he's there, you go sit across from him. I'll wedge him into the booth on the same side. I'll take the lead, OK?"

"Fine with me. I don't want to talk to him at all."

The two women went back to the table where Giovanni was sitting and sat down.

Giovanni checked out the space and faced Sara again. "Who's this?"

"My friend Anna," Sara said.

"You were waiting for her?"

"Brilliant," Sara said. "You didn't think I would talk with you alone, did you?"

"Did you tell anyone else that I'm here?"

"No," Sara said.

"Like who? The police?" Anna asked.

"Anyone. Anyone at all," he said. "I don't want to get us all killed."

"I don't want you to get us killed either," Anna said.

"Any one of us could have been followed," Giovanni said. "We have to talk fast."

"Fine by me," Anna said. "Let's get this over with."

"First," he said. "I want you to know that I loved Evy."

"Little good that does now," Anna said.

"I can't believe she's dead," he said.

"Please," Anna said. "So what?"

"That's why I'm here," he said. "It's the only way I could make things right."

"Make things right?" Anna snapped. "You can't fix things! Tell me this: Who do you work for?"

"Mainly," he said, sighing. "Myself," he added. "I have my own company, foreign exchange trading, based in Bangkok."

Anna sat back in a huff.

"It's called Cutting Edge Forex," he continued. "I founded it more than a decade ago. Now I have 11 employees."

Anna had been holding her left hand in a fist. Now she pounded it on the table. "Cut the crap!"

A few people turned to look at them again.

"It's not crap," he said. "It's the truth."

"Fine. Whatever. Something is missing here, and..."

"Yes," he interrupted. He sighed again.

Sara and Anna looked at each other.

"Get to the point!" Anna said.

Giovanni reached into his jacket pocket and removed two small booklets. He placed them on the table in a pile and slid them over.

Anna noted the blue jacket and cover design of the one on top. It was an American passport. The one underneath was maroon, like the passports from the E.U.

Giovanni nodded once and stared at her, a signal to look inside.

Anna took the top one, cracked it open and flipped to the photo page. There she saw a photo of the man sitting across from her, the name Giovanni Salazar, and the usual birth date, place of issue, and date of issue. She looked at him, and he nodded again. She took the second one, which had been upside down on the table. Instead of the European passport she was expecting, she saw Chinese characters on the cover. She flipped it open. The photo inside was the same as the one in the other passport. Giovanni's face. Instead of the name "Giovanni Salazar," this one said "Zhang Wei" under "name" in the English translation. "What's this?!" Anna demanded, sliding the passport to Sara. "You are American and Chinese?"

"Yes," Giovanni said.

"Is that even allowed? Dual citizenship with China?" Anna asked.

"I was with Chinese intelligence."

Sara's mouth fell open.

Anna, too, was dumbstruck at first. "You were working for Chinese intelligence? Why?"

"I am Chinese," he said. "Well, part Chinese."

"You are Chinese?" Sara said incredulously.

"I was born and raised in New York. So were my parents. My father's parents were both from Spain, and my mother's father was French. But my maternal grandmother was Chinese. The Chinese government took advantage of this when they recruited me."

More outraged than exasperated, Sara snapped: "Recruited you? You just went and worked for them? No big deal?"

"At first, I didn't want to do it," he said. "But eventually they convinced me of my obligation to China."

"What obligation to China?" Anna said.

"And what about your obligation to the United States?" Sara asked, whirling her hands around. "What about all this?"

"I didn't do it right away," he said, slouching. "But this man—this Mr. Gold—he got to me. He talked a lot about my family in China," he added, and exhaled hard. "My Chinese roots."

Sara looked suddenly drained of life, like she might pass out.

Anna asked, "How could you fall for that?"

"He pushed the right buttons," said Giovanni, hanging his head. "When we met, it was a bad time for me—I had just lost an enormous amount of money on some bad trades, and my grandmother had just died. Mr. Gold played on that relationship. My grandmother pretty much raised me. He talked about her good values—hard work, justice, patience, loyalty. You can say I was a fool or he was good at brainwashing. But the point is he convinced me to help him, so I started working for their military intel agency—the Chinese equivalent of the CIA. I know it sounds stupid now."

"You're right. It sounds stupid," Sara said, crossing her arms and staring at him with disdain.

"What did they have you do?" Anna asked.

"At first, I was only passing information. It seemed harmless," he said.

Sara put her hand on her temple. A headache ripped through her skull. "And what, one thing led to another, and you started killing people?" she said.

"I didn't kill people," he said.

"Except Evy? I mean, I don't understand," Sara said. "Why did Evy think you worked for the CIA?"

"Because I told her that—and she believed me," he said, closing his eyes.

"She bought that?" Anna asked.

"She bought it," he said, drooping his head

"She's not, she wasn't, an idiot. I don't see why," Sara said.

"I didn't think it would work, either, at the beginning," he said. "But it was my job to keep trying, and then it was, you know, fun, getting her to trust me," he stammered. "That's the most twisted part. I figured out what made her tick. I told her the CIA wanted to stop embezzlement at the World Bank, which was good, and cease illegal arms deals, which was even better," he said, talking faster. "She was into the idea of cleaning up the Bank. And I justified it to myself, because the embezzlement and weapons trades are not fabricated. They were real schemes."

"Wait," Anna said. "What real schemes?"

"Embezzlement of World Bank funds, used to purchase and ship arms to rebels along the western Chinese border."

"The Chinese knew about that?" Anna asked. "How?"

"China is constantly sifting through data, all the data, everybody's data, right? And by the way, the Chinese government is not the only one to do so, which you probably guessed. But anyway, China is analyzing data from its own citizens as well as foreign governments, NGOs, international agencies, everybody—whether the apparatus admits it or not. Chinese analysts were running routine reviews of international financial transactions, including the World Bank's, and anomalies popped up."

"Anomalies?" Anna asked.

"With the inflows and outflows. Something didn't add up. There were anomalies. That's how they detected the embezzlement. Even they never expected something this huge, though, a treasure trove in their lap. So, that part was the truth, and I told Evy that by ending the financial games and the arms deals, she could put a stop to considerable instability and violence."

"Sort of a tall order. What was she supposed to do?"

"Leak the story to the press."

"For that, you were going to pay off her student loans?"

"It may sound small to you, but it wasn't. Had Evy completed her mission, the entire balance of power would have shifted. The Chinese government was fixated on stopping the unification of the rebel groups, and it would have gained enormously if they prevented that. You see?"

"Wow," Anna said.

Perking up as she considered the veracity of his confession, Sara nodded. "A classic 'divide and conquer' strategy."

"Yes. The key was, by working with Evy, the Chinese could implement a 'rebalance without detection'," he said, using air quotes. "She was about to go to the press, be the perfect source. Had she done so, everything would have taken its natural course."

"Journalists love a good story, and the American public hates spending on international development. And secret arms deals," Sara said.

"Yes, and the World Bank is dominated by the United States. Thus, the Chinese would have killed two birds with one stone. They wanted the scandal to cripple the World Bank," he said.

"Manipulating the virtues of the American media against America," she said. "Nice."

"And do you see?" he said. "If the World Bank is plagued by scandal, it would have paved the way for China's Asian Infrastructure Bank to singlehandedly develop the entire region. This is no small goal. China has been fixated on replacing the World Bank with its AIB for a long time. All the AIB projects are developed according to Chinese specs—so afterward, Chinese supplies, parts and training are obligatory. This type of planning secures Chinese contracts indefinitely, while freezing out American and European companies."

"Wow," Sara said. "I see what you mean."

"Second, publicizing the scheme would prevent the arms flow, paralyzing the insurgency. The rebels would be as lost as they ever were, and China would cement its dominance in the region—over the natural resources, rivers, pipelines, everything throughout Myanmar all the way to the Indian Ocean," he said. "Do you get it? Evy's whistleblowing would have been invisible, silent—and revolutionary."

"But why involve Evy? Why not leak it yourself?"

"Evy asked the same thing," Giovanni said, smiling wistfully. "But the Chinese side felt that would not work. After I thought about it, I understood their point. Western journalists consider their sources carefully. American editors would have to believe the story, and

American journalists would not take information blindly from either a guy at the Chinese embassy or a random informer. If it fell in their laps anonymously, they would have been just as suspicious. There had to be a strong source, someone legit, believable, morally upright, someone reputable and without conflicts of interest—like Evy."

"That fits, then," Anna said. "So it's true. You didn't kill her."

Sara frowned.

"No," he said. "I didn't. You understand? The Chinese government didn't protect her well enough. That's true. Now that she's dead, their whole scheme is falling apart."

"What are you talking about, Anna? I thought he did it," Sara said, pointing at Giovanni.

"No," Anna added. "It wasn't him. Right before you texted me this morning, I met with a source who said Sasha Bolokov hired someone to kill Evy, and his story made sense. I believed him."

"Sasha? From the Bank?" Sara asked.

Before Anna could explain further, Giovanni interrupted: "And Sara, I must tell you something else. Now, the Chinese want you to take Evy's place."

Sara hit the table with both fists. "You must be joking! Giovanni Salazar or Zhang Wei or whoever you are," Sara spit out. She leaned forward on the table and shoved her face in his. "I am not doing anything of the sort. I don't want to be a source or assist Chinese intelligence, and I don't want to get myself killed!"

Chapter 53

Washington, DC – Mon., Feb. 24, 10:00 a.m. EST

Sara jumped up and headed to the front door of the café, planning to bolt just like she had done at the Portrait Gallery.

Anna rushed after her. "Sara, wait!" she pleaded. "Please sit down. We need to make a plan."

Giovanni trailed as well. "I didn't mean I thought you would do it."

Pausing by the entrance, Sara glared at him.

Filling the silence, Giovanni quickly continued. "They gave me a few days to convince you, but instead I came to warn you. Chinese intelligence anticipated many things—but they didn't foresee someone eliminating Evy. Since you are her best friend and work at the Bank too, the killer will assume you know something. Understand? You're in danger!"

Sara stood there frozen by fear, grappling with the ramifications of what he was saying.

"Please talk about this with me," Giovanni begged. "I even made this for you," he said, holding out a flash drive. "Let's sit down again, Sara."

Sara grabbed the flash drive and handed it to Anna, who tucked it in her coat pocket. Then Sara relented and returned to the table, with Giovanni and Anna following.

Seated again, Giovanni said, "Proof of everything I've told you is on there."

"Why would you help me?" Sara asked.

Giovanni studied his coffee. "Evy's death is already on my conscience. I don't need another."

Sara made a retching sound.

"Evy wanted to make the world a better place," he said. "Rule of law, fair elections, freedom of speech. Those things meant something to her, and now I want to stand for them too. I have to."

"Oh my God, you and your clichés!" Sara said, motioning her hand in the air, as if she was swatting a fly. Her breaths became shallow.

Anna waited, but Giovanni said no more.

All at once, Sara jumped up again. "I've got to get out of here. Fresh air," she gasped.

"Now what's wrong?" Anna asked, but Sara was already escaping.

Anna threw a twenty on the table, and she and Giovanni chased Sara out. Frowning at the commotion, Jean Claude waved goodbye as they left. Outside, Sara took quick breaths and tapped her hands on her thighs.

"You OK?" Anna asked. "Should I get something for you at the pharmacy over there?"

"No. Just wait. It's happened before," Sara said, still breathing audibly. "Pain down my left arm," she said haltingly. "Panic...attack."

"Should we walk?" Giovanni suggested, holding out his arm in a chivalrous gesture.

"This is such a nightmare, so hard to understand," Sara whispered, making an effort to inhale deeply. "Sasha, a bad guy? Why did Evy have to die? And Nou?" As she exhaled slowly and deliberately, Sara looked straight at Giovanni, assessing him. Then, the combination of his beaten-down demeanor, the stories he told about Evy, which rang true however corny they seemed, and the remorseful look in his eyes convinced her he was telling the truth—and she decided to take a chance on him. Looping her arm through his, she allowed herself to be led by the man whom only an hour before, she had believed was a killer.

"Aren't you too cold out here?" Giovanni asked her.

"No, the cold air is good," Sara said. "I'm feeling a little better. Come on, Anna. Let's go."

"Yes, we need to find a better place for Sara to lie low for a while," he said.

"One sec," Anna said, shuddering. "I have a funny feeling."

"What do you mean?" Sara asked.

"Oh. I don't know. I think I forgot something inside," Anna reassured her. "I'll be right there. You go ahead."

"Well, OK. We'll go this way," Sara said, pointing. "Don't be long."

"I'm coming. Don't worry," Anna said, looking around for the source of her unease.

Traffic was humming along Massachusetts. On the other side of the wide avenue, a dark-haired middle-aged woman in a parka with a fur-lined hood was walking a handsome hunting dog. Closer in, a young man carrying a brick-like law book rushed by, and in the parking lot, a fit, grey-haired man was getting into an electric vehicle with a bike rack, while a health aide was trailing a bundled-up grandma inching along with a walker. It all seemed pretty run-of-the-mill.

But Anna did a double take as she suddenly noticed another woman closer to her. Standing between two cars, the woman had on glasses and frumpy clothes—a dark green cloth coat and light grey sweatpants—and her hair was in a bob with bangs. She bent down to pick something up, when Anna said out loud, "Ha! The shooter from UMD!" But it was too late. The woman had already stood back up and was pointing a handgun.

A loud popping sound pierced the air. Someone screamed, and the dog barked. A man shouted, "Run! Active shooter!"

Across the parking lot, Giovanni pushed on Sara's shoulder. "Sara, get down!" he yelled. "Down! Take cover!"

Sara fell flat, and the cold concrete scraped her cheek. A second shot rang out. As a third one exploded, Giovanni draped himself over Sara. She felt his warm breath on the back of her neck.

"Shouldn't we run?" Sara asked. "What if there's another shot? What if they come closer? Giovanni, you're too heavy." Her right ear and cheek pressed against the ground. "Are you sure we should stay here?" Terrified, she clamped her eyes shut. "We're going to die!"

A fourth shot exploded.

What Sara couldn't see was Anna tackling the assassin from the side. Using the Krav Maga skills she had practiced faithfully for a decade, Anna thrust both of her hands forward beneath the shooter's outstretched arm, looped them around and hung on, weighing her arm down and redirecting the line of fire. Then she flew up, and with all the fury that had accumulated since spying Evy's lifeless body on that patio, Anna engulfed her in a defensive bear hug. The woman fired again, but destabilized and surprised, she lost control of her aim, fell to the ground and loosened her grip.

Anna grabbed the gun, flipped it and pummeled her opponent in the face. As the assassin fell slack, two police officers swooped in and grabbed her. Anna backed off and collapsed to a seated position on the ground. Pumped full of adrenalin, she propped her elbows on her knees, held her head in her hands, and tried to calm herself.

Meanwhile, Sara's own body plus the weight of Giovanni's crunched her right hand, which tingled beneath her chest. "What's going on? Where's Anna?" she asked him.

Giovanni shifted to the side, removing the burden of his weight from her back, though his warmth still radiated against her side.

"Thanks. You were so heavy," Sara said. A gust of wind chilled her face, and she saw Jean Claude coming closer—as if in slow motion, like a cartoon.

The café owner rushed forth. "*Mademoiselle*," he said. "You are OK! And, boy, can your beautiful friend fight!" he laughed, offering his hand to hers. "Here, let me help you sit up."

Sara pivoted to sitting. "What?"

"You seemed so scared back at the café," Jean Claude said, placing his hand on Sara's back. "I thought it was this poor French man. I thought he was threatening you. So I called the police. That's why they were here when that crazy woman started shooting."

Sara struggled to comprehend. "Giovanni?"

"*Mademoiselle* Sara," Jean Claude said, kneeling at her side and bending down to meet her face. "You will be OK now."

Chapter 54

Washington, DC – Mon., Feb. 24, 12:00 noon EST

Anna was dying to confront de Jeanbourg. For the last couple of hours, she had been consumed with her obligations at the crime scene. She had watched with satisfaction as the hand-cuffed assassin was shoved into a squad car, and regret had washed over her as Jean Claude placed a cloth over Giovanni's face and comforted Sara. Giovanni had probably not realized how literally he would end up protecting Sara, Anna figured. But he had redeemed himself in a most honorable way.

An officer had approached Anna and asked about her version of events. She discussed the attack with her, and pointed out its connection to the earlier one in College Park. When the questioning was over and the authorities deemed her free to go, Anna had emailed Tanner with an update, and she had been relieved to find Sara with steady nerves urging her to pursue the story right away, so she ordered a car. All the while, she was racked by de Jeanbourg's apparent betrayal.

Now whisking down Massachusetts Avenue, Anna finally had her chance. The moment de Jeanbourg answered his phone, she shouted, "What is wrong with you?"

"Nice to hear from you again, Anna," he replied.

"You almost got me killed!" she spit out.

"Luckily, you were able to handle it, Jones."

"You left half the story out!" she exploded. "Did you think I wouldn't find out?"

"At least now you have more of the pieces."

"You must be kidding me! Why didn't you tell me about Salazar? And why didn't you stop him?"

De Jeanbourg's line sounded dead.

"Charles!" she shouted.

He still didn't answer.

"Charles! Evy only knew about the embezzlement and the arms deals, because Giovanni Salazar told her! And she would still be alive, if you had stopped him!"

"Exogenous factors are never..."

"Bull shit!" she yelled.

"No, we—."

"Oh!" she interrupted. "Wait." A switch had flicked in her mind. "You didn't know about the Chinese scheme! And that's why you really couldn't have been Evy's killer. You had no reason to target her, because you were clueless!"

"I am afraid so, Jones," he admitted.

"But what the hell? Why didn't you tell me that either?"

"No one wants to broadcast their mistakes, Jones. The CIA failed to detect a Chinese mole. But, now that you figured it out, at least it should convince you that we didn't kill Evy."

"How could this happen?" she shouted. "It's like the Chinese intelligence service is sitting around playing chess with little American pieces, and you guys have no idea you're even on the board!"

"Here's another news flash, Jones: No one knows everything," de Jeanbourg said. "Not even the Chinese—with all their data collection and number crunching. In particular, they didn't know that Sasha was onto Evy. Which is why they didn't protect their asset better. They didn't predict anyone would go after her."

"When did you figure out Giovanni was working for Chinese intelligence?"

"If I say anything, it has to be on deep background."

"Tell me!"

"We didn't figure it out until after you called Garrett Zarribe. When Zarribe began snooping around, I caught wind of your investigation. That's why I called you to meet at Union Station. At that time, I told you the truth: I didn't know who Salazar worked for. All I knew was it wasn't for us. Until then, our algorithm had flagged Salazar for his unusual behavioral patterns, but his forex business was legit. We couldn't pinpoint anything else. Then, you told me he claimed to be a CIA agent. And that was it. We talked to a few more people on the ground in Thailand, tweaked our computer model. And bingo. We realized Salazar was working for Chinese intelligence. We also discovered who his handler was—a Chinese national living in Bangkok named Li Fang. Code name Mr. Gold. Turned up dead in Bangkok's red-light district. But Evy was not on our radar screen."

"That's incredible," Anna said. "You wouldn't have known without me—and Sara, and Evy. But...if you had known, you would have wanted Evy dead too. After all, it would have been bad for you, if she had been this whistleblower, this source or leak or whatever."

"I don't know. I wouldn't say that, necessarily. We could have worked with her," de Jeanbourg said. "But she should have stayed in her lane."

"That's not fair. Evy thought she was working with you, helping the American side. The more I think about it, the more it makes me sick, de Jeanbourg. She is dead, the Chinese almost got away with it, and you were bumbling around in the dark!"

"You're rubbing salt in the wound now, Jones."

"What the hell, de Jeanbourg! How does this relate to Channarong?"

"We're done here."

Chapter 55

Miami – Monday, Feb. 24, 1:00 p.m. EST

Lin sauntered up the gangway of the Angelfish followed by two willowy women, both taller than he was. One was wearing tight jeans and a black tube top with stilettos, the other strappy sandals and a short white dress. Hendrik greeted them and showed them to the upper deck, where Torenmaas was waiting.

"Theo! After all we've been through lately, I brought you a special present," Lin said, shaking Torenmaas' hand and glancing back at the women, one on each side. "Christal and Belle," he said. "You pick."

"Ladies," Torenmaas said, smiling at each. "Welcome to the Angelfish, my home away from home. See those lounge chairs on the lower level?"

They nodded.

"Hendrik will show you the way. Get some sun, have a drink. There's a changing room with bathing suits and towels, a bar and a fridge. Jimmy and I need to discuss some business alone."

The women sought guidance from Lin, who nodded.

Torenmaas tipped his chin at Hendrik, who escorted the women downstairs.

"You're no fun anymore," Lin said.

"I appreciate the gesture," Torenmaas said.

A twenty-something woman in a bikini top and thong arrived from a staircase on the opposite side of the yacht.

"This is Lana," Torenmaas told him. "My girlfriend."

Lin cackled. "OK, Theo. I see."

"Perhaps you misunderstand. She is actually my girlfriend, Jimmy, and she's a law student," he said. "We met at an art opening."

Lin raised an eyebrow.

Lana walked over and kissed Torenmaas passionately. "Nice to meet you, Jimmy," she said, shaking Lin's hand. "I wanted to check on my darling," she added, turning back to Torenmaas. "Do you need anything?"

"Not at the moment," Torenmaas said. "You study. It's fine."

Lana gave him another kiss and stroked his cheek. "You are so understanding." Facing Lin, she smiled. "Contracts exam." She sauntered back to the staircase and disappeared.

Hendrik came back with two scotches, which he left on a table.

"Let's catch up," Torenmaas said.

"What the hell," Lin said, waving toward the women. "If I'm not having that, I might as well have this."

They held up their glasses to one another and drank. Behind them, the high rises of Miami Beach glistening against the clear blue sky.

"What are you really here for, Jimmy?"

"What do you mean?"

"What else do you want?"

"You do have a point," Lin said. "I want to discuss the shipping date."

"No. I told you, Jimmy," Torenmaas said. "I am out."

"You can't be serious. With a few modifications, this deal can still happen. But we have to pounce the moment the rebel leadership regenerates—which in my estimation will take place within the week."

"Even if someone takes Keng's place, the rebels don't have enough money. The source has dried up. They're not going to be sticking their fingers in World Bank coffers again."

"Come on, Theo. You know how that works. They'll be back in the market by the end of the month, and when they dig around for shippers, we need to be there."

"I'm out. I've made up my mind."

"Not even to recoup your losses?"

"Make no mistake. I've thought about that long and hard, but I'm too old for this cyber shit," Torenmaas scoffed. "After you tipped me off about that asshole Bolokov, I had my team look into it, and they confirmed he was the son of the bitch responsible for that video of me with Channarong. He actually hired some jackass to take real videos—guilt by association. It's old school, and it's bad enough. But, Jimmy, we're in a world of deep fakes now. And all these bank hacks and analytics and AI—I don't need it. My cargo business goes on sale next month. I'm retiring. Raven wants to help me with the philanthropy. And, otherwise, there's Lana. So, you see, I'm done. You've heard of quitting while you're ahead?"

"You're not joking," Lin stated flatly, taking another swig.

"You never know how much time you have left, right? I'd rather spend it lounging on the Angelfish here with Lana and watching the partiers at the Iguana Pool on Venetian Island than scratching my ass with inmates in a prison yard. Understand? I can give you a few names, if you want."

"That won't be necessary. I wanted to finish this deal together, that's all. But I have my own contacts. I can move on."

"You do that, Jimmy."

Chapter 56

Washington, DC – Mon., Feb. 24, 1:00 p.m. EST

When Anna arrived home, she was still seething at de Jeanbourg. She knew he was capable of hanging up on her, but when he actually did it, her blood boiled. She jumped out of the car and rushed upstairs without so much as a glance at the lobby lounge. It was as if the people playing billiards, debating the latest social media storm and staring at their laptops weren't even there.

Entering the apartment, she dumped her bag on the floor and went to the bathroom. She needed to clean up as much as she needed to rest. After a long hot shower, she wiped the fog off the mirror with a hand towel and ventured a peek. There were rings under her eyes, but all her stitches were intact. She fixed the bandage on her leg, put on her silk robe and made a pot of Georgian black tea, which she brought to her desk.

For the next two hours, she combed through Salazar's flash drive and got her mind around his files. Pulling the pieces together, she made notes on all that had happened the whole crazy morning. When her mind became too foggy to process, she set her alarm for a twenty-minute cat nap, but the moment she sank into a deep sleep, the phone rang.

Angry at herself for failing to mute it, she held up the blasted device and stared at the display screen—an unknown DC number. She considered not answering, but too much was at stake, and her adrenaline was already rushing. There would be no napping.

"Hello," she answered. "Jones."

"Ms. Jones?" a man asked tentatively.

"Yes, this is she, Anna Jones."

"My co-worker gave me your card," he said. "By our loading dock?"

Anna flew into a seated position. "Oh!"

"Can we meet?" he continued.

"Sure," she said, thrilled her groundwork had finally borne fruit. "That would be great. Tell me when and where."

"I don't know," he said. "You tell me."

"OK," she said, as non-threateningly as possible. "What's convenient for you? Somewhere near the Bank?"

"There's an alley where the food trucks park at GW, a couple of blocks from here, over toward the Foggy Bottom metro station. You know what I'm talking about?"

"I do," she replied.

"I could be there in a half an hour," he said. "By the taco truck."

"Great. See you soon," she replied.

Thirty minutes later, Anna was sitting on a stone ledge a few feet away from the taco truck, wolfing down shredded pork and pickled onions in homemade corn tortillas. She was surprised how hungry she was. Another half hour after that, she was still alone. GW students in fashionable-yet-casual clothing shuffled past her in a steady trickle. A contingency of passers-by wearing scrubs probably worked at the hospital a few blocks further west. Mixed in were government workers and a sprinkling of the well-heeled embassy/international agency crowd. But no sign of loading dock guy. Anna tried calling him back on the number he had used, but the phone rang and rang.

Then a man pitched a taco wrapper into a garbage can pivoted toward her. "I'm the guy who called you. Can we go for a walk?"

"No problem," said Anna. His hair was short and brown, he wore coveralls, a plain winter jacket and construction boots, and he had five-o'clock shadow.

"My name is Mike."

"Nice to meet you, uh, Mike. You saw my picture online?"

"Yeah. Sorry."

"No, it's fine. Everybody does it," she said, nodding in encouragement. "Thanks for getting in touch."

"I have something for you," he said.

"Alright," she said.

He took off his backpack and unzipped it. "It's hard to talk about," he said. "Because I was the one who found him."

"Who?"

"Professor Channarong. I am the one who discovered his body."

"Oh. I'm sorry. That must have been awful," she said. "But I thought it was a woman? I mean, the police told my boss a woman found him."

"Right, Maria reported it," Mike said. He reached into his bag and pulled out two letters, which he shoved in Anna's face. "Here. Take them. I think the professor wrote them the night he died."

"Oh my goodness!" Anna exclaimed. In beautiful hand-written script, the top envelope was addressed to "Evy Poole." Anna pulled the bottom one out. She made a face. "It says my name!"

"Yes," Mike said. "I'm delivering it to you."

"Where did you get them?"

"That night, the night he died, I saw Professor Channarong in the hallway around one in the morning. He was going to his office—he often did that late at night, you know, to think. Our crew was running late. I told him we could clean his office later. He thanked me, as usual. I've done it before—flipped the schedule. It's not a big deal. In the early morning, I would go back to finish, and sometimes we would have longer conversations. He was nice, always asked about my family. Sometimes, he gave me advice." Mike trailed off.

Anna waited for him to finish.

"He clearly wanted to be alone. When I left, though, I was worried. He seemed shaky. I smelled alcohol, which was unusual," he said. "So, when we were finally at the end of our shift, I was anxious to check on him, and...." Mike stopped talking.

"And?" she whispered.

"And he was—dead. We were too late."

"I'm sorry."

Mike's eyes teared up. "I feel like it was my fault. I mean, I had a feeling, maybe I could have helped him—but I was too late."

"No," she said. "It wasn't your fault. You can't blame yourself. He had a lot going on. And I'm sorry to push you to talk about this, but who's 'we'? Can you tell me again, what happened, exactly?"

"I was with my co-worker Maria. I was carrying the vacuum, and she was pushing the supply cart—for his executive bathroom, you know. I unlocked, so I saw the body first. I told her not to look. It's not a good image to have in your mind. She's the one who called the police. They spoke to her first, but we were together. After, they talked to me too."

"What about the letters?"

"They were in his out-box. I saw them sitting there. I don't know why I took them, but I shoved them in my shirt. I never told the police, and Maria never knew."

"Why tell me now?"

"Maria is friends with that woman you met at the loading dock, and she was talking about you. When I heard the name from the letter, I had to bring it to you."

"No, I mean, why not open them, or throw them out?"

"Because it's not right," he said. "I wanted to help him, like he used to help me, but then I thought it might look like I stole the letters, and I got scared."

"Thank you for contacting me. I won't tell anybody how I got them."

"At least they're off my hands now."

"Do you want to read them with me?" she asked.

"No," he said. "I don't. You figure it out, Ms. Jones. I have to go."

As soon as Mike had disappeared, Anna marched across campus to a coffee shop she knew would be open but uncrowded. Inside the law school, the place was next door to the World Bank, and yet a world away. She would be invisible there. Anna bought a latte at the counter, sat down at a flimsy bistro table and took a minute. Convene with Tanner? Give the letters to the police? Open them right away?

Maybe it was the jolt of caffeine, but the next step became obvious. One of the letters is addressed to a dead person, and the other is to me, she thought. I have every right to read my own letter. And, given the circumstances, I can argue it's OK to read Evy's too. Reporter's privilege is on my side.

Anna grabbed a plastic knife sitting on the neighboring table and carefully slit open the envelope marked "Evy Poole." Inside, she discovered a tri-folded letter on World Bank letterhead. In beautiful hand-written script, it said:

Dear Evy,

You are a brilliant researcher, a thorough analyst, a true friend. You also possess that rarest of gifts—an independent mind. With so many assets, you are well on your path to becoming a global leader in sustainable development and a significant advocate for the poor. Stay the course. For now, keep working

with Anna—I believe you were right to trust her.
Together, you are sure to expose the wrongdoing.
Once the scandal blows over, do not look back. None
of this was your fault.

Forgive me,
Nou Channarong

Anna put it down and sat back. Channarong thought Evy would
continue his work? He would have been devastated to know her star had
burned out. But does it confirm suicide?

She picked up the knife and opened the other envelope. Inside it, too,
was a hand-written letter, signed in Channarong's careful hand. She read:

Dear Ms. Jones,

People will say I should not have taken my own life,
but only each soul can truly comprehend his own lot.
In my case, it is for the best, I assure you. My wife has
left me, my children are grown, and my life's work has
been destroyed. I am a pawn in a new Great Game,
for which I lack the rulebook. You could say I stood
up for the poor. God knows, I tried. But on balance, it
doesn't matter, because I failed miserably at detecting
schemes unfolding beneath my nose.
Ms. Poole tipped me off. She came to me with her
documents and data sets and suspicions. She
desperately wanted to figure out what was happening
and fix it. She took a big risk—I could have been an
enemy. Her instincts were good, though. I wanted to
help her. But I didn't understand any better than she

did. One thing was clear: someone had already set traps for me. Of course, I knew my own truth, that I was innocent of any machinations, but I was not innocent of the mismanagement. Now, I cannot bear the shame or guilt any longer.

You may wonder why I am sending this letter to you. My wife has not cared about me for a long time. Nothing good would come of revealing this to her. As for the Bank administration, I could not be sure whom to trust. It was Ms. Poole who chose you. She is convinced you are a brave and honest person of integrity, someone who will not back down until the truth emerges. By now, she will have told you everything, fed you every last statistic, and I am glad. You are a well-known correspondent, and I remember meeting you several times. As I leave this world, I do so knowing you will work with her to discover and report the full and complete truth. Feel free to share this letter with whomever you see fit. Godspeed.

Sincerely,
Nou Channarong

Anna carefully refolded the letters and returned them to their envelopes. Doing so felt like paying respect. What a terrible mess. Poor Evy! And poor Channarong, too. His death was equally pointless. That he believed Evy would set the record straight only deepened the tragedy. Anna marveled at the strange fate that had thrown them all together.

Her grief mixed with excitement, though, as she pictured getting the truth out. She had to find Tanner.

Chapter 57

Washington, DC – Mon., Feb. 24, 3:00 p.m. EST

With the Federal Reserve behind her, Anna darted into Constitution Gardens near the Vietnam Veterans Memorial. The wind was blowing, but the sleet had ended. Through the trees to her left, the Washington Monument obelisk glowed in the afternoon sun. Suddenly, she spotted Tanner sitting on a bench facing the Reflecting Pool and rushed over.

As soon as he saw her coming, Tanner nodded hello. When she got close, he stood up and gestured toward the Lincoln Memorial. "Let's walk," he said. "This is where I often come to be alone. Makes me feel unplugged."

Anna kept pace beside him.

"Nice walk from the bureau—a parade of history, don't you think," he continued. "The White House, OEOB, DAR, OAS, the Fed. The park here with its pond and American flags is restorative. In February, even better. Fewer people."

"Mm-hmm."

"This whole mess with you and BEAT, the deal you supposedly made, it's a lot to take. But you didn't think I'd let you go, did you, Jones?"

"I hoped not," she said. "But you know. Sometimes things don't work out."

"Those blockheads in New York have to cover their asses, Anna. You know that. We have better things to do."

"I am grateful you see it that way."

Tanner smiled knowingly. "And by the way, I didn't know there was history there—with Simonson and Garcia. Can't say how it would have affected my decision-making, but anyway, I was ignorant of that. Just to be clear."

"Thanks for telling me, but it doesn't matter. Forget about it."

"Bring me up to speed."

"Glad to, sir. Here's the amazing thing: Everyone was missing something—none of the key players in this whole scheme held all the pieces," Anna explained. "And lucky for us, too, because that was their downfall. They had blind spots, an incapacity to see the big picture. They were so absorbed in their own plans that they failed to observe others observing them, which led to mistakes."

"Lay it all out there for me."

"Sasha thought his scheme was a secret, right?" she said, as they continued walking. "But the Chinese were watching his every move, of course. For its part, the CIA had no idea about Giovanni. They completely missed the fact that Giovanni had been co-opted by Chinese intelligence. The Chinese, in turn, missed that Sasha was onto Evy. Then, neither the Chinese nor Sasha saw that Evy had turned to Channarong for help. Meanwhile, Ko had no idea Keng was working with Sasha. And, if that wasn't complicated enough, nobody predicted Channarong would crack. Nobody saw his suicide coming, so they didn't anticipate the ripple effects that could have."

"It was that very evening that Evy came looking for you, wasn't it?"

"Yes. She was already in danger—but Channarong's suicide is what triggered her to go to the movie theater that night. Now, with these letters, we know for sure," she added, opening her bag and taking them out. "Here they are."

Taking them, he at first handled them like they might break. Standing still, he read one, then the other. "Fuck. They sure do seem authentic."

"Told you."

"I'll get them verified, just to be sure," said Tanner, putting them in his coat pocket and resuming his stroll.

"And here's the flash drive I told you about on the phone," she said, passing it to him. "I already made copies."

"There are videos of Evy?" he said, taking the drive.

"Yes, nine, labeled sequentially. There are also five documents—Confession, ID, Gold, Meetings and Payments. Also, tons of photos in two separate files—one called Poole, the other Gold."

"In the videos, she's having a conversation?"

"Yes. Giovanni took them clandestinely as part of the recruitment process."

"Amazing," Tanner said. He pursed his lips. "Give yourself a pat on the back, Jones."

"I don't know," she said. "It was really Evy Poole. She's the one who got this rolling—and she paid for it with her life."

"Acknowledged," he said. "But, without you, there would be no justice for her either. You were the one she picked to tell—and ultimately that's why Sara turned up for you too. They saw you as a fair and honest broker. All that coverage of corruption in Moscow and Tbilisi has paid off in more ways than one. Great work, Jones."

"Thank you," Anna said. "Of course, there was also Raven's work in Chiang Mai. You've heard those incredible recordings she got of Sasha and Ingrid. They corroborate the pieces from Salazar and De Jeanbourg. And there's one more thing."

"By all means."

"Remember when I asked you if we could contact that NGO?"

"The digital forensics outfit?"

"Yes. Jeff in tech helped me out with that."

"And now you're going to tell me they found invisible yellow tracking dots embedded in your documents?"

"You heard about that?" she asked, laughing. "No, no, but this group helped Jeff comb through the metadata, tags, codes and such—and they found some things. First, the majority of Evy's documents were 'scrubbed'—that is, their metadata is missing. That means we don't know when or where they originated. My guess is these documents were furnished by the Chinese—since they would know how to do that. Second, some of them weren't scrubbed at all. That means it's obvious that they come from particular offices or workstations at the World Bank, and there is no mystery. But third, some of the files were poorly scrubbed. Specifically, two of them."

"Two? Only two?"

"Yes, only two. The video of Channarong dining with Torenmaas, and that spreadsheet," she said. "And they bear the electronic markers of one device—which belonged to Sasha's girlfriend Ingrid."

"Why am I not surprised?" Tanner said. "She wasn't as talented a hacker as she thought?"

"Precisely. You see, in the event that things turned sour for him, Sasha planned to put the blame on Ko and Channarong. These two files are part of the effort to frame them. Evy had real evidence, which the Chinese had given her, but she was also in possession of files like this video, which were decoys or fabrications, things Sasha planted. Sasha knew about the legitimate link that Channarong had to Torenmaas through their philanthropic work, and he was exploiting that. Evy hadn't figured out what was what, but she was working with Channarong to decipher it all when she was killed."

"Amazing," Tanner repeated, shaking his head. "Bolokov thought he had it all nailed down, didn't he?"

"Seems so. He thought his plans were foolproof."

"Thankfully, they weren't," Tanner said. "And now, I have something for you, too."

Chapter 58

Washington, DC – Mon., Feb. 24, 3:30 p.m. EST

Anna and Tanner reached the end of the Reflecting Pool and paused by the foot of the Lincoln Memorial. Anna detected a twinkle in Tanner's eye. "Is it about the *Mirror* article?" she asked.

"Yes, indeed," Tanner said, nodding and pursing his lips again. "Turns out Steven Brown, Senator Caleb's flack, admitted to planting the smear campaign about you. You'll never guess who put him up to it."

"I couldn't say," she replied.

"Sasha Bolokov," he said.

"That too? How do you know?"

"Brown told me himself," Tanner said, shrugging.

"He did?" she said. "Thank you."

"Simple blackmail," he continued. "Something to do with a certain high-priced call girl."

"Why would he tell you that?"

"We go way back! He couldn't help himself," Tanner said. "Besides, my interrogation skills are top-notch."

"Tanner," she whispered.

"No, that's not the reason," Tanner continued, chuckling a bit. "Actually, the flack over at FBI media relations filled me in. I've known him for years."

"My, my," Anna interrupted. "After all that, you do trust a flack from time to time."

Tanner smiled. "It's great fun to mock them, you know, but some are worth their salt. This guy I'd even call clever. Anyway, the FBI held Brown's feet to the fire, and Brown didn't want to go to jail. Brown confessed, in order to avoid being an accessory to Bolokov's crimes. Now, he's a blackmail victim. Pathetic victim. But a victim all the same. The bank account where you were supposedly receiving payments from BEAT was trumped up by Bolokov and Ingrid Jonsson."

"Wow," she said. "Wow," she repeated, staring at the sun a moment too long. Squinting, she returned her gaze to the trees by the reflecting pool. At first, she saw only black and white speckles. "Sasha Bolokov and Steven Brown. Both of them could have destroyed me. One of them I knew well, the other hardly at all. I don't know which is worse. And for what? I mean, why did Brown do it?"

"To save himself," Tanner said. "Self-preservation is a powerful motivator. What was that about the lack of moral fiber you were discussing the other day?"

"They make me sick," she said, staring ahead. Geese paddled around in the Reflecting Pool. One of them flapped its wings, as if preparing to take off, and settled down again. "I feel like I should tell them off, but what can one even say?"

"The story is your victory, Jones. You know that. Just tell the story. You've got the evidence from Evy Poole's phone," he said, pointing his right forefinger. "Giovanni Salazar's flash drive, interviews with Theo van Torenmaas and Charles de Jeanbourg," he added, pointing more fingers. "Garcia's recordings of Sasha Bolokov and Ingrid Jonsson, and the CIA statements, however lame they are," he said, holding out his entire hand. "Plus statements from Jordan Green and Steven Brown. It's time to crank this out."

Anna's phone vibrated, and she glanced at the screen. "It's Raven," she said with curiosity. "Raven, what's up?" she answered, putting the phone on speaker. "I'm with Tanner."

"Garcia!" Tanner bellowed good-naturedly. "Working 24/7 I see!"

"I'm glad I caught you guys," Raven said anxiously. "Things have been crazy, but the spokesman for the Royal Thai Police finally got back to me."

Tanner leaned down toward the mike. "And?"

"He confirmed that this guy Keng, who is the cousin of Ko Maung Mai, died when the military raided the compound—along with Sasha, Ingrid and 22 other people deemed terrorists," Raven said. "They arrested a further 27 people and confiscated a huge weapons cache—he even gave me a detailed inventory. Said the cousins have been working together to arm the rebels, both here in Thailand and in Myanmar," she continued. "It's all on the record."

"Terrific," Tanner said. "And my my. China will love that."

"But what about Ko?" Anna asked.

"They don't know," Raven added. "He was neither among the captured, nor among the dead," she added. "And the military spokesman said that with Keng, the mastermind, gone, a power vacuum has opened, and they expect a scramble for leadership."

"That's some amazing work, Garcia," Tanner said.

"That's flattering," Raven said. "But Ko is now at the top of the most-wanted list over here. The spokesman was more than happy to share this information. They'd like to see Ko behind bars, you know? In their effort to capture him, they're plastering his picture all over the media."

"Ko disappeared?" Anna asked.

"It must have been a close call," Raven replied. "The spokesman said Thai authorities were poised to arrest him upon the arrival of a large shipment of weapons and ammunition in Bangkok this week. But it never arrived, and he was not where they expected him to be."

"Crazy," Anna said. "The World Bank spokesperson in DC told me yesterday that Ko will be back in a month."

"That's never going to happen," Raven said.

Tanner interrupted. "Hey, both of you, listen! We can follow up on Ko later. It's time to run the story on Channarong and Poole. It's a go. Double byline. Got it?"

"Great, OK," Raven said. "Anna, OK?"

"OK," Anna confirmed. "I think we can pull this off. But what about my leave of absence? I'm not even supposed to be talking to you, Tanner."

"I'm working on that, Jones," Tanner said. "Just get the story done."

Chapter 59

Washington, DC – Weds., Feb. 26, 11:00 a.m. EST

When Anna walked into the conference room at the DC bureau of the *Daily Journal*, it was already full. A crescendo of claps, cheers and hoots filled the room. "Whoo hoo!" "Congratulations!" "Welcome back!" She smiled at everyone.

Tanner's hands were in the air with palms springing up and down, as if patting an invisible pet. "Alright! Alright! Settle down," he said. Marching to the head of the conference table, he left the chair that had been saved for him empty. He placed his hands in his pockets, took a deep breath and surveyed the room. Then he stretched his arms out and up. "It is my great pleasure to announce officially that our friends in New York finally see things my way—Anna Jones has been cleared of all accusations," Tanner said, reaching out to shake Anna's hand. "Welcome back!"

Beaming, Anna shook his hand. "Great to be back," she said, standing next to him.

"Now," Tanner said, making eye contact with as many of his reporters as possible. "This has been a trying nine days at our paper. And after four decades in the business, I venture to say the scale of this scandal was colossal, the lies epic. Amid this insanity, Jones lost her job—albeit temporarily—and she might have lost her life. But she did not give up. Instead, she took the lead in investigating the twisted scheme."

Cheering and clapping flooded the room once again.

"Jones' work was, needless to say, impressive. Also...," he said, pausing dramatically. "Credit is due to Raven Garcia as well. Garcia, join us!"

Raven stepped up. Nodding affirmatively, Anna watched Raven approaching. Tanner was then flanked by the women.

"Garcia," he said, shaking her hand. "You did some damned fine reporting out of Thailand over the last week! Glad to see you arrived from Bangkok safely!"

Eyes puffy but somehow as glamorous as ever, Raven smiled.

"Garcia, Jones, you make a marvelous team," Tanner said, waving his hand back and forth. "Together, you uncovered Sasha Bolokov as the rogue agent, the ultimate source of deceit, and the American and Chinese agents manipulating the situation. Really solid work! Your scoop on page one today was stunning. We, the citizenry, are all rewarded."

Raven and Anna nodded as their colleagues offered them one more round of applause.

"And now!" Tanner said. "For those of you who don't already know him, let me introduce Viktor Simonson from our Moscow bureau."

Viktor stood up from his seat along the back wall. "Greetings. Happy to be here," he said, looking around to acknowledge everyone.

"As you can see, Simonson has been released from the hospital. He's been cleared of concussion dangers, and is ready to get back to his post. And finally—Jones has one last surprise," said Tanner, waving his outstretched palm toward Anna.

"You must be wondering what happened to Jordan Green, the author of the infamous *Mirror* article smearing me," Anna said. "You might assume I couldn't stand her."

Stifled laughter passed through the room.

"But you'd be wrong," Anna continued. "Green is an aspiring reporter, a straight-A student with strong writing skills and some great clips. But she's young—just started college. She was actively misled at the *Mirror*. There's no way she could have known how she was being manipulated, and she didn't deserve to be put in that position. So, today I am pleased to say, she has accepted an internship with us." Anna smiled and gestured toward Tanner.

Tanner, who had walked toward the conference room door, opened it for Jordan Green.

Green, a petite Black woman wearing a smart red suit jacket, black pants and black shirt with chunky Chelsea boots, stepped up. Her makeup was plain, and her hair was styled in an intricate braided updo, which showed off large pearl earrings. "Thank you for the opportunity," she said, scanning all the new faces. "I'm looking forward to it."

"So, Tanner and I will be training Green," Anna continued. "Because—and I understand this is through no fault of my own—Raven Garcia will be moving on!"

"And if you'd like details about that," Tanner said. "Ask Garcia at Karl's tonight. Now, back to work!"

Chapter 60

Washington, DC – Weds., Feb. 26, 9:00 p.m. EST

A waiter rested his tray, loaded with five steins of beer and five glasses of bourbon, on the table next to Anna. Around her sat Viktor, Raven, Mel and Sara. The table was draped in a white tablecloth. A little plastic "reserved" sign stood in the middle.

"I can't believe you got Karl to take a reservation, Mel," said Anna.

"You're welcome," Mel said. "But let me be clear—the tablecloth was Karl's idea."

"What about the drinks? Was that Karl too?" Anna asked, as the waiter distributed the drinks.

"No," Mel said. "That was me. And now, I'd like to make a toast," Mel said, holding up her bourbon. "To finding—what did Tanner say?—the source of deceit!"

"Here, here," Raven said, as they all drank.

Anna took on a serious tone. "I'd like to add that we're deeply sorry for your losses, Sara. You must miss Channarong and Evy deeply. It took a lot of courage to pursue Evy's story."

The gravity of the events cast a pall over the table, and for a moment no one spoke.

Sara broke the silence. "It's true. It's pretty awful. But I'm grateful to you all. I had no idea what Evy and Nou were going through. Anna, you were awesome. Thanks for listening to me, and for tracking down Charles. You followed through. Not everyone would do that," she added, holding up her glass again. "To you, Anna, and to Evy."

All five clinked glasses and drank, as the waiter returned with appetizers, and they began to nibble on the food.

"What's this news, Raven?" Viktor said. "You're defecting?"

"I'm moving!" Raven said. "To Chiang Mai!"

"Really?" Viktor asked.

"Yes!" Raven said.

"What are you going to do there?" Mel asked.

"Ha! We'll see!" Raven said. "At first, I'll freelance. You know—write a travel blog, post pictures of food, do hotel reviews, all that stuff everyone does when they quit their regular job!" She laughed. "But, seriously, Tanner already talked to the editors in New York, and it sounds like I'll be able to do some meatier stories for them too."

"I'll miss you!" Anna said.

"You will not," Raven said.

"No, I will. You're a great reporter, and now that we really know each other, it's a shame," Anna said. "Cooperating with you actually works."

"Thanks," Raven said, tilting her head and shrugging. "I agree—about working with you—but, you know, sometimes you have to shake things up."

"Why, if you don't mind my asking, Chiang Mai?" Viktor asked.

"My uncle wants me to run his philanthropy over there."

"Are you sure that's the only reason?" asked Anna, squinting. Raven looked happier than she had ever seen her.

"No, it's not the only reason," Raven admitted, smiling. "Ice suggested it. He knows a place I can rent."

"And it's not too soon?" Anna asked. "After all, we know now that there's enough room at the DC bureau for both of us! And what about Apollo?"

"Actually, I'd been thinking I needed a change of pace for some time. This really is a chance I can't pass up. Besides, Apollo can come with me."

Anna nodded. "OK!"

"To life," Viktor said.

Once more, they toasted. "To life!"

"Maybe you can find out what the rebels are up to next," Anna said. "And what happened to Ko."

"That's what Tanner said," Raven replied. "But I'm sure Ko is long gone!"

Chapter 61

Bangkok – Thursday, Feb. 27, 9:00 a.m. local time (9:00 p.m. EST on Wednesday, Feb. 26 in DC)

His driver opened the rear door of the German luxury sedan, and Ko stretched his long legs out onto the red carpet. He paused before the main entrance of the Honor Park Embassy, brushed off his suit and straightened his tie. A tropical downpour—strangely early this year—had just ended. The air smelled fresh, and the trees and plants lining the semicircular drive glistened as they dripped dry. Patches of steam floated upward, like tiny clouds.

Two life-size stone elephants lurked among the banana trees on either side. Typical pandering to the tourists, Ko thought. Holding his head high, he strolled past the bellhops into the lobby.

The hotel manager immediately spotted him. Placing his hands in the traditional prayer pose, he approached with a wai. "This way, please, Mr. Mai. Your associates are waiting in conference room number three." Ko nodded and followed. The man smiled and offered another wai as he signaled which door. Ko grabbed the handle and went in.

Jesse and Joanna Martin and Charles de Jeanbourg were chatting as if they were at a cocktail party. Bottles of mineral water and an array of hors d'oeuvres were arranged in the middle of the table. The two men nodded and chewed, while Joanna held a champagne flute.

"You have been enjoying yourselves," Ko said.

Jesse barreled toward Ko and delivered a bear hug, which Ko accepted stiffly.

"Brother," Jesse said. "It is fantastic to see you again so soon," he said, patting him on the back. "But I am sorry to hear about your cousin. Please accept my condolences."

"Thank you," Ko replied flatly.

"It was a mixed blessing, though, wasn't it?" added Jesse, chortling.

Ko looked at him with a sparkle in his eye.

"Whoo-eee!" Jesse said, laughing. "My mother always said you would amount to something!"

Ko smirked.

"Keng reached the end of the line, my brother," Jesse said, nodding. "The cycle churns."

Grinning, Ko approached Joanna.

She tilted her head. Her lips turned up at the corners.

"Thank you," Ko said, offering his hand and nodding. "I understand now that you have been advocating my position all along. I owe you an apology. I didn't realize."

"Apology accepted," she said, shaking his hand. "Working with you is the logical choice. I only wish they had listened to me before, and you had been in position sooner."

Jesse slapped Ko on the back. "She is a sly one, Ko. I told you!" Jesse said.

Ko harrumphed.

"Anyway," de Jeanbourg interjected. "Mr. Ko Maung Mai! It is my pleasure to meet you, finally."

Ko nodded and shook de Jeanbourg's hand.

"I trust you have been well, Mr. Mai?" de Jeanbourg asked.

"Indeed. This land is my home, after all. It is good to be back. Your support has been appreciated," Ko replied.

"Your colleagues at the World Bank don't know what to make of your disappearance. Some even say you are in hiding in a 'rat hole'," de Jeanbourg said.

"Economist in a rat hole. Imagine that," Jesse said.

De Jeanbourg chortled. "Now, let me see. I have this little pouch here for our devices. Metal threads, special fabric—it blocks the signals. The Martins and I have already put ours inside. Would you be so kind as to join us, Mr. Mai? We must ensure our conversation is private."

Ko put his phone into the pouch.

"And, excuse the bother, but a few swipes with this, and I can confirm you have not forgotten anything," de Jeanbourg added, holding up a wand.

"Fine," said Ko, lifting his arms, while de Jeanbourg waved his detector up and down.

"Excellent. Excellent," de Jeanbourg said. "Nice to know you're not carrying additional devices. By the way, we also checked this meeting room beforehand. Just to be sure."

"Just to be sure," Ko said. "What about you, de Jeanbourg? How do I know you are not recording this meeting? What about your devices?"

"Do you want to do a sweep too?" de Jeanbourg replied, cackling.

"Wouldn't you do the same?" Ko asked.

"Shit!" Jesse bellowed. "You get him, Ko!"

De Jeanbourg hesitated. Then he held out the wand. "By all means. Take it."

Ko accepted it and scanned his interlocutors. "Touché," he said when he was done, and handed it back over to de Jeanbourg.

The four of them sat down.

"Let's get right to it, shall we?" de Jeanbourg said. "Your cousin, Keng Maung Mai, was a legend, a warrior, a giant among men. However. He was also undisciplined and unsophisticated—a loose cannon, a bull in a China shop, a peasant. As such, we had difficulties working with him. Now, we have a new 'landscape'," said de Jeanbourg, using air quotes. "And, given that, the agency is rebalancing its strategy in this theater. Thus, a chance arises for you, my friend. It is my understanding that you, Mr. Mai, would be a steady and reliable partner, one whose aims are in line with ours."

"Unlike Keng's, he means," Jesse added.

"I understand," Ko said.

"It will still have to be cloak and dagger," Jesse said. "But with your deluded nut case of a cousin out of the way, everything about these shipments from me and our CIA friends here to you and your rebels up north will be much easier."

"It isn't the Thai style to do so, but I too shall be blunt," Ko said. "Keng made some mistakes. He doubted me, his own family. He trusted Sasha—whom he never realized had been cut loose. And he went too far. His 'inclusion' plan was lunacy, pure fantasy. An independent NNT is possible. Yes, secession can work. But the NNT should not merge with Thailand," he said, pausing. "We are all better off with Thailand as a good neighbor, a bystander."

"Excellent," De Jeanbourg said, nodding. "Our view precisely. Simple secession. And our people determined the factions would stand behind you. Despite his delusions, your cousin had named you as his successor in the event of a crisis. That was an advantage he left you."

"The local leaders know me well. That is correct. I am familiar with the terrain. I know the strategy," Ko said. "Much of what we need is in place. However, some shipments remain undelivered."

"I have been in contact with Mr. Lin about that," de Jeanbourg said. "Apparently, he kicked Mr. Torenmaas out. Mr. Lin is lining up another cargo consultant. It is a lucrative contract, and he has someone in mind. It will not take long. Wouldn't you say, Mr. Martin?"

"God knows there is a lot to be gained, yes siree," Jesse said. "We can't be too careful locating a cargo man, but Lin is clear on that."

"I also need cash," Ko said. "It has to keep flowing in the villages. Otherwise, the local leaders will turn toward the East. The alliance is strong, but there is only so far we can go."

"Not to worry. The agency sees the need. The director is negotiating. I hear talk of a new 'loophole' in the black budget," de Jeanbourg said, again using air quotes. "You'll get your money."

Jesse leaned forward on the table. "Now, Ko, what about your family on the other side of the Thai border? That's one thing Keng got right—the arbitrary nature of that line."

"Yes. My great regret. Many of the ethnic groups have spread out, live across more than one national boundary—even in China," he said, looking down for a moment as if in prayer, then quickly up to face them squarely. "We can't untangle that now. All we can do is create a new space. An independent and united NNT in control of its resources would give our people freedom. With the violence and repression in the past, we could clean up the landmines, end the checkpoints, build schools and clinics, more forward with economic development. Over time, the expatriated could move back."

"That's a pretty picture, brother," Jesse said.

Joanna added, "Mm-hmm, God helps the downtrodden to rise."

"Yes, He does. My father used to preach about that too. You remember that, Ko?" Jesse said, wide-eyed. "It sure has been long in coming. But your time is now, Ko. Clear skies ahead. God is smiling upon you. I can feel it. You're being smart about it. And you picked the right partners."

"Yes, Mr. Mai, with our help, you will prevail," de Jeanbourg said. "And not to worry. We're in it for the long haul."

Chapter 62

Washington, DC – Thurs, Feb. 27, 10:00 a.m. EST

When Anna woke up, Viktor's side of the bed was empty. She put on her robe and walked into the kitchen. He was leaning against the counter, drinking espresso. The toaster oven was humming, and its power button glowed orange.

"Good morning," he said. "You look amazing. Oh, wait, you are amazing," he said, sidling up to her and putting his hands on her waist. "And brilliant."

She wrapped her hands around his neck. They kissed, interrupted by the ding of the toaster oven.

"I wish you were still in Moscow," he said, holding her around the waist, pushing his body against hers and staring into her eyes. "Or I didn't have to go back so soon."

Anna smiled at him, as a thousand thoughts charged through her mind.

"Your eyes are sparkling," he said.

She put her hands through the hair behind his ears, careful not to disturb the wound on the back of his head. "I'm just glad you are OK. I can't believe you nearly got killed again."

"I didn't, Anna. It was not such a big deal this time. I can't believe I was stuck in the hospital, while you were in danger. That's what was killing me. You were out here alone."

"Thanks, Viktor," she said. "But I can take care of myself."

"That's not the point. I like to take care of you," he said, gently letting her go, then handing her the latte he had just prepared. "I almost forgot."

She took a sip. "Thanks. It's perfect."

"Are you sure you aren't still upset about Raven?" he asked, as he turned to fetch the bagels he had placed in the toaster.

"I'm not," Anna said, shaking her head. "Really. The whole thing with Raven doesn't matter anymore. You should have handled it better, though," she said with a theatrical side glance, as if she were squinting in the bright sun.

"I know," he said, nodding as he spread cream cheese on the bagels. "I should have told you about her, before you heard it from someone else. I get that."

"True," she said, nodding playfully. "Anyway, now I consider Raven a real friend—it's too bad she's leaving."

"You two together! If she stayed, I'm not sure I could handle it," he said, taking capers, dill and lox out of the fridge.

"You better get ready," Anna said, widening her eyes. "We're planning on keeping in touch."

"I'll watch my step, then," Viktor replied, eyebrows raised. "You two are a force to reckon with."

"Maybe I was being rash by throwing you out."

"No," he sighed, returning to her side. "You had every right to get rid of me. You were in a tough spot—you sensed something was wrong, and you were right—I was avoiding telling you everything, and meanwhile, Raven had lied to you, even if it was on Tanner's orders. You can be proud you sensed something was off. A great skill for anyone—especially a journalist."

"I wish I'd had that sense about Sasha."

"Everyone gets fooled sometimes. It's inevitable. And he was a master manipulator. The point is, you figured it out."

"I appreciate the vote of confidence," she said. "But the truth is that even one person bent on twisting the truth can inflict a lot of damage, not to mention several simultaneously, and I could never have seen what was really going on without help—a lot of help—you, me and Raven, plus all our sources, the ones we tracked down and the ones who found us. We had to team up to get it right. That's why you and I have to be honest with each other—always, always. We have to be able to trust at least one other person."

Viktor approached Anna again, grasped both her hands and looked her straight in the eye. "I won't lie to you. I never have. But I also promise that I won't keep you in the dark—ever again. I am really sorry."

"Apology accepted," she said.

"I'm really glad you took me back in last night," he said softly.

"Who else would prepare me such great midnight snacks?"

"Oh, so you just keep me around for my culinary skills?"

"Definitely, just for your great culinary skills," she said, laughing.

"Well, come on, then. Brunch is ready," he said, placing down the plates with the bagels, lox and toppings.

"This looks gorgeous, Viktor. When did you even have time to get this stuff?"

"Maybe there are some secrets I'll have to keep after all."

The room brightened as the sun came out from behind the clouds.

"It's a sign," she said.

"To keep secrets?"

Anna laughed. "No. Maybe just that we should go outside today—not waste our rare day off together."

"Absolutely. Bike ride or a hike?"

"But first, I've got another idea."

"Good thinking."

"Not that. Not right now, anyway! What I meant was, I wanted to ask you something. I'll be covering that European-American security conference in Dublin next month. Why don't you come? It's a short flight from Moscow. What do you say?"

"You'd have me lounge around in your hotel room, pining away until you finish filing long stories at the end of your grueling days?"

"You could use the hotel gym, and the sauna. Sample all the local stout, whiskey, whatever you like. Bike along the Liffey? Meet me for dinner? You can get some great venison. After the conference, we could take a few days."

"How could I resist that?" he said, holding up his espresso cup. "To Dublin!"

"To Dublin."

SOURCE OF DECEIT

ABOUT THE AUTHOR

Wolf Bahren is the pen name used by the writer Kristi Bahrenburg
Janzen for her fiction. In 2016, she published her first espionage thriller,
Agents of Suzharia. She has been a writer for more than 25 years,
including working as foreign correspondent, reporter, managing editor,
editor, freelancer and fact checker. She has covered international finance,
business, trade, economics, agriculture and food. Currently residing in the
DMV (Washington, DC-Maryland-Virginia metro area), Wolf has also
lived and worked in New York and Europe. Her website is
www.wolfbahren.com.